## THE HUNTED

I raised my eyes to find the hunter watching me.

Moisture glistened on his lower lip, making his hard features arrestingly sensual. His amber eyes held an almost dazed quality, one of indulgence and—if I read him right—satisfaction.

He dipped his head slightly, in a courtly gesture of greeting, and leaned uncomfortably close. My fingers trembled against my switch stars as the beat of the music anchored me to the here and now. I breathed in the light, spicy scent of him, mixed with the sulfur of the demon.

"I wasn't expecting one so early," he said, his voice husky from the kiss of the succubus he'd just destroyed. "Thanks for distracting her."

Early? I drew back. It was nearing midnight. And as far as what he'd done... "What are you?"

His mouth spread into a toothy Matt Damon grin, which would have completely disarmed me if I hadn't known exactly what he was capable of. He held out a hand, palm up. "You must be Lizzie."

"Who are you?"

"Call me Max," he said, his warm hand closing on my arm. "Come with me, and I'll tell you everything."

Other *Love Spell* books by Angie Fox:

**THE ACCIDENTAL DEMON SLAYER**

# CRITICS PRAISE *NEW YORK TIMES* BESTSELLING AUTHOR ANGIE FOX AND *THE ACCIDENTAL DEMON SLAYER*!

"With its sharp, witty writing and unique characters, Angie Fox's contemporary paranormal debut is fabulously fun."

—*Chicago Tribune*

"This rollicking paranormal comedy will appeal to fans of Dakota Cassidy, MaryJanice Davidson, and Tate Hallaway."

—*Booklist*

"A new talent just hit the urban fantasy genre, and she has a genuine gift for creating dangerously hilarious drama. Fox has created her own unique flavor of the supernatural, and it's a weird one!"

—*Romantic Times BOOKreviews*

"Fox's rollicking, paranormal romance is absolutely full of laugh-out-loud humor, heart-pumping action and uniquely quirky characters."

—Romance Junkies

"*The Accidental Demon Slayer* was an unexpected frolic filled with smart-mouthed geriatric witches, a talking terrier, and a drop-dead sexy griffin. I read this book in a day; it was hard to put down. Pick it up for yourself and see."

—Night Owl Romance

"In the uber popular genre of paranormal romance, just about everything has been done before, yet *The Accidental Demon Slayer* keeps it fresh and unique, carving out a place for itself."

—CK2S Kwips and Kritiques

## MORE PRAISE FOR
### *THE ACCIDENTAL DEMON SLAYER*!

"*The Accidental Demon Slayer* is a jackpot read for the paranormal lover. Angie Fox offers up a plethora of hardened yet screwball characters, wild and bizarre situations, spells and danger and powers galore, and let's not forget a simmering pot of sexual tension."

—Once Upon a Romance

"Filled with colorful characters, this is not a Buffy rip off. It's a fun romp with a definite hillbilly twang that will leave you in stitches. If this is the start of a series, readers have a lot of laughter to look forward to."

—Eternal Night

"Oh my, *The Accidental Demon Slayer* is a fun book! Angie Fox's world and adventures had me laughing as the vivid and hilarious scenarios got funnier and funnier."

—Merrimon Book Reviews

"*The Accidental Demon Slayer* is an entertaining ride."

—Romance Reviews Today

"Funny and action-packed with quirky details that make it a very interesting debut...well worth a read."

—The Book Smugglers

# ANGIE FOX

## The Dangerous Book for Demon Slayers

LOVE SPELL  NEW YORK CITY

*To my daughter Madeline, who wants to be a
princess fairy author when she grows up.
I'd like to be one of those, too.*

LOVE SPELL®

May 2009

Published by

Dorchester Publishing Co., Inc.
200 Madison Avenue
New York, NY 10016

ISBN 10: 0-505-52770-7
ISBN 13: 978-0-505-52770-7
E-ISBN: 978-1-4285-0676-3

The name "Love Spell" and its logo are trademarks of
Dorchester Publishing Co., Inc.

Printed in the United States of America.

10 9 8 7 6 5 4 3 2

Visit us on the web at www.dorchesterpub.com.

# ACKNOWLEDGMENTS

This book wouldn't have been half as much fun without Jess Granger, my first reader and great friend.

A big high five to Harley rider Brad Jones, who keeps the Red Skull biker witches on the straight and narrow, and of course to Harley Boy and Cletus, the biker dogs who taught Pirate how to ride. Now if they only hadn't taught him to ride so fast...

Thanks to my brother, Mike Fox, for designing my web site and also to Kit Smith for setting up the *What's Your Biker Witch Name?* online quiz. Without you two, it would be impossible to tell a Mantrap Marcie Steel Butt from a Wino Wally No Brakes. And we all know how important that is.

Thanks also to Leah Hultenschmidt whose support for this series has just been amazing. To Jessica Faust, who pulls off the combo of savvy and nice in a way few people can.

Last but not least, I'm blessed with an amazing husband Jim, who only occasionally uses my early manuscripts as coasters, along with wonderful friends who (mostly) keep me in line: Aileen Crowe Nandi, Ben Terrill, Shirley Damsgaard, Joanna Campbell Slan, Ann Aguirre, Diane Freiermuth, Teresa Bodwell, Kathye Marsh, Matt Bernsen and Scott Granneman. And of course to Sally MacKenzie who is always the first to pop into my e-mail inbox when there is good news to be shared. Thanks, guys.

# THE
# Dangerous
# Book for
# DEMON SLAYERS

# PROLOGUE

I've had more than my share of those dreams where I show up somewhere naked. My high school reunion, my cousin's wedding reception, double-coupon day at the Piggly Wiggly—my goodies are on display. And in every dream, I've dealt with it by pretending I wasn't the only leafless tree in the forest. I'm not sure if it ever fooled anyone, but it got me through.

It's when I'm awake that the real trouble starts. I'm a demon slayer—as of two weeks ago.

Lord help us all.

For me, being a demon slayer is kind of like showing up naked everywhere I go. I have to let it all hang out and do my best with what I've got. Because if I fail, I could get somebody killed . . . or worse. Believe me, I think of that every day.

# CHAPTER ONE

The Hairy Hog biker bar stood on an acre and a half of scrub brush, right off Highway 40. The beer was cold, the pool table fixed and the jukebox jinxed to play two-for-one Lynyrd Skynyrd. Not that we'd been able to enjoy it for long.

We were blowing through Defiance, New Mexico, with my grandma's gang of witches, the Red Skulls, on a somewhat sensitive, definitely secretive rescue. Good thing the biker code didn't leave room for our hosts at the Hairy Hog to be asking a lot of awkward questions.

We'd stopped long enough to buy a few rounds downstairs before bunking in the attic. Well, some of us. I crept back into the bar with the sunrise and saw that the rest of the "Freebird" crowd had opted simply to pass out in their wooden bar chairs and on the stained concrete floor. From the look of it, not to mention the smell, they'd spilled as much booze as they drank.

I fiddled with one of my silver stud earrings like I did every time I was nervous. Just my luck the sleeping beauties weren't going anywhere.

*Jesus, Mary, Joseph and the mule.* I hadn't wanted to do this in front of people, unconscious or not.

"Pardon," I mumbled as I braced one hand on a rust-flecked cigarette machine and eased a black boot up and over the very hairy man who seemed to be using the selection knobs for a pillow. His mouth slacked open and a snore rumbled in his throat. Of course he wouldn't have noticed if I'd tap-danced across his whatnots, but I was raised as a good Southern girl and, well, old habits die hard.

I blew out a breath and smoothed my purple suede skirt. Things would work out. They had to. I didn't even want to think of what could happen otherwise.

Instinct had pulled me out of bed at dawn. I'd dressed quickly and strapped on my weapons. My new demon slayer mojo gave me an insane attraction to trouble. Right now, it was leading me to the long, dark hallway that ended at the kitchen of the Hairy Hog. I cleared my throat against the stale cigarette smoke crowding the narrow space, as if the worst wasn't right around the corner.

My heels struck the floor like gunshots, but there was nothing I could do. Chances were, whatever was in the kitchen knew I was coming.

*Focus.* I touched one hand to the rough wood planks that lined the hallway. The other, I rested on the round, flat switch stars at my belt. They were the demon slayer weapon of choice, and let's just say I didn't go anywhere these days without them.

My heart pounded. I focused my breathing, prepared for the attack. I could see the danger like a dot of light in my mind.

A grinding, screaming machine kicked on. *Demonic robots?* I ran the last three yards, kicked my way past a plastic trash can and threw the kitchen door open.

"Eeeeeya!" I hollered, ready to strike.

Grandma lurched away from the sink, clutching a handful of her *Hairdo by Harley* T-shirt. "Criminy!" she hollered in a rusty Southern twang born from years of Metallica concerts and Jack Daniel's straight from the bottle. "You want me to reach seventy-nine?"

"Stay where you are." Grandma wasn't the type to let herself get ambushed. But there was something very, very wrong in here.

I scanned the small industrial kitchen. An exhaust fan rattled over the stove. Dented pots hung from nails tacked into the wall and an ancient refrigerator huddled in the corner. Crumbs littered the counter, along with empty pretzel bags and a half-collapsed beer-can pyramid. The place reeked of overcooked grease and sour mayonnaise. At least I didn't detect the sulfuric stench of demons. "Cut the disposal," I said.

"Oh for the love of Pete." Grandma shoved her long gray hair out of her eyes and flipped a switch. The metal monstrosity grumbled to a stop.

"Keep back," I ordered. A large pot rumbled on the stove. Perhaps full of imps or other minions of the devil? I stalked the stainless steel vessel of evil.

Grandma threw a skinny yet surprisingly strong arm in front of me. "Don't open that. Those poached eggs have at least another minute left."

"Well geez, Grandma." How could she be worrying about eggs at a time like this? I surveyed the kitchen again. I had to be missing something. The chill along my spine, the fear at the back of my throat, my basic demon slayer instincts had never lied to me before.

"Did you know your left eye is starting to twitch?"

Grandma asked. "You need to chill out. You're tighter than a bull's ass at fly time."

Sure. Relax. If I'd done that last week, Grandma would still be in the second layer of hell. I was the slayer of the group—the only one who could kill demons. I was also insanely attracted to anything that could chop off my head, steal my soul or wipe out North America. And right now, no one seemed to care but me.

I blew out a breath.

Problem was, I was still fine-tuning my supernatural compass. That meant my apocalyptic-danger radar also tended to zone in on poisonous snakes, rabid bats and telemarketers.

And now a dirty kitchen, a pot of poached eggs and—Grandma.

A wave of suspicion swept over me. "What are you up to in here?" Knowing Grandma, it didn't stop at breakfast. She believed in a loosey-goosey fly-by-the-seat-of-your-pants magic. For the longest time, she hadn't had much of a choice. Her coven had spent the last thirty years on the run from a fifth-level demon. They'd gone from borderline hippie to, well, biker.

I'd recently killed the demon who'd chased them all over kingdom come. Still, I supposed old habits died hard. If Grandma thought that meant I'd let her get away with this, she'd been breathing diesel fumes for too long.

Grandma blustered like I was the one driving her crazy.

I ignored her and slid past a can of cooking grease. "What were you grinding in the sink?"

"None of your beeswax," she said, cutting me off with a flick of the disposal on-button. The machine screeched to life.

I kicked my way past a trash can. Grandma blocked me with her butt. Too bad for her stubbornness ran in the family. I thrust a leg past her. She maneuvered her body between me and whatever she had going in the sink.

Her hair tangled over her shoulders and hid her face. "Lizzie, I hate to say it, but scram," she bellowed above the grinding as she shoved an ominous wad of *something* down the disposal.

"Grandma," I warned.

"I'm fixing your problem." She grabbed another wad of yellow from her back pocket and jammed it down the drain. "Thirty seconds and the clanging in your head will be gone."

Why did I get the feeling that was more bad than good? I flicked off the machine. "They have four trash cans in here," I said. All overflowing with beer bottles from the night before. "Why is it so important to mash a wad of—oh help me Rhonda."

The gold seal of the Department of Intramagical Matters (DIM) clung to the top of the soggy, chewed-up mess of paper. I'd only been a demon slayer for two weeks, but I knew you didn't want to tangle with those guys.

I inhaled sharply. "Are those tickets?"

Grandma puffed her hair out of her face and the phoenix tattoo on her arm sagged like the jowls of a bulldog. "Told ya you shouldn't have looked," she said. "Now why don't you mosey along and let me get rid of these for you?"

I about choked. "Those are mine?" I scrambled past her to dig the mangled mess out of the sink. I nicked my fingers on the blades of the disposal, knocked my wrist against the drain. My stomach knotted. "Impossible!" These couldn't be mine. I'd never even had a speeding ticket before. I'd never had a library late fee. I always showed up at least thirty minutes early for my teaching job at Happy Hands Preschool. I did everything right.

Until I became a demon slayer.

Hands shaking, I pried apart the sopping wet charges: *Unlicensed Exorcism,* two counts of *Unsanctioned Demonic Warfare,* at least eleven counts of *Unauthorized and Overt Magical Destruction.*

God bless America.

"Now don't you wish I'd shredded 'em?" Grandma said, flicking part of a ticket from the sleeve of her T-shirt. She coiled a thumb through the silver-studded belt at her waist. "You wouldn't have passed the licensing exam anyway."

"Licensing exam?" I was supposed to have a license? Two weeks ago, I hadn't even known my family was magical, much less come face to face with demons, werewolves and that particularly nasty creature who lived in the back of my demon slayer utility belt. "How am I supposed to pass a licensing exam? You haven't taught me anything."

Most slayers trained their whole lives. I got zip.

"Hey." Grandma brought a finger up. Her silver raccoon ring glinted with the rising dawn. "I'm a big believer in on-the-job training."

"Fan-frickin'-tastic," I said, panic rising, water from the tickets dripping off my elbows. "I'm glad that works for you. But let me ask you one very, very important thing—how is that going to help me?"

Grandma's eyes darted toward the doorway and I followed her gaze just in time to see Dimitri, my strong-as-sin boyfriend, lean up against the doorframe, his large hand wrapped around a steaming mug of coffee. He raised a brow. "Is there a problem in here?" He ran a rough hand through his tousled hair and my body warmed as I remembered exactly how it had gotten that way.

Dimitri couldn't help—not with this. He'd already taught me what he could. Grandma was supposed to be my true mentor, the family member I needed to fulfill my heritage, grow stronger, avoid demon-slaying violations.

She gave Dimitri the stink eye. The man was six feet of raw Mediterranean heat and power. He also happened to be a shape-shifting griffin and—don't ask me why—witches loved griffins. Well, every witch except Grandma. She popped open her claw-shaped pinkie ring.

"We don't have time for this," I told her as a skunk-like scent filled the air.

Naturally, she didn't listen. Grandma dashed a fine yellow powder at Dimitri. "*Superio casuico retractum!*"

Dimitri had the nerve to be amused. He crossed his arms over his chest and challenge shone in his eyes. "Even if it shrank, it'd still be quite formidable."

I didn't want to know. "Can we get back on topic here?" I asked.

"Aw, for the love of . . ." Grandma rushed over to the stove and yanked the lid off the pot. Steam billowed out as she poked at the eggs with a fork. "Dammit. They're overcooked."

"We don't have time for breakfast anyway," Dimitri said. "I've got the witches lining up. Except for about ten stubborn souls, everyone's relatively cognizant. We need to get moving. Lizzie, your dog wants to ride with Crazy Frieda." He must have seen my spirit deflate, because he winked and added, "She's been slipping him beef jerky."

It did make me feel a bit better. Pirate tended to think with his stomach.

My fingers went to the emerald pendant Dimitri had given me. "Why didn't you tell me about the Demon Slayer Licensing Exam?"

"Exam?" He seemed genuinely puzzled. Well of course he didn't know. How could he?

How could I?

Dimitri eliminated the space between us and folded me into his arms. I closed my eyes, letting his warmth wash over me.

"We'll worry about it later," he said, kissing me on the top of the head. "You can't plan everything."

No, but I could sure try.

He gave me a squeeze. "I'm going to unlodge the Defiance road captain from under the pool table so I can thank him for his hospitality. You two, be out in ten."

"Fine," I snapped, suddenly cold and royally annoyed that he had everything under control. As always.

Meanwhile, the all-powerful demon slayer didn't know what she was doing. "How am I supposed to pass this test?"

Grandma brushed past me, dumping the ruined eggs onto a platter, presumably for the bikers who were too hung over to know better.

"You won't pass the test," Grandma said, sliding the platter into the fridge. "Forget about it. We'll head to Vegas. You'll be in and out before they even know you're there."

"I think they know I'm here already." I clutched the sorry-looking tickets until even more water dripped out. "What am I going to do?"

Grandma eyed the garbage disposal.

"Except that," I said.

I didn't have money for a bunch of fines, even if the instructions to pay hadn't been recently pulverized. My eye caught a particularly troublesome line: *All unlicensed demon slaying activity must cease, or . . .* I gulped. "They're going to shoot me on sight?"

Grandma pried a pair of silver-framed reading glasses from the back pocket of her skinny jeans. Rhinestone clusters in the corners twinkled as she peered at the death threat. "Oh, yeah. I forgot about that part. Maybe you do need to get your license."

# CHAPTER TWO

That afternoon, I stood in line at the Greater Nevada Department of Intramagical Procedures (DIP) office, about a half hour outside of Las Vegas. We didn't have time for me to get caught standing in line to fill out forms to get permission to stand in a different line. Then again, I didn't want to get shot, either.

I'd changed into one of my new demon slayer outfits—black leather pants and a sleek lavender corset top. The top was a nod to the purple prairie flower, the symbol of my demon slayer line. Told you I was a planner.

I wiped a smudge of axle grease from my wrist. I didn't know what I was going to do if I didn't pass their exam.

DIP officials had enchanted the office to look like a dry cleaner's from the outside. Inside, I'd immediately gotten flashbacks to my last visit to the DMV. The air smelled like metal folding chairs and industrial cleaner. The entire facility consisted of one room, done in gray, beige and more gray, with a plastic desk that ran along the back. A few magical posters dotted the walls. *Safe Shifting Is Everyone's Responsibility. Don't Jinx Yourself: Alcohol and Witchcraft Do Not Mix.*

A burst of Harleys thundered past, rattling the glass

doors behind me. Leave it to the Red Skulls to be having fun.

I took a deep breath and let it out slowly. If only I'd had time to prepare. I didn't even like to go to Target without a typed list.

A few manuals sagged in a brochure stand. Most of them had to do with basic witchcraft. Nothing for demon slayers. It figured. We were rare. It had taken Dimitri years to find me when he'd needed me. I didn't even know where I'd look for another one of my kind. In a world where everybody tries to stand out and be special, what no one really thinks about is how lonely it can get, especially when the pressure is on.

I focused on deep, even breathing as I clutched my Demonic Licensing Exam paperwork.

"Now that's just wonky," said the round-faced witch behind me. The wooden beads on her dress clacked together, and one of her blonde dreadlocks tickled my neck as she checked out the official forms I'd brought. She huffed like a steam engine. "You think they could have called it the Demonic *Slayer* Licensing Exam." She looked me up and down with a critical eye. "You are one of the good guys, right?"

A doe-eyed woman behind her took a step toward the door and nearly ran into the large, woodsy-looking fellow at the end of the line. Yeah, well with the Red Skulls popping wheelies in the parking lot, she and the mountain man were much safer inside.

"I am most definitely one of the good guys," I said, folding my wad of paperwork and stuffing it into my black leather utility belt. I never hurt anybody, except for a homicidal werewolf and a fifth-level demon, but that was self-defense.

She sized me up before evidently deciding to give me the benefit of the doubt. "I've been here three times for my Express Voodoo License. 'Cause you know folks these days can barely wait to microwave a burrito at the Quick Trip, much less hang around for a full-fledged magical incantation. I would have passed the first time, but I keep getting the old Dragon Lady." She pointed a long, gold fingernail at a five-foot-nothing Vietnamese woman with poufy black hair and wide glasses straight out of the '70s.

The Dragon Lady's plain beige uniform didn't have a wrinkle on it, not even at the matching cloth belt. She stood ramrod stiff and blended with chameleon-like precision into the colorless office. Even the other workers gave her a wide berth.

"Gives me the heebie-jeebies just looking at her," my new friend said, adjusting the gold and red shawl at her shoulders. "Bet she eats steak with a spoon. They say she's been here for thirty years and only passed two people."

"That's ridiculous." I hoped. Because unlike the witch behind me, I couldn't afford to fail. I had to get into Las Vegas yesterday.

It seemed my Uncle Phil, who should have just signed up with eHarmony, had taken up with the wrong woman. And, no, I don't mean a gold digger or the flavor of the week at the Double Trouble Gentleman's Club. He'd fallen for a she-demon. Literally. A succubus, who'd charm a man silly before draining the poor guy of his life force and sometimes even his soul.

I tried to hide a grimace and failed. Succubi were the worst kind of demons because you couldn't see them coming. Supposedly, they looked like beautiful people, right up until the time they drained you. I'd like to think—hope—I'd sense them. But right now, most of what I knew about succubi, I'd learned on Wikipedia.

In fact, most of what I'd learned about the magical world, my powers, everything—I'd learned through the back door. It had better be enough. Uncle Phil couldn't afford to wait for me to master the Practical Demon Slaying Exam.

"See now," the witch said, tapping me on the shoulder. "You want the Yeti." I followed her chubby finger to a portly gentleman with tufts of snow white hair bursting from the vee in his uniform shirt. The same hair curled around the bald spot on his head and peeked out of his shirtsleeves.

I nodded. *Come on, Yeti.*

The bored-looking clerk at the only open window motioned me over. I handed my paperwork to Bradford, a mousy man whose name tag said he was happy to serve me.

*Now or never.*

Without a word or even so much as a glance in my direction, Bradford slapped a thin, pasty hand on top of the stack. "*Veritas probatum,*" he said, like he'd been asked to read the dictionary, "*dedecus impedio.*" The area where his hand touched the paper glowed an orangish green. He sighed. "This would be a lot easier if you wouldn't lie on your application."

My breath caught in my throat. *He was going to flunk me before I even got started.* "Everything in there is *true,*" I insisted. "I did make it to the second level of hell and back."

He lobbed me a patronizing glance as he rifled

through my stack of paper, ripping off the pink "anti-demonic practitioner" copies. "You weigh one-ten?"

I felt the color creep into my cheeks. "I did in high school." After I'd had mono.

He made a notation on the form and handed me my packet. "Step outside the metal door to test area 3A and wait for your examiner."

The metal door opened into a long, narrow yard fenced in with gray cinder blocks. The hot desert sun warmed my face and I could smell the acrid remains of magic in the air. The walls reached at least two stories high and I wondered why they didn't enchant the yard like they had the front of the building. Then again, maybe they had. Unease settled over me. The cinder-block enclosure might not be there to keep random people out, as much as it was to keep creepy things in.

White stenciled markers divided the lot into three distinct sections. I walked through the sand of test area 1A and tried not to think too hard on the small jets of steam erupting like minigeysers. I edged past the dug-out water pit (I wouldn't call it a pool) that was test area 2A and made it to an expanse of black-top pavement with what looked to be ancient runes carved into the surface.

Harleys rumbled on the other side of the wall. I wished I could scale the thing and join them, even if it meant watching Ant Eater ride in that too-tight red leather halter top.

Just to have something—anything to do—I counted my switch stars. Five. The same as there were on the way over here. The same as I had this morning. Five.

I usually carried five, mainly because they fit comfortably on my utility belt. Heaven knew if that was the correct number. I supposed I'd find out.

I was about to check out a trench that ran along the outside wall when something down there growled.

I took three steps back, thought about it, and took two more.

Times like this, I wished for my old life back. I'd kept a tidy condo, a 10:00 P.M. bedtime and a secret stash of Junior Mints for when I felt naughty. My adoptive parents and I tolerated each other from noon to 1:30 P.M. every other Sunday, and I never, ever had to worry about she-demons or things that snarled under the parking lot.

Footsteps rang out behind me. I turned and saw the Dragon Lady.

Oh Sheboygan.

Spending the past seven years as a preschool teacher made it impossible for me to cuss, even in my head. But now would have been a good time to start.

The air itself seemed to heat another ten degrees as the Dragon Lady sauntered straight for me, with absolutely no mercy in her eyes.

She'd better not be a real dragon.

She was short—tiny even. It only made her scarier. She brandished her clipboard knowing she held my magical fate in her hands.

"I am Officer Ly." The wrinkles around her mouth deepened as she scowled. "You are here for the Practical Demon Slaying Exam, Part A, with waivers C, D and E."

I found myself nodding for no particular reason. A

cool wind whipped the hair at my neck, but didn't even seem to touch her.

"Stand away from the targets," she commanded.

I followed her to the back edge of the lot and waited while she wrote something on her clipboard.

Her sharp eyes caught mine. "This exam is for basic slaying only. If you violate this, the Department of Intramagical Procedures will be forced to enact corporal punishment."

As if I didn't know.

She tilted her dyed black head over her clipboard. "Lizzie Brown?"

"Yes."

"Prepare your switch stars."

I nodded. Switch stars reminded me of tricked-out Frisbees. I rested my hand on top of a star. My worn leather utility belt felt cool against my black leather pants. No matter what, the belt seemed to hover at about eighty-five degrees. No one knew why.

The switch star warmed as I slipped two fingers into the delicately carved holes in the center. It was flat and round, about the shape of a small dinner plate. Five blades curled around the edge. They'd been dull. When I touched them, they glowed a light pink.

Officer Ly eyed me like I'd taken too long. "What is the average standard velocity of a switch star as it impacts a target fifty meters away when said target is attacking with thirty-two metric tons of force?"

My heart skipped a beat. "Can you repeat the question?" I asked, swallowing an involuntary squeak.

She did. And it didn't make any more sense the second time around. Nobody told me I needed to know these kinds of things. Grandma's idea of studying magical theory involved a keg of cheap beer and a Ping-Pong table. And Dimitri? He'd been too busy helping me learn how to throw switch stars through the air instead of into the dirt. We hadn't made it to math problems. My hands started to sweat. I had to work to keep a good grip on my switch star.

*Fifty meters was about one hundred sixty-five feet, and who cared how fast something was attacking as long as I could kill it?* I was still trying to do the math in my head when an orange plastic target flew up out of the ground.

"Fire!" the Dragon Lady roared.

I half tripped, half spun and hurled the star fast and strong—straight into the ground ten feet in front of us. Chunks of asphalt spattered across lot 3A and the smaller bits rained down on us. I tried not to wince as a few pebbles of the testing area nestled in the Dragon Lady's stack of black hair.

The officer pursed her lips, plucked a chunk of asphalt out of her hair and started writing on her clipboard.

"Wait." I said. "I'm sorry about that. You caught me off guard."

"A demon will catch you off guard."

True. But it was a completely different mind-set going into a demon attack than it was standing in a blacktop lot next to a growling creature in a ditch while trying to convert feet to meters in my head as the instructor from hell (I should know, I've been there) decided whether to let me into town in time to save my uncle's life.

"Let me try it one more time," I insisted.

Without waiting for an answer, I hurled a switch star for the target. This time, it flew hard and straight, slicing the target straight down the middle. Ha! I practically did a jig as the switch star arced back to me. I caught the razor-sharp disc on my finger and gave it an extra spin.

Dragon Lady wasn't amused. She wrote something down on her chart. "Remove your shoes and climb the ladder."

"Excuse me?"

The Dragon Lady pointed at a rickety ladder at the edge of the lot. I'd barely noticed it because there wasn't much to see. Made of dark wood, with age-blackened joints, the thing belonged in a museum rather than a testing yard. Besides, it stood about fifteen feet tall, which was higher than I wanted to be.

"Go," Officer Ly ordered.

"Sure." I eased off my Harley boots and chanced a look at the wooden ladder. "Why not?" I stuffed my socks inside my boots. I was dating a shape-shifting griffin. He'd taken me flying a lot higher than fifteen feet. Of course, Dimitri would never let me fall.

I gripped the sides of the ladder and planted one bare foot on the bottom rung. The whole contraption wobbled. I ignored it as I climbed another rung, and another.

Dragon Lady reached into her pocket and pulled out a small cloth sack. "Name the Three Truths of the demon slayer."

Okay, I rolled my shoulders and kept climbing. I knew this question. "The truths: *Look to the Outside. Accept the Universe.*" I gripped the ladder tighter as she spread a handful of nails—pointy side up—on the ground underneath my ladder. "*Sacrifice Yourself* and . . . what are you doing?"

"This is the levitation test."

"Wait. Demon slayers can levitate?" My first thought? *Nifty!* Followed swiftly by concern—I'd never done that.

Or maybe I had.

I'd certainly broken a fall in hell. But did the rules of physics apply in the underworld?

*No question they'd apply here.*

"I don't think I can levitate." I mean drift to the ground effortlessly? Balance in thin air? Land amid the nails? I could barely walk in high heels.

I rubbed my lips together. Those nails looked really sharp—rusty too. I didn't even like it when I got my ears pierced. And what business did they have injuring test takers?

"This isn't fair. I'll jump, but no nails."

Didn't they have the magical budget for something better than nails? Not that I wanted to meet any conjured-up nightmares, but nails?

"I conduct this test per Rule 89d of the *Updated and Unabridged 2009 Department of Intramagical Procedures Practical Demon Slaying Exam Manual*," she said, scowling over her glasses. "If you don't complete the test, you will fail."

I pinched the bridge of my nose between my fingers, even as the ladder wobbled. "There's no way for me to get into Las Vegas without getting this license?"

"No."

Not unless I wanted to be shot, which she would no doubt enjoy. I winced as I took another look down at the nails.

Son of a sailor.

I held my breath and stepped up onto the top of the ladder, my toes curling over the edge. Fifteen feet wasn't overly high, but it looked that way from where I stood. I really could break my neck doing this. A slight breeze cooled my ankles as I stared at the nails scattered below. There was no way to land without cracking something or slamming down on at least a dozen nails.

Officer Ly clicked something on her watch. "Go now. Ten seconds."

Wait. I needed to prepare. "Why do you need to time me?"

"Eight seconds."

Oh geez. I had to do this. My uncle needed me. My friends were champing at the bit to get into Vegas. They couldn't face a demon by themselves.

"Five seconds."

I stared down at the parking lot below and the rusty nails ready to slice me to ribbons. Maybe I could levitate. If not, well, I'd land barefoot on the nails and be no good to anybody.

"Three!"

But I wasn't going to be good to anybody if I didn't make it in to Las Vegas. *Sacrifice Yourself.*

I held my breath, said a prayer and jumped.

# CHAPTER THREE

I landed hard. Intense, vibrating pain shot through my heels and up the back of my legs. I stumbled forward and pitched shoulder first onto the pavement, teeth rattling at the impact. *Hell's bells.* I rolled sideways, the whole left side of my body on fire.

What in the world made me think, consider, *dream* I could levitate?

Then again, I never thought I could face down a demon until one had appeared on the back of my toilet bowl.

I cradled my shoulder and let the pain come. In a way, I deserved it. I didn't even like to jump off the high dive and now I suddenly thought I could fly? For most of my thirty years, I'd gone to great lengths to get things right. I studied, I planned—I flossed my teeth twice a day. That's right. I'd never even had a cavity.

Now in the magical world, all I did was screw up. And crash into things. I stretched my legs, numb from this latest impact. If it wasn't for a bunch of powers I had no hope of controlling—much less understanding— I'd have been taken out by the demon I'd met in my bathroom, or that werewolf from Memphis, or heck, twenty seconds ago when I thought I had any business vaulting off a rickety ladder onto a bed of nails.

Gritting my teeth, I eased my head back on the warm asphalt and stared up at the cloudless desert sky. Oh for the days when I didn't feel the need to prove my antigravity capabilities to a tiny Asian woman who may or may not be a dragon.

She frowned down at me, interrupting my view of the heavens. Her oversculpted eyebrows jabbed at me like accusing fingers.

I took a deep breath. It was time to try and salvage this test. Somehow.

"I'm good," I said to the Dragon Lady, not expecting a response. Careful of the nails strewn everywhere, I pulled myself into a sitting position. Hard to believe I'd missed each and every one of them.

The Dragon Lady scribbled on her clipboard. "Outside magic is illegal."

"You think what I just did was magical?" I asked, prying a small rock out of my bloodied left shoulder. Dang, that stung.

New rule: no looking at that shoulder until I could do something about it.

"You fail."

"What?" I braced my hands on the pavement as a new kind of pain punched me in the head. I couldn't fail. I never failed. "Hold up," I said, lurching to my feet, ignoring the way my legs threatened to buckle. "I may not be great at levitation, but I aced that target back there." On the second try, but she didn't say I only had one chance. My heart stuttered. "This is a matter of life or death."

She looked at me as if I suggested she dance naked through the street.

"You fail."

*Fail?*

"That's it? That's all you can say?" It couldn't possibly be over this fast. "Is there anything I can do? Extra credit? Another test?"

She didn't even have the courtesy to respond.

"How long until I can take the test again?"

"One week," she said, handing me a red slip.

"A week? I don't have a week." My uncle was in trouble now. And even if I could learn to levitate in a week, I didn't know if I could pass the rest of the test anyway.

She skewered me with an exacting glare, as if she could pull me apart right there and examine my worth. Yeah, well I didn't amount to much right now if I couldn't even rescue my uncle.

Harleys thundered on the other side of the wall. What was I going to tell the Red Skulls?

Stone-faced, the Dragon Lady eased a long purple rod out of a side pocket in her pants. It had to be two feet long, jagged in spots, smooth in others. "You hold still," she ordered as she came at me with the thing.

Yeah right. I could have run to Cleveland with the excess energy I was trying to hold back.

I forced myself to stay put as she came at me. The rod swirled with a life all its own. My shoulders tensed. I'd wondered where the magic was. Now I regretted wondering.

Whatever she was going to do with that thing was not going to be fun.

She touched it to my ear and I felt a cold energy seep through my head, down through my neck and arms.

"I thought you said the test was over," I said, fighting not to flinch. Sure, she was stone-cold and possibly evil, but I didn't think she'd hurt me. *Probably.* I fisted my hands and forced them to my sides, my fingernails slicing into my palms.

Get a grip.

This had to be standard procedure. If I was getting ready to face a soul-stealing she-demon, I could handle the dragon lady and her oversized stick. She gripped my chin with a chilly, freakishly strong hand. I clenched my teeth as she forced the rod farther into my ear canal.

I never thought anything would make me miss those standardized tests at the DMV. Those stubby pencils and—"Yow!" The rod stung like an icicle. I cringed, trying to ignore the low *thwom, thwom, thwom* of the gadget from hell.

"What is that thing?"

"You stay still."

Easy for her to say. Something gooey trickled into my ear. My right hand eased down to my switch stars, just in case. Of course leveling a switch star at my DIP Examiner wouldn't bode well for my licensing efforts.

Boots crunched up behind me. I tried to turn, but the rod in my ear made it impossible.

I heard a chuckle, which was almost worse than the *thwom, thwom, thwom.*

"Very interesting," said a smooth male voice behind me.

"She failed."

"I saw," he replied. "It was like pitching a semitruck off a cliff."

He moved to where I could see him, a man in his early forties with an overlong face, thick gray hair and a little too much amusement in his eyes. At least he looked human. He wore a standard beige DIP uniform and nodded at me like I should somehow know him. "You avoided a nail pit back there. That takes skill."

"Enough to pass the test?" Maybe this was Dragon Lady's boss. "I need to get my license in order to—"

His grey eyes twinkled. "I know why you're going to Vegas, Miss Brown."

"How?" I stammered.

"That doesn't matter." He dipped a hand into his front pocket and cocked his head sideways. "Officer Ly?"

She drew the rod out of my ear and I found myself rubbing at the spot where it had been.

He handed me a Kleenex. "You're off the charts when it comes to natural ability. I've never seen the divining rod go blue before."

I turned to see the Dragon Lady wiping it down with an alcohol swab. Sure enough, it sparkled with an eerie, ice blue light. And it had shrunk about a foot.

"What good is that going to do me if I can't get my license today?"

The Dragon Lady balanced the rod on her clipboard and began scribbling. "According to your reading on the Augur Rod, you are in fact a demon slayer and therefore entitled to a Demon Slayer's Learner's Permit, to be used in the presence of an instructor as per the Demonic Licensing Code, subset C."

Relief whooshed through me, along with the distinct feeling that I'd somehow regressed back to age fifteen. "So I can go to Vegas on some kind of a supervised program?"

She frowned. "You have an instructor?"

"Yes." Grandma qualified. For the most part. "An excellent instructor," I said, wishing I was right.

"You will wait inside for your permit to be printed, at a cost of twenty dollars, payable by cash, check or credit card."

"Fine." Pride is overrated anyway. At least I could finally do my job.

"You will leave the testing area." The Dragon Lady turned on her heel, and I was about to follow her when the gray-haired man touched my arm, setting off a new wave of pain down my left side.

"With me," the man added. "I'm Senior Officer Reynolds." He delivered a smile designed to reassure, and I felt a warning tickle in the back of my brain. He reminded me of my high school principal, who had a way of making me feel like I'd been scheming, even when the wildest thing I did was play five card stud for pennies during lunch.

Reynolds winked, like he knew what I was thinking, and I decided right then and there I didn't like whatever kind of power he had.

"If you'd like to step into my office, I have a proposal for you."

Of course. Dread slicked through me. Everybody wanted something, although I wondered what Senior Officer Reynolds could possibly want from a demon slayer with a learner's permit.

He led me through the side door of the DIP office and down a hallway behind the main customer area. Traces of magic lingered below the stained yellow ceiling tiles and I could almost sense something above. "This place only has one story, right?"

Officer Reynolds didn't answer. Instead, he motioned

me into a cramped gray room with a small industrial desk and two hard-backed folding chairs. "Have a seat," he said, wedging himself between the desk and a potted plant he'd ambitiously placed between it and the cinder block wall.

I sat, arms over my chest, feeling the tug as a messy scab began to form on my chewed-up left arm.

Officer Reynolds leaned forward, his hands clasped together. "I understand why you're suspicious. Everyone wants something from a demon slayer, right? Well, I promise I won't delay you or put you in any more danger than you're already in."

How comforting.

He ignored my apprehension. "Word is that you're heading into Las Vegas to take out a succubus."

I nodded. "One has her claws in my uncle."

He tented his fingers. "With a learner's permit, you are allowed to attack if provoked—in the presence of your instructor, of course. However, I suggest you lure her out of the city before you attack."

"Why?" Spilling demon blood could disrupt gravity for a few seconds, maybe startle a couple of folks in the immediate vicinity, but quite frankly, that was the least of our problems.

"I'm sure you understand that we've always had a succubi issue in Las Vegas. It's what lends the city its charm, really, that 'devil may care' attitude."

I stared him down, refusing to believe a demon could be charming.

"Nevertheless," he said, straightening in his chair, "it's gotten a bit out of hand. We started with six. At last count, we had thirteen."

Holy Hades. I couldn't clear out that many. Not that he'd asked.

With a start, I realized why he'd suggested I lure my uncle's she-devil out of the city. If the succubi learned of a slayer in Las Vegas, they'd swarm me. I'd have no shot—not against that many. "How'd it get so bad?"

Officer Reynolds cleared his throat. "Time, a lack of options. The Department for Intramagical Welfare has studied the situation extensively and determined it isn't worth the risk. The demons police themselves . . . somewhat," he said, fingering his collar. "Never mind."

These bureaucrats were insane. "You think it's easier to ignore thirteen demons than it is to deal with them?"

His cheeks colored. "I don't make the rules. I follow them. But it is true. I don't know how we'd uproot the demons. To tell you the truth, I'm not sure the American public would want us to. They lend a certain air of unpredictability. What happens in Vegas . . ." He cleared his throat. "Anyhow, I'm certain you're aware of this," he said in a tone that suggested the opposite. "As a demon slayer, you can sense how many are in a single location."

I wasn't following.

"You can get a head count if you will."

"Okay," I said, unwilling to admit that was news to me. Then again, I'd never been in the presence of multiple demons. And of course telling me in advance wouldn't help me to prepare because—let's face it—I had no idea what I was doing.

"We'd prefer that you not contact any of the Greater Nevada Magical Governing Departments while you're in Las Vegas. We'd rather not be involved if things get messy."

"Oh sure." Scary thing was I was used to this kind of thing. *Be a good little demon slayer and help us out while we leave you high and dry.* If I had a switch star for every time . . .

Well, unfortunately, I did.

Reynolds delivered a wan smile. Yeah, he knew what I was thinking.

"We'll send a plainclothes representative to you. One of the fairies."

I have to admit I lit up at that. I'd never known fairies existed, much less met one.

He smoothed his short gray hair. "If you'd be so kind as to tell us how bad the problem has gotten," he said, sliding open the top drawer of his desk, "I'll let you keep this, ahem, guide until your next exam. You can study up," he said as he flipped through the official *DIP Guide to the Demonic Licensing Exam, Volume 3.*

Guide? This was an antique, done in purple mimeo type. I picked it up and flipped through the yellowed pages. "Is this your latest version?" I asked. "There's a diagram of a garter belt switch star holder in here."

Officer Reynolds had the decency to look embarrassed. "The book was printed the last time we had a slayer in town. A pair of them, actually—back in 1936. After that?" He shrugged.

Yeah, yeah. I knew. Everybody wanted a demon slayer—nobody wanted to train one.

I knew there weren't a lot of us out there, but, "Why is there no updated instruction book?" I asked. "How is it you have printed pamphlets out in the lobby for basic witchcraft, exorcism"—Reynolds snorted, but I kept going—"Heck, the library stocks spell books. Ever heard of *Divination for Dummies?* I have. Then there's *Voodoo for Dummies, Druids for Dummies, Alternative Magick for Dummies.* I can learn how to brew up "protective" bath bubbles, but when it comes to saving people from the scourge of hell, I have to wing it?"

He raised a finger. "You don't wing it," he said, the lines on his face deepening. "You listen to your instructor."

If I'd listened to my instructor, I'd be in Vegas right now, probably being ambushed by about a dozen she-demons. We'd almost messed up. Bad.

I was tired of taking chances.

I always had a plan—except when we ran into scary magical creatures that wanted to kill us. No more. I was going to take control. I'd start a diary. No, a guide. I'd seen *The Dangerous Book for Boys* in every store from Mississippi to here. I'd create my own manual. *The Dangerous Book for Demon Slayers.*

In it, I'd record everything I knew (not much) and start filling in the gaps from there. The more I thought about it, the giddier I became. I could study how fast and far switch stars could go. There could be a whole section on magical creatures, forbidden and otherwise. I could make modifications to my utility belt, starting with the critter that lived in the back and liked to chew holes in my nightshirts. I could find other slayers. I knew we were rare, but it was all the more reason to stick together. When we supported each other, demon slayers across the world could fight harder, be more efficient.

*I could control my life and my destiny—one color-coded binder at a time.*

The 1936 handbook would offer a decent start. I flipped through the old book. Sure, I could probably lose the section on demonic jazz clubs and demon activity at the dedication of Boulder Dam. Maybe keep parts on how imps had been trained to drive cars. I hadn't realized they were so smart.

I squinted. Lo and behold. "Are these recipes in the back?"

"Don't let the outmoded wording fool you. There's some good information in there." He hesitated. "I know you're desperate."

"Look, I might not be able to levitate—" and maybe I'd seemed a bit frantic when I thought they were going to refuse to let me into town . . .

His smile was grim. "You're bringing a griffin into Las Vegas. I know you're desperate."

"Never mind how you know about Dimitri," because somebody was certainly a snitch, "but why shouldn't I bring a griffin into Las Vegas?" As far as I could see, my strong, steady boyfriend was my best shot at getting out of there alive.

"Griffins are of the sun, the light. Energy, power flows from them."

He had that right. My body warmed just thinking of Dimitri.

Officer Reynolds leaned across his desk, hands clasped, his expression somber. "Griffins are a succubus's favorite snack."

My heart slammed in my throat.

Dimitri had done it again. Maybe it was a griffin trait. I wanted to understand, but I couldn't help it—it drove me crazy every time he'd run off and try to solve everything himself. It usually involved sacrificing himself for what he perceived to be the good of the group. He had no right to do it, especially when he didn't even have the decency to tell me where he was going.

Reynolds looked at me like he was seeing me for the first time. "Ahh, so you're not bringing a griffin into the city to act as a sort of locator beacon?"

"Stop it," I said. I didn't know what Officer Reynolds was, but enough was enough. "Why would anyone use a person like a locator beacon?" *That's horrible,* I thought. On purpose. To test him.

At least Reynolds had the decency to look embarrassed. "It used to be standard practice. Griffins can even fight succubi, for a while. Surely you know the story about the two griffin clans that defended London back in 932 AD? The ones honored on the London coat of arms?" He shook his head. "Never mind."

"Do griffins know about this? What succubi can do to them?"

"Of course. Griffins avoid them at all costs."

Except my griffin.

Forget the succubi—I was going to kill Dimitri myself.

# CHAPTER FOUR

I stormed out of the DIP office, a Demon Slayer Learner's Permit in my back pocket and fire in my eyes. Dimitri had a lot of nerve to put himself at risk without telling me. Sure, I wanted to help my Uncle Phil, but not at the expense of the man I think I might love. Not that I was in the mood for any romantic confessions. Right now, I'd just as soon chuck Dimitri off the Dragon Lady's ladder as kiss him.

Biker witches jammed the parking lot roasting weenies and burning rubber. Some joker was playing Van Halen's *Runnin' with the Devil* on a boom box. I didn't see Dimitri right away. If we wanted to work together—heck, if we wanted to *be* together, he'd better start leveling with me.

Pirate, my Jack Russell terrier shot out of the crowd like a miniature thunder clap. "Lizzie!"

Ever since I'd grown into my powers as a demon slayer, I could hear my terrier talk—and talk and talk.

Pirate ran smack into my knee, bounced off and jumped up again. "I'm Sidecar Bob's barbeque helper! Want a hotdog? They come in two flavors—raw and cooked."

I scooped him up before he could hurt himself. He wriggled against me as I planted a kiss on the back of his neck. Pirate was the one thing in my life that always made sense.

"Have you seen Dimitri?" I asked, brushing Cheetos dust off his back. Leave it to the witches to feed him junk food. When Pirate wasn't half orange, he was mostly white, with a dollop of brown on his back that wound up his neck and over one eye.

"Dimitri? Sure! Dimitri taught me blackjack! It would have been easier if I could count. Want me to show you? I know you always wanted me to be able to do tricks."

True, although I'd been aiming more along the lines of sit and shake. Maybe a nice roll over that didn't take place within the picketed confines of my adoptive mother's award-winning Daisy Bess rose garden.

"So where's Dimitri?" I asked, scanning the hot parking lot. With the witches so spread out, not to mention the strip mall's regular customers, it was hard to see who went where.

"Ohhh  you mean now," Pirate said, jamming his wet nose into the crook of my elbow. "I don't know where Dimitri is now. I *was* with him, and then Bob opened up a bag of Flamin' Hot Cheetos and after that, things get a little hazy."

"Come on." I ran a hand through Pirate's wiry fur as I pushed my way through the crowd. Dimitri had to be here somewhere, although it would have been nice of him to be there for me half as quickly as my dog.

If possible, the biker witches had multiplied since I'd left. They'd taken over an entire section of the parking lot, lounging around their mini-Weber grills, playing cards and—oh my word—they'd duct-taped their traveling dart board to a metal light pole.

Had I really been inside that long?

"Lizzie!" Grandma waved from her perch on the hood of a silver BMW, her motorcycle boots planted on the front bumper.

She directed her attention back to a blindfolded witch in pink leather pants, currently aiming a dart at a parked highway patrol cruiser.

"Go left! You got it," Grandma hollered. "Fire!"

"Stop!" I called to the blonde witch, known as Crazy Frieda, who was about to take out the fuzz. "Grandma's going to get you arrested!"

Frieda dug a pink fingernail around her blindfold. "Wouldn't be the first time." She blinked her eyes twice, sunlight glittering off her rhinestone-tipped lashes.

"What is this? Las Vegas Bikefest?" I said to Grandma, who looked entirely too amused. I'd bet anything they'd whipped up some kind of cover spell to keep the party going.

She stretched her arms over her head. "What can I say? Life is about catching that magic moment."

Ah, yes. The Van Halen life philosophy. Come to think of it, I didn't really want to know if they'd voodooed the lot or not. "Where's Dimitri?"

"You pass the test?" she countered, sliding off the car and doubling back behind me. "Ah hah!" Grandma plucked the permit from my back pocket and holding it up for everyone to see. "Call Oral Roberts—it's a miracle! Lizzie passed!"

I felt the pink rise to my cheeks.

The Red Skulls let out a series of whoops and cheers. Frieda enveloped me in a hug that smelled like Bengay and cigarettes.

"Aw, now that's nice," Pirate said, wedged in the

middle. Frieda's bracelets dug into my raw left side and I pulled away.

She chomped at her gum, beaming at me. "I'm proud of you, sweetie," she said. "Now excuse me while I kick your grandmama's ass."

"First things first," I said, raising my voice for the benefit of the parking lot crowd. I was starting to worry. "Has anyone seen Dimitri?"

"Kiss him in Vegas," Grandma said to a cascade of whistles and at least one catcall from some smart aleck in the back. She winked at her friends and clapped me on my good shoulder. "Just don't do it in front of me."

A tickle of fear ran up my neck. "What do you mean Vegas?"

He couldn't. He wouldn't.

"Can your pumpkins," she said, accepting a charred hotdog from one of the witches. "Dimitri decided to ride ahead."

Sweet mother. And nobody stopped him? "You let a griffin go into Las Vegas?"

"Sure." She shrugged, taking a bite. "He's a big boy. Besides, he was getting on my last nerve."

Oh great. Grandma, my esteemed instructor, didn't know what a succubus could do to a griffin. I was screwed two ways to Sunday. "Listen," I said, trying to keep Pirate from jumping into her arms. "I talked to a Department of Intramagical Welfare guy in there. He said the she-demons will corrupt Dimitri, suck him dry."

Grandma's eyes widened to saucers.

Frieda gasped. "Maybe that's why he couldn't stand still while you were in there. It was like he had termites in his pants. Couldn't stop looking down the high-way."

This was bad. "He must have sensed them. There are at least thirteen succubi."

"At least?" Grandma scoffed. "Dammit, Lizzie. You'd better count them and make sure."

How did everyone know about that but me?

I dialed Dimitri's cell number, but it went straight to voice mail.

"Round up the Red Skulls," I said. "We're leaving." Maybe we could overtake Dimitri before he reached the city.

Yeah, and bats ride bicycles.

"Not so fast," Grandma said. "We need to get your Uncle Phil first. Dimitri can take care of himself."

I knew Dimitri was good in a fight, but still . . . "He's up against multiple demons."

"Yeah, but he's not the target. Phil is. Besides, if any-body can avoid a demon, it's a Red Skull. Ant Eater!" Grandma called over her shoulder, eyeing me the whole time. A monster truck of a witch with curly gray hair and a red leather halter jogged up. Her gold tooth glinted in the sunlight as she smiled and gave Grandma a mock salute.

Thank goodness Grandma was beyond fun and games. "Ant Eater, I need you and the Red Skulls to catch up with Dimitri. Lizzie and I will take care of Phil."

"Fine," I said, heading for my bike. She was right. Annoying, but right.

"That's what I'm talking about," Pirate said as I buckled him into the glorified baby carrier that served as his bike harness. The black leather contraption looked like it belonged in an old Kiss video, but it worked. Pirate wasn't the only Harley biker dog out there, but he considered himself one of the most stylish.

"You know I was thinking I might learn how to drive," Pirate mused as I dialed Dimitri again. It went to voicemail. Of all the dumb things for him to pull, heading into a mess of succubi had to be at the top of the list. I was mad. I was worried. If they so much as breathed on him . . .

Pirate wriggled in his harness. "Yeeeeeesss!" he hollered as I gunned us out into the open road.

The drab brown of the desert whipped past at speeds that would have made me go pale a month ago.

Doubt crept over me. Who was I kidding? I still didn't know what I was doing. And after the debacle with Dimitri, I wondered how much Grandma knew.

She acted like I'd asked to be a demon slayer. Like I'd chosen it. Okay, well I did have a chance to get rid of my powers and I didn't take it. But still, none of this would have happened if the original Demon Slayer of Dalea, my mom, hadn't foisted her powers off on me. My mom had received detailed instruction from a range of top teachers. I got what we could do on the run—what Grandma remembered.

This whole thing—me being a demon slayer—had been a complete and utter accident. I'd never felt it as keenly as I did today—knowing I was expected to levitate, to know the science of switch stars—heck, to know when I was leading my lover into a trap. Now Dimitri might be in mortal danger. Uncle Phil certainly was, along with the citizens of Las Vegas if we drew a demon attack, and I still didn't know what I was going to do about it.

I glanced at Grandma on the bike behind me and motioned to her that I was taking it up a notch. She'd be thrilled. It took anything over ninety miles per hour to really blow her hair back. I, on the other hand, usually liked to work under the assumption that speed limits were there for a reason. Besides, Pirate tended to throw me off balance when we went full throttle. Pirate had a need for speed. He liked to pretend he was running.

Pirate's tail thumped against my stomach as I hit the gas. "That's what I'm talking about!" he cried. "Let's pop a wheelie!"

"Let's not." I ducked my head around a flailing paw and kicked it up to ninety-five.

Ever since we'd gotten back from hell, I'd been on edge. I didn't know if it was the sheer terror of facing a fifth-level demon or the fact that I'd quietly given up part of my essence to save Dimitri's life. Probably both.

When I cradled Dimitri's bloodied head in my lap, when I made the choice to bring him back, Grandma told me there'd be consequences. Unfortunately, she didn't know what they'd be. At the time, I didn't care. Of course I'd do it all again. Still, I felt like I was walking around waiting for the other shoe to drop.

Maybe I should've told him I saved his life. Then again, that could open up another whole can of worms.

As we stormed toward Vegas, I began to feel the succubi. It started out as a heaviness, like a cascade of worries raining down. I gunned my engine harder.

Oh yes.

I wanted to feel them, needed to see them. The closer I came to Las Vegas and its demons, the more I knew I had to be there. I could almost touch them with my mind. And there weren't the original six devils anymore. Not even the thirteen that DIP Officer Reynolds predicted. Oh no. There were at least two dozen of them.

*Excerpt from* The Dangerous Book for Demon Slayers: *Beware of live spells. They may look cute, but most have minds of their own. Case in point: a two-inch-tall flutter of black and gold named Beanie. His job is to fetch Starbucks coffee for the bikers too embarrassed to be seen in a place without neon beer signs on the walls. They like him. I don't—not after he filled my favorite black leather boots with pumpkin spice latte.*

# CHAPTER FIVE

Uncle Phil lived in a working-class neighborhood about ten minutes south of Las Vegas. Iron gates wrapped around gravel front yards. Mismatched 1970s ranch houses sweltered behind the occasional brittlebush or chokecherry tree.

His modest gray home hunkered under a television antenna that took up half the roof. Statuettes of the Seven Dwarves marched through a rock garden that was more sand than anything else. A woman two doors down ushered her children into the house as we shut down our Harleys.

*Please don't let her know something we don't.*

If we could get Phil out of here—fast—well, I hoped we could avoid trouble.

Pirate inspected the lawn chair on the porch while I rang the doorbell once, twice. I felt Dimitri's teardrop emerald warm against my neck. He'd given it to me because it held protective magic. Too bad Dimitri was the one in need of protection now.

The bronze chain began to hum as it slid down my neck. In a million years, I'd never get used to Dimitri's go-anywhere, do-anything jewelry. In the past, it had turned into a breast plate—right before a witch aimed a loaded rifle at my chest. It had morphed into a bronze collar around my neck, right before a werewolf used it for a handle. And I'd never forget the bronze cap that had kept my head safe from a skull-shattering blow.

I held my breath as the metal slid down my side to form—a bronze butt plate? I felt the heavy metal encasing my hindquarters. Maybe Dimitri's magic was suffering along with him.

*Don't think about it.*

I leaned on the doorbell. "Please be home." We didn't have time to hunt down Uncle Phil.

"Damned lying she-devil," Grandma muttered behind me. "I'll bet she's got her hooks in him right now." She motioned me away from my assault on the doorbell. "Hold your horses, Lizzie. Deep breath." She held her arms out to the side, her silver bracelets clattering. "Now, open yourself up to the universe. Let yourself go. Can you feel her?"

I glanced over Grandma's shoulder at the curtains fluttering in the window of the house next door. She didn't know the half of it. I could sense each demon that had invaded the Las Vegas metro area. All twenty-five of them.

No way I could kill twenty-five.

I blinked hard, tried to focus. "I can feel them. But I don't know which one is her." How could I possibly get a lock on a demon I'd never met? "Please say you can teach me."

Grandma shook her head, her hair tangling around her shoulders. "That's a sense you have to develop on your own. It'll come. In time."

Yeah, well we didn't have time. Phil didn't have time. And Dimitri? I didn't even want to think about it.

At least there were none in the house. I tried to rub the tension from my forehead. I could feel their rage and the absolute darkness they held. Something horrible was going down in Vegas, and there was nothing I could do to stop it. It was steaming toward us like a freight train and the only thing I could do was get Uncle Phil out of the way—if we could find him.

*Focus.* I braced my hand on the door and willed myself to think rationally. If we could get inside, we had a shot at figuring out where Phil went with his demonic floozy. Maybe, just maybe he left his door open. People did all the time down South. I twisted the handle. Unfortunately, we were a long way from Georgia.

"Okay, Grandma?" She had plenty of spells. Maybe one of them could open a lock. "For the love of switch stars, tell me you have something—anything—that can get us in there."

"Sure." Grandma charged out to the rock garden, seized one of the Seven Dwarves and heaved it through the front window. The glass shattered, leaving a Dopey-sized hole.

"What are you doing?" I clutched my head to keep it from spinning. We needed to be smooth, not suicidal. She was going to get us arrested. Property damage, breaking and entering—I'd never even had a speeding ticket.

And who breaks through the front window in broad daylight?

The curtains swayed next door. We had to get out of here. We couldn't do Phil any good from jail.

"Pirate?" Where was my friggin' dog? He'd been sniffing Uncle Phil's daisies not two minutes ago.

"Get your panties out of a wad," Grandma said, digging around in the front pocket of her jeans.

"Oh because you've got this whole thing planned out. Well tell me who's going to save Phil, *and* get Dimitri out of here if we get sent to the pokey!"

"Who calls it a pokey?"

"Grandma!"

A skinny man in a bathrobe burst out of the house next door. His sparse, graying hair sprouted from his comb-over like unruly weeds. His mustache twitched with excitement and—oh lordy—he brandished a rifle. "I'm calling the cops!" he squeaked.

"Oh yeah?" Grandma scoffed. "Then what the hell are you doing out here?" Silver rings flashing in the bright desert sun, she yanked a chain out from under her *Hairdoo by Harley* T-shirt.

She'd brought her pets.

Several Ziploc bags dangled on safety pins from the chain. Inside, living spells hovered, practically falling over themselves as they vied for her attention. They refashioned themselves at will—flattening, lengthening, twirling as the mood saw fit. One spun itself in shimmering corkscrews before mashing flat against Grandma's palm, rubbing at her like a cat.

Grandma tore open a bag and let the spells fly. Globs of goo ricocheted off each other like the Crazy Balls I used to play with as a kid.

They were Mind Wipers. Heaven help us.

"Sic 'em, Gene! Ace, Paul, Peter!" Leave it to

Grandma to name her spells after the original members of Kiss.

"Duck!" I hollered as a pointy black one zipped straight for Grandma's head.

She sidestepped and caught it as it veered past her left ear. "Aw, come on, Gene. I thought I had you trained." She tossed the spell toward the neighbor with the rifle. "Go get 'em, tiger."

The man bolted back inside, his robe gaping to reveal a pasty white chest as he slammed the door. Curtains fluttered up and down the street.

"Geez, Lizzie, don't just stand around with your mouth hanging open," Grandma said, hauling me toward Phil's broken window. "Get in there before the cops come!"

Right. Go ahead, break in. Don't worry about the man with the gun. Or the police who are without a doubt barreling right for us, handcuffs ready. I needed to make sure I was actually inside the crime scene when they arrived. In the meantime, we pin our hopes on Gene, the Mind Wiper, who couldn't seem to tell the difference between Grandma and a rifle-waving crazy with a comb-over.

Cold air streamed out into the dry, desert heat. I reached through the jagged hole and unlocked the window, careful of the glass littering the marble sill. I yanked a couple of cushions off the brown plaid couch in front of the window and, shaking them off as best as I could, laid them over the worst of the glass. My butt would be fine, but I didn't want to catch glass anywhere else.

"Move it, princess!" Grandma hollered as Phil's neighbor got off a shot.

Oh sure. Like I flung myself through broken windows all the time. And why had I thought it was a good idea to wear stiff black leather pants? For Dimitri. And while I was busy looking sexy for him, he'd left me with Grandma and the Mind Wipers.

I planted my rear on the cushion and straddled the window sill, one leg in, one leg out. Broken glass crunched underneath the pillow and where my right foot dug into Phil's couch. I ducked inside, eyes adjusting to the cool, shaded interior of the house when I saw it. My legs went limp.

"Jesus, Mary, Joseph and the mule," I said, staring at the coffee table in front of me.

A mess of picture frames crowded the long wood table. Which wouldn't have been strange, except for a certain person in almost every picture—me.

I was so shocked I almost slid right down onto the glass-covered couch. There was no way Phil could have been there to take pictures of my college graduation, my stint as a molar in *Tommy and the Toothbrush*, the time I'd trashed my dollhouse in the name of science.

Impossible.

Illogical.

The glass crunched under my bronze butt plate as I leaned over as far as I could. There I was at the sixth-grade science fair, powering up my dollhouse with a potato, and was that my old retainer, on his bookshelf, encased in glass? Of all the things I could have expected, this wasn't it.

I braced my hands on the pillow and concentrated on taking long, even breaths. There had to be a logical explanation for this.

Yeah, right.

I'd never even seen Uncle Phil, technically my great-uncle. He was part of the package that came with meeting my real family. And that had only started happening a few weeks ago.

Legs shaking, I scrambled off the couch to inspect a picture of Pirate right after I'd picked him up at the Paws for Love pet adoption event. Phil had been there.

Grandma hadn't known how to find me until I'd grown into my powers. You'd think Phil would have helped out, or heck, introduced himself. In an eerie way, I didn't know whether to be wigged out at the idea of him following me all of these years or to be glad someone, anyone—besides my parents' housekeeper—had actually made it to some of the most important events in my life. My adoptive parents, it seemed, always had a party or a charity function or a tennis match. Unless it was a "see and be seen" kind of event. Then they'd spend the whole time talking to other people.

From the look of it, Phil had been there for everything. And he'd certainly brought plenty of film. But why hadn't he said anything?

More albums crowded two tall bookcases that flanked the entrance to the kitchen. I walked over to take a closer look and—holy moly. He had copies of my diaries. Every journal I'd kept since I'd learned how to write. I pulled one off the shelf.

Pages and pages of badly drawn horses—mine—from the days when I'd wanted to be a jockey. That was before I grew hips. And a butt.

I slammed the book closed.

"Aw, hell." Grandma poked her head through the window behind me, her long gray hair tangling around her shoulders. "I was wondering what took you so long to open the door."

I turned to her, diary in hand. "You're not going to believe this."

"Try me."

I unlocked Phil's door and flung it open. "Uncle Phil is an insane, lunatic stalker."

Grandma didn't look convinced. "Nah. He's just your fairy godfather."

"Fairy what?" I asked, scarcely believing what I'd heard.

"Not *that* kind of fairy."

"Excuse me?" This didn't make any sense.

"You need me to draw you a picture? Uncle Phil is your fairy godfather. You know, a guardian type, a do-gooder, bibbity bobbity boo and shit."

I opened my mouth, then closed it. I didn't know what to think.

A flicker of warmth caught hold of me. I thought I'd been all alone. For years, it was simply me. Then it was me and Pirate. I didn't know anyone else had truly cared.

"I have a fairy godfather," I said, letting it sink in. I was sooo not Cinderella.

A black and silver Mind Wiper buzzed past Grandma's ear and dive-bombed me. I dodged and flicked it back into the front yard. "Out!" I told the wiper. Those things better leave my dog alone. Pirate chased spells like they were fireflies.

Dread tickled the back of my neck. "Where is Pirate?"

She snorted. "Playing rescue dog."

I stared at her incredulously. "You mind-wiped my dog?"

Grandma looked offended. "Of course not," she said. "He ate Peter."

Dang it. Reason #512 why live spells are a bad idea. I scanned Phil's barren front yard for any sign of my dog. When I didn't find any, I squeezed past Grandma and dashed for the back of the house.

"Oh, come on, Lizzie. Pirate's having a ball." Grandma jogged behind me. "My Mind Wipers make you forget everything but who you'd most like to be."

Sure enough, right past the rusty barbeque pit, Pirate had already dug a hole the size of his head. Dirt flew up behind him as he burrowed into Phil's backyard. "Don't worry, Timmy! I'll save you!"

I knew I shouldn't have let him watch *Lassie* on TV Land.

"We're running short on time," I told Grandma.

"I might have hit the old man with a Mind Wiper," she said, kicking the door closed behind her. "It's hard to tell."

I fought the urge to roll my eyes. "Well if you didn't," and if this block had any sort of a neighborhood watch, "the police could be here any time." My stomach dropped at the idea of being handcuffed in the back of a police car, having a mug shot taken, having a record. It would be the end of my dignity, not to mention my teaching career.

Bits of glass crunched under my feet as I stalked through my uncle's cluttered living room. "We have to find something in here that tells us how to find Phil. You take this room." I'd already seen enough. "I'll go back to the kitchen. Then if we don't find anything out front, we can check the bedroom in the back."

I headed straight for Phil's refrigerator and began scanning past the year's worth of pizza coupons, newspaper clippings and, egad, pictures of me plastered all over the door.

"Come on, Phil," I muttered, fingering the mess on the refrigerator and sending a couple of slot-machine magnets clattering to the floor. All we needed was a phone number, a calendar, anything to tell us where he might be.

"You never told me you wrote poetry!" Grandma hollered from the next room. I could hear her clomping around on the hardwood floor, from display to display. Phil had more mementos than my own adoptive parents. Although to be fair, my adoptive mom, Hillary, did have mounted displays of my report cards, until she'd opted to use the antique wood frames for her equestrian certificates.

"Focus," I said, rifling through a stack of lunch receipts and pay stubs from the Hoover Dam. "I can't believe you knew about this."

She'd dragged me halfway across the country without all the facts. If she wanted to have me as a partner, she'd better well start treating me like one.

I stared at the decade's worth of dance recital photos crowding the side of Phil's fridge. My adoptive parents hadn't even made all of those performances. He'd been there for me, even if I hadn't realized it at the time. I just wish I knew how to save him.

My stomach dipped when I saw the jar on top of the refrigerator. Were those my baby teeth?

Couldn't my parents even handle being the tooth fairy?

On the other hand, it explained why my friends had gotten silver dollars and I'd gotten inspirational notes and fairy beans. No wonder my adoptive mom hadn't been pleased when I planted my fairy beans behind her Carolina jasmine arbor. But most of my wishes had come true, except the one about Luke Duke coming to my birthday party. And even as a six-year-old, I knew that was a stretch.

I blew out a breath in frustration. Nothing in this kitchen gave me the barest hint to where Phil had gone. Until I saw the St. Simmions Church calendar tacked up next to the yellow wall phone, and what was scrawled across today's date. "Grandma, he took today and tomorrow off work at the dam." A knot formed in my throat. "For a wedding."

Something shattered in the next room.

No kidding.

"Where?" Grandma demanded.

I raked a hand through my hair. "I don't know." This didn't make any sense.

Grandma burst into the room and began riffling through the calendar herself.

"Do succubi even get married?" I asked.

"No," she said, staring at the entry I'd found. "Never." She looked at me, eyes wild. "Let's see what else we can find."

Grandma hurried back to the front room and I kept at it in the kitchen until there was nowhere else to look. I'd gone through the last of Phil's junk drawers when Grandma appeared in the doorway. "Bad news, Lizzie," she said, holding up a massive Las Vegas Wedding Guide. Post-it notes sprouted from the book.

She tossed the guide onto the kitchen counter with a *thunk*. "Forty-three chapels, every one marked as a possibility. We're screwed."

So he *was* getting married.

*Why?*

I reached for the book. We couldn't possibly check out that many places. Unless—"What are you doing?" She'd begun chanting quietly to herself.

Balancing the book on my knee, I began flipping through the entries. Phil had indeed marked everything from the Little White Wedding Chapel to Cupid's 24-Hour Drive-Thru Weddings. I stared at the pages until I found myself looking right past them. This was bad. In fact, I had a feeling that I couldn't begin to comprehend the awful event that could be taking place at this very moment.

If I knew what I was doing, if I were a better demon slayer, I'd be able to handle this. As it stood, I didn't have a clue.

I heaved the book onto the counter and to reassure myself that something good was happening in the world, pushed aside Phil's kitchen curtains. The kitchen overlooked the backyard and sure enough, I saw lots of flying dirt and a tail. Give him long enough, and Pirate would dig a hole to China.

Grandma clomped up behind me. "I tried to summon Phil's spectral trail."

"What?" I had no idea what that was.

"It'd take a day to explain."

Fine. "Did it work?"

"Not that I can tell."

We headed for Uncle Phil's simple white-walled bachelor bedroom, praying for a break, a hint, a clue as to where he might be. A mattress hunkered in the corner under a mess of green-striped sheets. More picture frames crowded a single dresser. But there was no trace of my uncle.

No clues.

No more rooms.

No way to find him.

I stared at the dust bunnies on the floor.

"Try to look at the positive," Grandma said.

"What's that?"

"I don't know. You're the one who's good at all the pansy-ass shit."

I plopped down onto Phil's bed, elbows on my knees. At least we hadn't been arrested for breaking and entering. Yet.

Grandma started rooting through the mess of pictures on Phil's dresser. "We'll go back to the hotel and channel him."

Oh sure. Why not?

I looked at her sideways. "Channeling scares me."

"Why? Because last time I ended up in hell?"

"Bingo."

The mattress sagged as Grandma sat next to me. "It'll be okay. You'll see. Besides, Phil is worth the risk. He's a hell of a guy."

"So if Uncle Phil's always supposed to be here for me, where is he now?" I was getting pretty miserable pretty fast. Speaking of tough times, "Where was he when we ran into Vald, the fifth-level demon, last week?"

"Oh he's been living it up. When you turned thirty, his job was done."

My heart sank. I'd lost him before I even knew I'd had him. It wasn't fair.

"What'd you want?" Grandma asked. "Demon slayer powers and a fairy godfather too?"

I didn't want anything, except to help out the guy who'd obviously put a lot of time into looking out for me. "Uncle Phil and me, we have to have some kind of a connection, right?"

"Nope." Grandma shook her head. "He's free as a bird."

"And now he's in mortal danger." I scooted off the bed. "Okay," I said, pacing the small room. There had to be a way. "He has to have some ties to me, right?" Or else why all the pictures? The diaries? The shrine to my retainer? If I were him, I would have boxed that nasty thing up the minute the clock struck midnight.

Maybe I could use that. He hadn't been able to let go completely. I had to reach the part of him that still held on, before it was too late. I closed my eyes and wished with all of my might that my fairy godfather would appear. I clenched my fists until sweat pooled in my palms, I focused on my fairy godfather, on my family, on my need to see him *right now*. It had to work.

My bangs fluttered as the air around me hissed.

Grandma chanted off to my left, "*Vis fero tuli latum, vis fero tuli latum*," deep and hard. Whatever she was conjuring, she'd better belt it out with everything she had. We were in a battle for Phil's life and I refused to let him down.

*Come on, Phil.*

I focused, pushed, reached out to the guardian I'd never even met. Hope bubbled through me as I clung to the thought of the one family member who could be there, who was there for me.

*Let me see you, Uncle Phil. Come back. Just this once.*

*Ffffzz-bit!*

I jumped two feet as Phil the fairy landed in front of me in a puff of silver sparkles. At least, I hoped it was Phil. Through the haze of glitter, he reminded me of Andy Rooney, from his bushy eyebrows to his red nose to the way his pointy ears looked like they'd been crammed on as an afterthought. He caught his balance and straightened his sugar-white tux over his round stomach. In his other hand, he held two rings, looped around his pointer finger, as well as a cup from Taco Bell.

"What the . . . ?" He stared at the cup before setting it on a mud-brown dresser. "Must have grabbed on to it when I felt myself going," he muttered to himself. "Never felt anything like it. Helluva tickle."

"Uncle Phil?" I struggled to see him through the glistening embers surrounding him. "Oh my God." Recognition slammed into me. "You were the one who pulled me out of Lake Newman when I was eight." Goose bumps skittered up my arms. It was him. I'd been reliving that moment in my nightmares for the last twenty years. I'd almost drowned.

"Lizzie!" His face lit up when he saw me. He batted his way through a cloud of fairy dust and pulled me into a soft, smothering hug that smelled like cinnamon buns. "At last! How's my girl?" He chuckled, his laugh almost musical, as he took me in like a proud great uncle. "You're even prettier than I remember."

Grandma sniffed. "What? From last month? I hate to interrupt the lovefest, but we have to get out of here," she said, sneaking a glance out the front window.

"Actually"—Phil captured me in a one-armed hug—"we'd better fetch my fiancée. Serena's going to be sopping mad."

Just what we needed—an enraged she-demon.

"Get on over here." Phil dragged Grandma over for a hug, sprinkling her in fairy dust. "You're both invited to the wedding."

Grandma wiped the glitter from the tip of her nose. For a second, I thought she was going to punch her half brother in the gut. "Over my dead body."

A puzzled expression crossed his features.

"Come with us," I said. He'd been mind warped by a she-demon, a succubus. From what I'd seen in the 1936 guide, his brain would be like a scratched-up CD, mostly intact but skipping over key parts. It should be fixable—if we could get him out of here.

"We'll explain everything," I said, dragging him away from Grandma. He was going to be okay. I hoped. "Can your fiancée track you?"

"Well, she has my cell phone number," Phil said, confused.

"Where is she?" Grandma asked.

Phil drew his brows together. "Right where I left her. At the Love Eternal drive-through wedding chapel." Phil's eyes widened. "Holy smokes! I left her at the altar!"

Grandma scowled. "She'll get over it."

"I hope so." He clasped the wedding rings tight. "She has an awful temper."

"About that," I said, trying to broach the subject of she-devils.

"No time," Grandma said, shoving him out the door. I hauled Phil out back to find my rescue dog while Grandma searched for her wandering Mind Wipers. Before we could get too far, I felt the sudden, intense, insane urge to run back into the house and see exactly what was shimmering along the baseboards. I could almost taste the evil.

"Grandma," I called, hustling Phil and Pirate down the driveway. "We have to get out of here. Now."

*Excerpt from* The Dangerous Book for Demon Slayers:
*Some things in life you just take for granted. They might
not make complete sense, but life feels better when you
believe them. Case in point: I never understood why a
lot of hotels don't have a thirteenth floor. It's the twenty-
first century. Surely we're not that superstitious anymore. Well, we're not. It turns out most every hotel does
have a thirteenth floor—it's the way they keep the magical folk away from everyone else. And that can be a very,
very good idea.*

# CHAPTER SIX

"Move, move, move!" I grabbed Phil by the belt loop
of his white tuxedo as he tried to sniff the hibiscus
along the circular drive of the Paradise Hotel. As far as
I was concerned, it had taken too long to get Phil off
the back of Grandma's bike. The sooner we got him
inside, the better.

Wrought-iron railings lined the front entrance and
the balconies of the art deco building. According to
Grandma, this was one of the oldest hotels on The
Strip. It also boasted a magical floor, not that I'd ever
seen one of those. I hoped Dimitri and the Red Skulls
would be waiting for us there.

As curious as I was to see the hexed thirteenth floor
of the Paradise, if we were lucky enough to find our
friends in the lobby, I'd be even happier to skip out of
town.

Pirate nosed the inside of my arm. "You mind letting
me down?" he asked, still dangling from the biker

dog carrier strapped to my chest. "A dog feels better when he's on all fours."

"Hold on, bub," I told him as I took Phil's elbow and squeezed the three of us into the same partition of the hotel's revolving door.

Pirate licked Phil's hand. "Mmm, you taste like pancake syrup. Oh, shoot. You just gave me a craving for the Shoney's breakfast bar."

Phil rubbed his sausagelike fingers over Pirate's head in a smushy pet. "I knew a fairy once who tasted like buttercream frosting."

We made our way past the curtain-draped lobby and into the heart of the Paradise. It reminded me of a tropical explosion.

"Pretty!" Pirate said, with the same awe he reserved for the Three Dog Bakery.

Bold floral wallpaper competed with gold lamé accents and a barrage of bright lights from the overhead signs cramming the walkways. Feathers sprouted from oversized vases and sky blue velvet curtains framed the entrance to a loud, clanging casino that instantly swallowed us whole.

I doubted the biker witches would come back without Dimitri. "You see them?" I asked, scanning the lobby. Luckily, the Red Skulls would be hard to miss.

"No," Grandma said, checking her cell phone. "No word from them, either." She shoved the phone into her back pocket. "Okay. We'll hole up on the thirteenth floor."

Pirate ran his nose along the inside of my arm. "Well as long as we're waiting, I think I might have a snack."

"When we get upstairs," I told him. Heck, I'd even pay minibar prices to get out of this lobby. Danger tickled at the back of my brain. I focused hard on the room around me, opening my demon slayer powers as much as I could. This place made it difficult to instantly spot something odd.

A slight tingling in the air stopped me. Grandma felt it too. I reached for the emerald that had—thankfully—morphed back around my neck. *Of all the times for Dimitri to go off on his own . . .*

Grandma saw my worry. "Dimitri's a big boy, Lizzie. He can handle himself."

"Yeah, well right now, he's screwing everything up."

I didn't want him in town if he was susceptible to the she-demons. I didn't want him trying to risk himself for me or for Phil or for anybody, and I really didn't appreciate him running off like he did. We'd be able to hit the road now if we knew how to find him—or the Red Skulls for that matter. As it stood, we were stuck in a hostile city with twenty-five succubi, not to mention an angry demon fiancée on our trail.

Pirate's tail thumped against my stomach. This probably wasn't the best time to have him attached to me. I unhooked him, and he belly flopped straight into Phil's arms. So much for doggie devotion.

I brought a hand down to my switch stars. The last time I'd faced a member of Satan's unholy army, he nearly killed me. And that was just one demon. Twenty-five would require serious backup. I had nothing but a geriatric biker witch, a disloyal dog and a fairy godfather who smelled like a Cinnabon store.

"Let's get out of here." Grandma beat a path for a row of slot machines decked out to look like rejects from a gypsy caravan. She stopped in front of a particularly gaudy machine, shellacked with glittering purple paint. *Play Forever. Stay Forever,* the sign on top beckoned.

Oh please. I realized we were in Vegas, but nervous energy or not, Grandma should've known we didn't have time for this. I was about to enlighten her when my demon slayer instincts jolted me again.

I glanced around the casino. A huddle of fifty-somethings eyeballed the latest turn of a roulette wheel, while dealers wearing pink bow ties flipped crisp playing cards onto blackjack tables. Slot machine patrons, like lone rangers, manned their stations. I felt uneasy, like I should be seeing something I wasn't.

Whatever this was, it didn't want to kill us, at least not right now. But it felt altogether wrong at the same time.

Grandma lined her hand up with the bejeweled gypsy hand on top of a crystal ball. The slot machine clanged to life, clanking and spinning until its picture wheels rested on two moonstone rings and a black cat.

It spit out two topaz blue cards. The hotel's key cards, I realized, as Grandma handed me one.

"Son of a gun," I said as she shoved the other card into her back pocket. Another good thing to add to *The Dangerous Book for Demon Slayers*—how to check into your basic magical hotel. I didn't understand how anyone could be expected to just know this sort of thing.

"At least while we're waiting, we'll have time to work on Phil," Grandma said.

"What do you mean? Unplug him from the she-demon?"

Grandma nodded.

I didn't even know we could do that.

Well good. I reached out and gave him a comforting rub on the arm. I couldn't help worrying about him. Besides, his close ties to Serena the demon wouldn't exactly enable us to travel incognito.

"Something's not right," Phil said, furrowing his bushy brows together. "Or is it me?"

I was trying to decide on a nice way to put it when I noticed the absence of a certain furry companion. "Where's Pirate?"

"He said you'd be okay with him wandering."

"He lied," I said, annoyed with Phil (and myself) for losing track of my dog.

I spotted Pirate down an aisle of island-themed slots and scooped him up.

"Hey now!" He craned his head back as I beat a hasty retreat with him. "I was only stretching my legs after the long ride over here. I mean, you did strap me into that pet carrier and you know I don't like being strapped down. My fur's smashed and I got bugs up my nose."

"Not now." Something was wrong. I couldn't quite put my finger on it, but I didn't want to stick around the lobby any longer than we had to.

"Elevator's this way," Grandma said, glancing behind us. We followed her toward the row of golden elevator doors.

"We'll be safer once we hit the magical floor," Grandma said, corralling our odd little party into the elevator.

I hoped she was right.

The doors eased together, trapping us as the elevator jerked and began its slow climb.

The presence grew stronger, even as the doors

opened onto our floor. I took a deep breath and stepped out.

A pair of beige wingback chairs flanked a glossy brown table. On top of it lay fancy-looking books that were probably glued down. Sprigs of lavender, dry and lifeless, huddled in a plain glass vase. I didn't feel magic. Only evil.

Phil drew a lavender stem from the vase and tucked it into his jacket pocket, like he didn't have a care in the world.

"Come on, kids." Grandma led us down a seemingly endless hallway. We passed a normal-looking couple and their three (presumably) human children, off to the pool it seemed.

"What are they?" I asked Grandma, but she was several feet ahead of us, and making good time.

"New Yorkers," she called back to me.

"Oh," I said, eyeing the back of the man's shirt. Red curling script read: *Famous Ray's Original Pizza*.

I hoped Grandma knew what we were doing.

"I need to call Serena," Phil murmured, rubbing his ring finger.

"You know she's a succubus," I reminded him gently.

"Nobody's perfect," he said.

"We'll fix that as soon as we hit the room," Grandma said. When she finally stopped, it wasn't in front of one of the cookie-cutter hotel doors lining the endless hallway. She opened the industrial Exit door at the end of the hallway and motioned us into the stairwell.

I wrinkled my nose at the stale, metallic air. "You have a magical card from a slot machine that told you to go to the stairwell?" Maybe this wasn't magic.

Let's see, Grandma was born in 1931. I started counting backwards.

"Cut it, Lizzie," she said, digging the key card out of her back jeans pocket. "This is our entrance."

"The wall?" I stared at the cinder block in front of us. "Are we going through?"

Grandma rolled her eyes. "Sure, Hermione, whatever you say." She slipped her key into the maintenance closet door and shoved it open.

Instead of vacuums, mops and jugs of industrial carpet cleaner, I saw a glittering hallway. "Oh my galoshes." I couldn't take my eyes off the carpet. It shone like a lake on a sunny day. "Can I walk on it?"

"Unless you want to string a rope from the ceiling," Grandma said as she tromped right in. Incredible. I'd never seen anyone walk on water.

"Come on, Lizzie. This entrance is private for a reason."

I stepped onto the liquid floor. It felt solid under my feet, even as I stared down into crystal clear waters. Schools of flat, impossibly bright yellow fish darted among twisting black eels and large puffer fish. Spindly sea urchins clung to coral reefs ablaze with color. I dipped my fingers into the warm water. It looked and felt like a tropical lagoon, but when I lifted my fingers away, they were dry. "This is amazing."

"Yeah, it is pretty," Grandma agreed. "You forget what it's like to see it for the first time."

The door shut behind us, and I felt the wards close in. At last. They were the magical equivalent of covering up in a warm blanket after a long, hard day. I glanced at Phil. Too bad we still had work to do.

Grandma led us down the porcelain white hallway.

The brightness of the place, paired with the reflections from the water, made me wish I had my sunglasses handy. Every few feet, alcoves cut into the wall held bright burning orbs. "Are these for light?" I asked.

Grandma laughed. "Look up, buttercup." A series of ornate chandeliers lit our way. "These balls of fire are Skeeps. A concierge service, if you will. Pluck one from the wall, ask him his name and then ask him to do your bidding. But remember, if you use one, make sure to give him very, very good instructions. You don't want these little suckers filling in the blanks."

I'd remember that.

"Oooh!" Pirate scrambled out of my grasp, his doggie claws scraping my arms. He splashed down onto the carpet and raced into an alcove. "Snacks!" Pirate adored vending machines.

"Hey," he called, "Why are there crickets next to the Cheetos?"

"For the harpies," Grandma answered.

"Let's just find our room," I said. We had bigger things to think about—like recovering Dimitri and fixing Phil.

"Right," Grandma said, two steps ahead of me. She shot me a look over her shoulder. "We'll take care of Phil's, er, problem." I followed her gaze to Phil practicing the wedding march behind us. Grandma shook it off. "She's got hold of him all right. Why she feels the need to marry him? Well, we'll find out soon enough."

"What do you mean by that?" I asked, watching Phil wind two gold rings around his finger and straighten his tuxedo tie. We couldn't possibly know why a demon would want to marry my uncle. And he was in no condition to tell us.

"I have an idea," Grandma said.

Oh no. "Let's keep it simple, okay?" We had enough to worry about with unhooking Phil from the succubus and getting Dimitri back.

Grandma ignored me. "What those demons don't realize is we can use their link to learn a few things."

"But we're going to break him free, right?" I was all for knowledge, but Phil needed his brain unscrambled, the sooner the better.

"We'll disconnect Phil as soon as we see what's got hold of him. Trust me."

"We know what's got him—a succubus in a wedding dress. I don't need to know anything else."

"Yeah, okay, Einstein," Grandma stopped at our door and dug the key card out of her jeans. "I didn't survive all those years against Vald without learning a thing or two." She pointed the key at me like a warning finger. "Information is power in this world, and until we know why a sex demon wants to get all holy at the altar, we're behind the eight ball." Grandma huffed. "I don't want any surprises. Do you?"

Pirate danced and nipped at our heels as we opened the door to a surprisingly ordinary hotel room. Frigid gusts of air roared from a unit under the window, causing the gauzy white curtains to billow and goose bumps to break out all over my skin. Whew, the place reeked of carpet cleaner. Pirate gave a big, wet doggie sneeze that landed on my foot. Lovely. I rubbed my arms against the cold and fought the urge to wrap myself in the well-used hotel comforter.

"Serena's not here," Phil said to the empty room. Quilts in muted green and blue covered the two double beds. A hotel-issue lamp sat on an unremarkable desk.

I dumped my travel bag onto the bed nearest the window and reset the thermostat from an inhuman fifty-eight degrees to a livable seventy-five. The afternoon sun hung low behind the towers of New York New York. It was just dark enough to see the light pouring from the top of the Luxor pyramid.

Phil worried me. He wandered the room, running his hand along the low TV stand, peering into the ice bucket, attempting to straighten the picture of the iris that I didn't have the heart to tell him was probably bolted to the wall. He seemed utterly lost, his forehead crinkling between bushy eyebrows. Finally, he said, "I can't stay here."

"We'll call down and get you your own room in a minute," Grandma said, tossing her backpack onto the bed closest to the door.

He reddened. "Oh, no. I have to find Serena."

"Right," Grandma said, watching me.

"Someone left us a present!" Pirate jammed his nose into the snack basket next to the television.

I dug through my bag and put on an extra shirt. "Is Phil going to be okay?" He was going downhill fast. At least I hoped my uncle didn't routinely sprinkle dust from his pockets while calling for she-demons.

"Don't worry," Grandma said. "He can booty call her until he loses his mind for good. Which he might unless we fix him. But either way, there's no way a succubus can get up here. Too many wards."

"What if she has friends?" I said, thinking about the creepiness downstairs.

"Yeah, let's fix this," Grandma said, rifling through her pack and pulling out a pair of fat crimson candles.

She raked one of the candles against Phil's fingernails, like a cat on a scratching post. My poor uncle merely mumbled as he watched the wax curl from under his nails and fall to the aqua carpet. Whatever hold Serena had on him was affecting his brain. I didn't know how long a person could hold on in those kinds of conditions, but I didn't want to find out.

Grandma spared a glance at Phil, before focusing once again on her task. "Watch and learn," she said to me. "I'm going to open the pathway before we cut him loose." Her voice dropped. "Then you can use that demon slayer mojo of yours to see what's gone wrong in this city." She eyed me from my uncomfortable leather pants to the *Don't Mess with Texas* T-shirt I'd tossed over my lavender bustier. "Look. Don't touch. We only want information."

I nodded, tucking my hair behind my ears. It's not like I could take on every succubus in Vegas.

Grandma dumped the clawed-up candles on the bed and unscrewed the top of the silver eagle ring on her middle finger.

Not possum tongue again. "Is this for Phil's ceremony?" I asked.

A girl could hope.

Grandma dug out a finger full of rust-colored pulp. Maybe she was going to lend her stinky power to the man who had saved my life. And, I realized to my dismay, the man currently enlisting my dog as a ring bearer.

"Hold still," she said, her breath tickling my bangs. She aimed the musky sweet goo for my forehead, hitting me square above the left eye. It felt sticky, wet and it smelled like roadkill. "You need all the help you can get."

"Thanks," I said, my learner's permit burning a hole in my pocket.

"I have to go," Phil said, breathing heavily as he leaned both hands on the windowsill. "She needs me. I need her. I need . . ." He trailed off, confused.

"Don't worry, bro. We're gonna fix it." Grandma tossed a packet of dental floss at my head. Oral-B Superfloss, mint, to be exact. "Give me two long strips, Lizzie."

I knew better than to ask.

Glad to be focused on Phil, instead of worrying about Dimitri, I unwound the floss until it curled at my feet.

"Now where's my Scope? Blasted travel size sinks right to the bottom," she said, digging past her spare jeans. "I hate to be a candy-ass, but sometimes I miss staying in one spot. Back in the day, we blessed a wood cabin in the garden behind the coven house. Ant Eater planted mint, motherwort, sage all around. They're the pit bulls of protective herbs, smell nice too." She whistled through her teeth. "Good times."

Before the coven was betrayed. Before my mom shirked her duty and the witches were forced to run, go biker. I'd never realized Grandma missed her old home. She played the part of the road warrior so well.

I handed the lengths of floss to Grandma. She nodded, stuffing the candles under her arm. She jerked her head toward the bathroom and, past the travel Scope bottle in her mouth, said, "Thwiss way."

She dumped the candles into the bathroom counter and spit the Scope bottle into the sink while I turned on the light. "No," she flicked the lights back off. "We have to do this in total darkness, so you might as well get used to it." She glanced at the door. "It's the best way I know to see what the hell is after him. And us."

Phil peered inside the bathroom, confused.

"Oh good," Grandma said, filching his white bowtie. "Focus object," she said, twirling it around her finger.

"Maybe we'd better get rid of Serena and be done with it." I wasn't a big gambler. Sure, I wanted to learn about what I'd have to face in the supernatural world, but not if it endangered Phil. As far as I was concerned, we needed to free him and get him out of here.

"Patience," Grandma said, easing Phil into the other room before she closed the door on him. She placed the candles on either side of the sink, with the bowtie in the middle. Then she lined the strips of dental floss above the mirror and broke open the Scope. "Mint," she said, sniffing the bottle. "It may not look as pretty as fresh herbs, but it'll work."

"The floss too?"

"This is road warrior magic. We have to use what we've got," Grandma sprinkled the Scope all over the sink, adding a liberal dose around the base of each of the candles. "Mint on the altar is good for protection. It'll help draw the magic too."

I studied the plain hotel sink. So this was our altar.

Grandma tossed me the Oral-B packet. "Why don't you floss up the place while I go find some matches?"

I wrapped the mirror in dental floss. I wound it in long strips over the top third of the hanging glass, letting some dangle like Christmas garland to get more coverage. Then I set to work, draping the sides until I'd used all two hundred yards of the stringy green trim.

Pirate *clickety-clacked* across the tile floor. "Say, that looks pretty, Lizzie! I always said you knew how to decorate."

"Out," Grandma ordered, sliding past him.

"Don't worry. I won't make a peep," Pirate said.

"I'm sorry, baby dog," I said, nudging him out the door. Whatever we were doing in the near-dark with the mint and the candles had to do with Phil's unholy connection to Serena. Once Grandma found out what she could, we'd cut the demon off cold. I wasn't sure how it would go down, but I'd rather not have Pirate anywhere near.

"Hold tight, Phil," Grandma called before she closed us into the pitch-black bathroom.

# CHAPTER SEVEN

I couldn't see a thing. "You forgot to light the candles," I said, hearing my voice take on a slight echoey tone.

"I'm getting to that, Lizzie," Grandma said. "You follow my lead, okay?"

I nodded, as if she could see it in the dark. For all I knew, she could. Grandma might not be the smoothest person around, but she could do things I'd never dreamed about until I met her.

She struck a match and held it in front of her. Our reflections shone like apparitions in the mirror.

"In this looking glass," she intoned, shadows falling into curves of her face, "I see more than there is to be seen."

She dipped the match to light the thick red candle on the right. "I call to the spirits who guide us." The wick caught fire and Grandma blew out her match. I could almost taste the sulfur. She glanced at me and I wondered if she was thinking the same thing.

"I call to the spirits of vision," she said, lighting the second candle from the first.

Her hands warm and strong on my shoulders, Grandma positioned me next to her. Her breath tickled my ear. "Now chant after me. Three times."

I nodded, watching my reflection in the light of the two candles.

"Bloody Mary," Grandma said solemnly.

Oh she had to be kidding. I remembered playing that as a kid. But as I watched her clenched jaw and determined stance in the mirror, I knew this wasn't a joke.

"Bloody Mary," I said, as solemn as she had.

I almost didn't want to know. I watched my nose wrinkle as we said it together.

"Bloody Mary."

The temperature of the room plummeted.

Holy hoo doo. I about fell over sideways when a scarlet liquid streaked down the mirror—from the other side. I couldn't have touched it if I wanted to, which I *absolutely* did not want to. I clenched my hands, my nails digging into my palms as I stared at my reflection through the murky red glaze.

Grandma slapped her sweaty hand around my chilled, shaking one. "Now for the money shot," she said.

"Bloody Mary," we repeated together.

My pulse pounded. The liquid on the mirror beaded and shifted like droplets of mercury until a narrow face appeared. Foul liquid streamed from the wide-set eyes and bubbled from the ugly gash in her neck. I held my breath, repulsed yet terrified to look away. Bloody Mary stared right back at us.

She opened her slash of a mouth. "What do you want?" she demanded in a thick, wet voice as crimson splashed from her lips, splattering the white sink and countertop.

The light from the candles cast deep shadows in

the lines of Grandma's face. "We need to see who controls Phil Whirley."

Bloody Mary faded and we saw Phil's living room. A shrunken, razor-toothed *thing* burst through the front window. A swirling gray cloud encompassed it as it clambered over the glass-strewn couch on black clawed feet. Serena? It had to be.

It smashed straight through the coffee table, heading for the bookshelf. The succubus punched through my retainer case, glass tinkling to the floor as it seized the framed photo behind it. It tore the frame like an envelope and ripped out the picture of my college graduation. It hissed, spittle clinging to its blackened lips. Rubies dangled from its scraggly ears. My picture crumbled into dust in its hands. Oh yeah, the demon knew who had Phil.

Well, too late now. "You lose," I said, bound and determined to make that true.

It whipped its head around, as if I'd walked right into the room. Could it see me? Impossible. Still, I practically felt its scarlet eyes on me. It cackled, low and throaty and the image in the mirror faded away.

That's when everything went to hell.

We heard the hotel door crash open. "What the—?" I searched for the demon in the mirror and found Bloody Mary instead. Terrified for Pirate and Uncle Phil, I scrambled for the doorknob.

"It's locked!" I said, twisting hard, wrenching my wrist.

"Let me see." Grandma barreled past me. She rattled the door with all she had while I watched the face in the mirror. What in the world had she summoned?

"Cookies!" Pirate said. I could hear his delight even through the door.

"Don't eat anything!" I hollered out at him.

"Aw now, Lizzie . . ."

I wanted to claw my way past the door. We should have cut the tie immediately. If we had, this thing wouldn't be in my room, with my dog. Why did I listen to Grandma?

"What's happening?" Grandma barked.

"Now watch it. This is a rental," Phil admonished.

It had to be the succubus.

"Phil!" I screamed.

Grandma pounded on the door. "Open up and fight like a woman!"

No one answered.

"Pirate!" I hollered. My stomach rolled over. If anything happened to him, it would be my fault.

"Phil!" Grandma yelled over me.

"Pirate!" I repeated. The apparition in the mirror chuckled, drops from its slashed neck sizzling down on Grandma's fat red candles. "What do you know?" I demanded, not worrying anymore about something awful happening because our afternoon had gone to hell anyway.

The face disappeared into the mirror, replaced by a vision I could have done without. Gray stone steps led down to a circular room devoid of windows. Heaps of men's rings, wallets and other jewelry choked the small space.

They weren't stealing energy anymore—they were killing people.

Watches were strung up along the wall like war

trophies, their faces smashed in, as if Serena stopped them the moment she murdered their owners. A brunette stood, her back to us, in a cloud of ash. A white minidress clung to her curves and a matching jangle of bracelets ringed her tiny wrist. "Phil, darling!" she called. Serena. I'd bet my last switch star.

*Please don't be there. Please don't be there.*

If I could call him to me, I hoped like anything I could also drive him away from her.

"Sugar lips!" Phil rushed down the gray stone steps. He wore the same white tuxedo I'd seen him in right before we'd corralled ourselves in the bathroom. The dried lavender drooped and fell from his coat pocket.

Son of a witch.

Phil's nose glowed bright red, and he couldn't stop smiling.

Tingles shot down my body. I wasn't sure if they were from shock or from the fact that one of my favorite childhood television stars turned her head and winked through the mirror at me.

"Agent Ninety-Nine!" I stammered. I felt like I'd walked straight into a TV Land rerun. Serena was the spitting image of Maxwell Smart's savvy brunette girlfriend, right down to her kicky 1960s hairdo and her kohl-lined eyes. Never mind that her eyes burned with an unearthly fire and sparks danced across her French manicure. I winced at the rubies dangling from her ears.

She stood next to a positively glowing Phil.

Grandma harrumphed. "He always had a thing for Barbara Feldon."

Serena's white plastic bracelets jangled as he dragged

her to him for a sideways hug, "I missed you, babe."
Phil planted a kiss on his fiancée's cheek.

Serena brushed her breasts against Phil's arm and
nibbled his earlobe. He stiffened and sighed as her nails
dug into his neck, leaving bloody scrapes in their wake.
"Phil, darling, you know you shouldn't have left me."

Phil seemed confused for a moment. He shook it
off, a trace of doubt lingering in the creases on his
forehead. "My goddaughter called. I had to go."

"Not anymore." With a flick of her French-tipped
nails, garlands of black jonquils sprouted from the
four corners of the room. Sickly sweet and unlike any
cemetery flowers I'd ever seen, the slender vines surged
up the walls and across the ceiling. Greasy green leaves
twisted with twinkling red lights, in a sort of macabre
wedding canopy.

A scraggly bone wedged its way out of the apex of
the canopy. I didn't know if it was alive or attached to
something or what. Bits of leathery flesh clung to the
tip as it heaved and hitched itself into place. More dis-
jointed parts snapped and scurried together to form a
grisly chandelier, complete with six bloodred candles.

Flames burst from the candles on the chandelier, ig-
niting stray bits of flesh like spider webs. "Oh that is
disgusting," I murmured.

"Do you like it, darling?" she asked my uncle. "I
made it from the bones of my enemies."

Enough. I wanted to reach through the blood-smeared
mirror and throttle the woman. "That's insane."

"She is the bride," Grandma said, her face lit in the
red glow from the mirror. "If she wants a chandelier
made from the bones of her enemies, well . . ."

I couldn't believe it. "How are you okay with this?"

Her jaw twitched. "I'm not. But I don't see what we can do to stop it."

Yeah, well maybe I did. I'd called Phil once before.

I focused my emotions—scattered as they were. Now was the time to prove to everyone, including myself, I could do this. I concentrated on Phil. Even though I'd barely met the man, I could picture him perfectly. I imagined his heavy-lidded eyes, his laugh, the smell of cinnamon.

*Please work.*

"I need my fairy godfather *now*."

Phil's ears perked. I saw it. At least I thought I did. He gave no other indication he even sensed me. Serena laid a possessive hand on his arm.

Oh no, she'd better not. I tried again, calling up every bit of power I had.

The flames in the candles danced as I focused on my fairy godfather. I watched him with her. Black smoke swirled and a squat-figured man with gray dreadlocks appeared. He wore red, flowing robes and held an ancient book. It was a demon. I knew it without even smelling the sulfur.

Phil took Serena's hands in his and spoke as if he were in a daze. "I take you as my bride. I am yours." He reached for her with the ring, stopping only inches away. I could almost feel him fighting it.

"No!" I yelled, my voice echoing off the tile. "I summon you now!"

Nothing happened.

"Now!" I hollered, heart pounding, head swimming.

Serena jammed her finger into the gold band. So much for free will.

Her beautiful face twisted into a sneer of pure

triumph. "I take you, Phillip Rosewood Clausen Whirley. For eternity." She grabbed his hand and screwed the ring onto his stubby finger.

I felt the energy build. Heard it in the way the bones on the chandelier clacked together. A sulphurous wind blew through the fortress of a room, sending jonquil leaves and petals cascading down.

"Man and wife," Serena grated. I felt the rush of power as she wrapped her fingers around the back of my uncle's head and yanked his mouth onto hers.

The red candles blazed high. "Are you sure this is real?" I asked, not really wanting to know.

"Yep," Grandma said hoarsely.

Serena released Phil's lower lip with a long, lingering suck. She stole energy from him, from the marriage, from her unholy victory. She curved her chin, shoving Phil backward with a finger to his chin.

Her crimson eyes settled on me.

*Holy hellfire, could she see us?*

I could feel her rage, her hate. Triumph burned in her eyes. "Leave us alone, demon slayer," she spat, "and I'll only kill him when I'm finished. Push me and I'll take his soul."

My stomach lurched. "What am I going to do if I can't go after him?" I asked Grandma. I couldn't be responsible for Phil surrendering his soul. Or for what the demons would do with his power, or . . .

Grandma clutched my arm and said something I'd never heard her admit before. "I don't know."

# CHAPTER EIGHT

The candles snuffed themselves, leaving us in a freezing, pitch-black bathroom. It was the least of our problems. In my short time as a demon slayer, I'd dealt with renegade witches, black magic and the wrath of corrupted souls, but nothing had prepared me for a choice between letting my godfather die, or risking his eternal damnation.

Dead if you don't. Damned if you do.

I couldn't let them have him, could I?

Even if I did, I didn't honestly believe the succubi would leave us alone. Something big was going down in Vegas and I had a feeling this was barely a glimpse of the horrors we'd face if we stuck around.

"You ladies ever coming out of there?" Pirate sniffed under the door. "Cause Phil already left."

With that, the door swung open. "Pirate!" I scooped up his impossibly warm little body. At least they didn't get him. "Are you all right?"

"Oh, I'm fine. I was all set to bite the guy in the shiny pants, but he gave me these." He whipped his head toward a bag of half-eaten Doritos on the bed. "And Phil seemed to know him and I felt sorry for him, you know, being a succubus love slave and all." Pirate paused to study me. "Gee, Lizzie, you look stressed. You want to rub my belly?"

I buried my face in the scruff of his neck. "Just give me a second." I couldn't believe things had gone downhill so fast.

"Aw, now that's nice," Pirate said, licking my hand.

"How many were there?" Grandma asked.

Pirate's expression fell. "You know I can't count."

Grandma launched her backpack at the wall. "Dammit!" She stood, fuming. "I would have bet my bike the wards wouldn't let succubi up on this floor," Grandma said. "I forgot they had slaves."

"Great," I growled. I didn't know what the hell I was doing and Grandma forgot.

"We really screwed this up," I said, *we* meaning her.

Here we were, fighting for my uncle, trying to save him the way he saved me; not to mention clearing the way to get out of Vegas before something even worse happened. I'm laying everything on the line and Grandma gets sloppy. Worse, I had no idea how to fix it. I didn't have the knowledge. She did. And it looked like I couldn't always count on her to think things through.

Her eyes narrowed. "You want to tell me something, sport?"

Oh yeah, I did. Lucky for her, we didn't have time to argue.

"They're not just sucking energy. They're killing people," I said. Uncle Phil would be next as soon as they got what they wanted from him.

"How does it work?" I asked Grandma. "We know their power is growing. What we don't know is if that's attracting demons from other places, or,"—I really didn't want to think about this—"if they're using that power to draw more of their numbers straight out of hell."

Could they even do that? It would take a lot of energy. But I couldn't begin to imagine how else their numbers could increase so rapidly.

"I don't know," Grandma said, clearly not wishing to dwell on the topic any more than I did. Well tough. We had to figure this out. I hunkered at the foot of the bed and rubbed Pirate's ears as if that was going to give me any ideas.

"Um, Lizzie," Pirate nosed my wrist. "I don't mean to interrupt your thinking there, but I have some business to attend to as well."

It took me a second to even know he'd spoken. "Say what?" I asked.

"Oh you know what. I spotted a nice grouping of palm trees next to the pool."

I took him to an empty lot behind the hotel. It clung to the very edge of the parking lot, a forgotten smidge of land—big enough for Pirate, but too small to do much else with.

Night had fallen, and Pirate danced in and out of the circles of light from the parking lot. I rolled my shoulders as I double-checked my switch stars.

Pirate sniffed at a tuft of weeds with tiny yellow flowers. "Oooh, now these are nice."

"You mind shaking a leg?" I asked. The menace in the air hadn't let up. If anything, it had gotten worse.

Pirate let out a long, wet snarf. "I'm just appreciating my environment. That's the great thing about being a dog. We know when to stop and sniff the flowers. And the rocks. And the dirt. And the grass. And ooh and here's a lovely crushed-up can of . . . hmm . . . I don't know what that is."

I stared up at the clear night sky. I tried to use the moment to clear my brain, focus my energies. But all I could think about was Dimitri—where he was right now, and why he wasn't here with me. I pulled my phone out of the top front right pocket of my utility belt. I'd begun to text him. Again. When I heard a sandy voice behind me.

"You call those turtle knees? These here are turtle knees."

"Battina?" Grandma's head apothecary specialized in hard-to-find ingredients.

"Who's that?" Battina's head popped up from behind a white PT Cruiser. Red glasses perched on the end of her nose and her ash blonde hair fluttered in the night.

"It's Lizzie," I called.

She plucked her glasses off and let them dangle from a silver chain around her neck. "Oh hey, Lizzie. You mind giving us a hand over here?"

"Pirate," I said to my dog, who stood completely immobile for no particular reason. "You stay here."

"Mmmmm," he said, savoring the air, his nose pulsing like a heartbeat. "Done and done."

I jogged over to Battina and found her huddled over two six-packs of soda bottles and a half dozen empty sun tea jars. She was with Spinebreaker, Jan Elkins, the library witch. Actually Jan preferred to be called the Library Hag. She wore her hair in pink braids today. The witch refused to go gray, and changed her hair color to anything but on a regular basis.

Jan lifted a bottle of chocolate-flavored Jones Soda

out of the case like it was liquid gold. Then I noticed the cork in the top. That wasn't soda.

"What's up?" I asked. "Did you guys find Dimitri?"

Jan dug through the rest of her bottles until she found another one she wanted. "Ant Eater tracked him down," she said, holding up a bottle of Grape. "Phoned it in to your Grandma right before we headed over here."

She handed it over to Battina, who uncorked it.

Phew, my nose burned. "What's in that thing? Lighter fluid?" My heart stuttered when she lit a match.

Wait a second. "You think that's a good idea?" I asked.

Battina chuckled as she tossed a match into the bottle and planted the cork back on top. "It's not really grape soda. We wouldn't ruin a good bottle of Jones. These are pickled turtle's knees. Very good in antidemonic wards. Only you have to toast them." She rattled the bottle. "Like this." A small curl of smoke escaped from the top.

Jan picked up a cork-topped bottle of ginger ale. "And this here is fresh Georgia creek water." She dumped it into a sun tea jar. "Nothing but the best."

"No kidding." I'd never seen these two at work before. "What's in the bottle that says Gravy?"

Jan tucked a lock of pink hair behind her ear. "Oh that actually is gravy soda," she said. "It's a special flavor. They only make it at Thanksgiving, so I stock up." She popped it open and took a long swig. "Mmm . . . gravy-licious. Want to try it?"

"I'll pass. Now what about Dimitri?"

Jan shrugged. "He said he's got things to do and he'll be back tonight."

That's it? Things to do? I'd like to do a few things to him right now—none of which he'd enjoy.

"So . . . what?" I asked. "You let him go?"

Battina took a peek into the turtle knees bottle before dumping out the gloopy black contents—match included—on top of the creek water in the sun tea jar. "What did you want us to do? Sit on a one-hundred-eighty-pound griffin? Actually, Ant Eater tried, but he shifted and flew off."

"Jerk," I muttered.

Battina shrugged. "He's your boyfriend. Now you mind helping us lug these spell jars over to the hotel? We had to toast the turtle knees over here. They're not very stable when you mix them with kerosene. But really, they're for the outside walls of the place."

"Extra protection?" I hoped.

"It sure ain't for the smell." Jan snickered.

Pirate joined us as we spent the next twenty minutes throwing protective wards at the walls of the hotel. They weighed a ton and smelled like the inside of a gas tank. It's a wonder we didn't get arrested.

"How long will these hold?" I asked Battina.

She rubbed her fingers along the wall and sniffed them. "Oh we'll be out here every two or three hours checking. You can't be too careful."

"You want a helper?" Pirate danced in place.

"Why not?" Battina said. "You need to get out of the hotel every once in awhile. Jan and I could use a guard dog."

Jan rubbed him on the head. "You can be in charge of guarding my bottles."

"Hear that, Lizzie? I'm in charge!"

"Thanks," I said. These witches might be rough

around the edges, but every one of them had a good heart. "I owe you one."

Battina studied the wards, and glanced back at Jan's soda-bottle cases of ingredients. "Get us out of here by tomorrow and we're even."

# CHAPTER NINE

We'd barely made it back to the room when a hollow
knock sounded at the door.

Pirate about hurt himself dashing for the door. "It's
company!"

The good kind, I hoped.

I opened the door to a scowling little man who could
have been Danny DeVito's brother. He was shorter
than most, balding, with a round body and hair that
circled his head like a wiry black halo. Glitter tumbled
onto his shoulders like a bad case of dandruff and he
reeked of bubblegum.

He held on to a cheap gray document case with
one hand and flashed a badge with the other. Beige
lettering splashed across the silver emblem— SID FUZ-
ZLEBUMP, DIP INVESTIGATOR. He gave Grandma a once-
over. "You Lizzie Brown?"

She should be the one with the learner's permit. I
spoke up. "I'm Lizzie Brown. And what do you mean

DIP? Are you here about the succubi?" Officer Reynolds had said they'd send someone.

Maybe he knew something. Maybe he'd seen something. Frankly, I didn't know what to make of this strange man with glittery ring-around-the-collar. I braced a hand on my black utility belt, in case we ended up needing a switch star or two.

He scowled at my defensive posture. "I'm with the Department of Intramagical Procedures. I'm the expendable guinea pig, here to see if you got off your precious demon slayer tuchis long enough to get a count of the succubi in Vegas."

Oh great. A bureaucrat. "What do you know about the demon love slaves running around town?"

He had the nerve to look offended. "Lady, what you do on your own time is your business."

Now I really did want to switch-star the little weasel.

I ushered him inside and after a quick look down the eerily vacant hallway, I closed the door. "We have a situation here. Does your department monitor enslaved people? Demonic kidnappings?"

The officer looked at me like I had a screw loose. "You think we want to get close to a demonic kidnapping?"

Of course not. They simply made me get a permit if I wanted to do anything about it.

Officer Fuzzlebump rolled his eyes. "I don't know what you're yammering about, but Officer Reynolds with the DIP office sent me over to get the official demon level. That's it. Kaput. Finito. I need to have my report in by six o' clock on the dot or there won't be anybody around to read it. So what do you say?" he asked, resting his briefcase on the floor and pulling out a stack of powder blue documents as thick as a paperback novel. "I'll need you to sign off on your official number. It's more than thirteen, isn't it?"

I took a deep breath. "Try twenty-five."

His bushy brows shot up, deepening the cascade of wrinkles etched into his forehead. "Hold up," he said, straightening back up, moving slowly from the shock of it. "Are you talking demons—in Vegas?"

"Yes."

He shook his head. "That can't be right."

"Their power is growing. I can feel it," I said, fighting off a shudder. "One just kidnapped my uncle and drank from him, but that's not the worst part. You know they're killing people, don't you? They're taking everything now. What do you imagine they're going to do with all that life energy?"

He glanced at Grandma. "I don't think I want to know."

I could feel the pressure build. "Something is trying to break through as we speak. It's time to call in the troops and deal with it. Now."

"Listen. I see plenty of this town. I drive an airport cab on the side. I also drive a Budweiser truck."

"So?" Grandma interrupted.

The fairy bristled. "So this town is crazier than ever, but it's not twenty-five-demons crazy."

"I didn't set the number," I said. "I'm just telling you what you're dealing with."

"Yeah? Well what if you're wrong?" he demanded.

"What if I'm not?" I might not know how to pass

some of the Dragon Lady's tests, but I knew what I felt in my gut. So far, that had been the one thing keeping me and everybody else alive.

His sweat-slicked forehead betrayed him. "You're scared, aren't you?"

He wouldn't look at me. "Sign here." He handed me a stack of unbound papers and a cheap plastic pen.

I braced the mess on my leg and filled in the official demon count on Form 233A, Form 666Z and, well, I lost track there were so many sheets and attachments. It didn't help that the number of succubi changed halfway through. I jerked the pen across the page. "Twenty-six," I gasped.

The portly fairy tried to clear his throat and choked instead. "Oh, like another demon just popped up from where?"

Grandma gave a low whistle. "Where? Now that's the question. No way she took the bus. Only way they could pop up like that is if they're coming straight from hell."

My stomach belly flopped. I hated when she was right.

I looked Officer Fuzzlebump straight in the eye. "You have to have somebody who deals with this," I said, because I sure couldn't handle that many.

Officer Fuzzlebump didn't look optimistic. "We don't have anybody but you." He scoffed at my dismay. "What? You think demon slayers grow on trees? We didn't even know you existed until you showed up. And I hear you're on a permit . . ."

I felt my face flush. "Exactly."

I'd try to make whatever difference I could, but

right now that meant getting Dimitri and Phil out of here. Not to mention Battina, Jan and the rest of the witches. I had obligations of my own.

He rubbed his chin. "We've got a vigilante running around. A rogue hunter. The guy's half nuts from what I hear."

"But is he a slayer?" We couldn't afford to be picky at this point.

Grandma cleared her throat. "Hunters are a different breed. Right, Sid?"

The DIP officer nodded.

"I've heard of them," Grandma continued, "but I never saw one before. I say keep your distance."

Sid scoured a hand over his forehead, visibly shaken. "The lady's right. This one's dangerous and unlicensed. Ly wants to shoot him, but so far, nobody can catch him."

Dangerous or not, I couldn't help wondering whether this "hunter" could help me with Phil. As far as I could tell, if he was hunting succubi, he was on our side—and doing more than the official magical establishment. He might even be able to tell me more about Serena. I had a feeling she was special.

"How would I find him?" I asked.

The fairy cocked an eyebrow at me.

"What's it matter to you? You've got your number."

He shot me the stink eye. "Suit yourself. His name is Max Devereux, a real dandy boy. He hangs out at the Pure nightclub in Caesar's Palace. You'll know him when you see him."

I nodded, hoping he was right.

Officer Fuzzlebump zipped his briefcase. "All right," he said, backing out of the door. "I'm out of here." He paused, like he was thinking twice about what he was about to say. "Just so you know, I'll keep an eye out on my cab run tonight."

He shrugged, stuffing his badge into his pocket. "Six was okay. Thirteen we could handle. But twenty-five?"

"Twenty-six," I corrected. "The Department of Intramagical Procedures needs to address this."

He gave me a look that suggested it was my fault before he turned and splashed down the hall, scattering schools of fish as he went.

"What are you going to do?" I called after him.

Officer Fuzzlebump cursed under his breath. "You're asking the wrong person, demon slayer," he called back to me. "What are *you* going to do?"

*Excerpt from* The Dangerous Book for Demon Slayers:
*All demons, no matter the breed, seem to be fond of deception. Succubi, however, take the act of deceit to a new level by becoming their target's fantasy. While searching for a new victim, or in their "predatory mode," they are faceless, formless beings similar to department store mannequins. This blank-slate approach doesn't seem to be noticed by nonslayers. As soon as a succubus has her target in sight, she morphs to become her victim's ideal woman and commences the seduction. Succubi prey on both humans and magical beings. Further study seems improbable as I intend to kill the next succubus I see.*

# CHAPTER TEN

I couldn't believe it. Grandma decided to sleep on the issue. Sleep! As if I could even sit still. I refused to think there was nothing we could do about it tonight.

The Red Skulls poured themselves into their rooms shortly before midnight. They'd had the nerve to go gambling and, from the smell of it, drinking again. On the upside, Ant Eater and the gang had trailed a flying griffin for thirty miles down Highway 95. That had to drive Dimitri nuts. On the down side, they lost him somewhere.

He'd told the Red Skulls he had pressing business. "Business?" I asked Pirate for the third time in less than a minute. "What business?"

"Something important enough for him to go flying

down Route 95. Good thing them nonmagical folks can't see that. It'd be pan-de-monium. Like my new word? Pan-de-monium." Pirate circled twice before curling up on the carpet, his chin resting on his paws.

"Lovely," I said.

What kind of business could Dimitri possibly have with a succubus? Much less a whole army of them?

We were making a big mistake. I could feel it. I paced between Dimitri's room and my own a few dozen times. Naturally, he hadn't returned. He wasn't answering his cell phone, and whatever he was doing certainly wasn't worth risking his life. Jerk.

Pirate followed me, two steps behind. Luckily, he'd given up on offering solutions.

My leather bustier itched with sweat, and I wondered for the twentieth time why I even bothered with it since I seemed incapable of wearing it without a T-shirt to make it more modest—or dumpy, depending on your opinion and my mood, which was pretty rotten right now.

When I'd had enough of stomping, I decided to do something a little more constructive. I planted myself at the writing desk by the window.

Forcing down my frustration, I tried to work on *The Dangerous Book for Demon Slayers* with a half-dead hotel pen and a few sheets of Paradise Hotel notepaper, but gave up almost as soon as I started. Number one—I was done half-assing anything. Number two—I was too mad to think straight. I yanked off my *Don't Mess with Texas* T-shirt and hurled it into the corner near the bathroom. Then because, okay, yes it was driving me crazy, I stalked back over, yanked it up and, hands jerking, folded it neatly.

Grandma snorted and rolled in her sleep. She'd taken the bed closest to the door, her face smashed into the down pillow.

Instead of smothering her with it, I ripped open the curtains and stared out at the lights of The Strip.

If I really wanted to think about it—which I didn't—I knew I should have taken charge before this happened. We should have cut Phil's ties to Serena immediately. Then I should have taken Phil with me and gone after Dimitri myself. I'd had my suspicions about the wards protecting this place. I could blame Grandma for making a bad decision, but I hadn't trusted my gut and pushed for anything else. I stood by, like most people do when there's trouble around, thinking Grandma knew what she was doing. But I was a demon slayer now, and, yeah I might be on a permit, but I couldn't afford to hold back.

It wouldn't happen again.

I wound my fingers into the cool leather belt at my waist. Grandma couldn't help. The magical bureaucracy wouldn't help. I had to start trusting myself. It might not make life easier, but then again, I doubted demon slaying was supposed to be a cakewalk.

A voice trilled from the hallway, dragging me out of my thoughts. "Miss Lizzie!" A warm glow shone under the door before a bright orange Skeep wriggled underneath.

He burned like a miniature fireball. "Meko at your service. Forgive the intrusion," the mystical concierge said, hovering under the knob, "but you did tell me to fetch you the minute the griffin in 1302 entered his room."

I nodded, edging past the dead-tired dog curled at

my feet, saying a quick prayer of thanks that Dimitri
made it back okay.

Meko glowed with pride. "I assume it has been a
minute and a half, roughly, since I had to fly down
the hall and summon you."

"Thanks," I said, wondering how to tip an orb.

He tittered and shot back under the door. I stuffed
my key card into the back pocket of my kick-ass
demon-slayer pants and hurried down the hall.

The splish-splash of the water in the hall felt cool
and eerily dry against my naked toes. And even though
it was half past two in the morning, someone had ordered pizza.

I'd barely knocked on Dimitri's door when he
yanked me inside.

"Quickly," he said, closing the door behind him
with the swish of something that sounded like Velcro.
Had he been expecting me? Knowing him, I wouldn't
doubt it.

Thick, dark hair tumbled onto his forehead, setting
off his angled features and giving him a deceptively
GQ look. I knew better. The man was 100 percent
raw power.

I gasped as soon as I got a good look at him. Red
cuts marred the taut olive skin of his chest. "You're
hurt!" He looked pale, almost gaunt, which was impossible considering I'd given the man a thorough inspection the night before and found him in amazing
health. My body warmed at the thought.

Square jaw clenched, he turned from me, but not
before I saw the crimson stains on his jeans. He'd bled
heavily, or someone else had.

"We need to talk." I followed him past the bed. "I

can't believe you ran off like that," I said to the angry purple bruises on his back as he dug through his traveling case. "I was half out of my mind. I didn't know if we'd find you dead or sucked dry or possessed or—" I captured his arm. "Are you even okay? Look at me."

He whipped his head around, and I nearly fell over backward. His eyes burned yellow like a cat's, and the skin around them had turned ashen.

Fear shot through me, and I instinctively yanked my hand away. "What in Hades?"

I saw a flash of something vulnerable in him. Hurt?

Dimitri gripped my wrists. "Let's say succubi have an unpleasant effect on me," he said, his voice strained.

I found myself wanting to break his grip. It's not that his grip was painful. No, it was worse. He made me feel weak. I was powerless to move, powerless to stop what corrupted him. He was in danger because I'd needed to come here and there wasn't a darned thing I could do about it.

My heart sped up as pulled me toward him, slowly—deliberately.

I gasped. "When were you going to tell me?"

The side of his mouth tugged into a wry grin. "I think I just did."

I scraped my hand down the rough stubble on his cheek. His skin felt different, rougher almost. Part of me wanted to drag him out of Vegas and handcuff him to the pool table at the Hairy Hog biker bar. I'd have tried it if it had any shot of working. The other part of me was glad to have him with me however I could.

Power radiated from him, not the warm, steady energy of the sun he usually exuded. Something else entirely had a handle on my noble griffin. Dread settled in my stomach. We had to break him free of the evil that was draining him of his very self.

I dragged my thumb over his lower lip. "We'll get you out of here, babe. Soon."

He smelled like smoke and seasoned leather. Before I knew it, he was kissing me, hard and fast and with everything he had. He kissed me with his entire body, his arms crushing me into him. He moved one hand up to caress the curve of my neck, sending heat searing down my spine.

More. I let him push my head back while his other hand gripped the curve of my butt. He showered me with hot, open, wet kisses while he forced me even tighter against him. His chest, his legs, his thighs—everything felt tight, warm and delicious.

And—my body chilled. Different.

I dragged my mouth away from his. "Wait," I said, refusing to give in as he trailed scorching kisses up my neck. I squeaked as he nipped the tender spot behind my ear. "Stop." I brought my fingers to the spot and my heart quickened when I saw he'd drawn blood.

"I need to know. What's happening to you?"

He dragged the bustier down, exposing my breasts. "Do you like it?" He flicked a tongue across my nipple.

"Yes," I gasped. "I mean, no."

Desire swamped my body to the point where I never felt so free, or exposed. Like I stood on the edge of an immense chasm, teetering on the verge of discovery—if only I had the courage to let go.

Dimitri shot me a wicked grin. Then he took turns with my breasts, licking and sucking them until I thought I was going to melt right there. I tried to push him away, but he was too strong.

I gripped two handfuls of his rich, dark hair as he continued his delicious assault. "We have to get you out of here."

He kissed the tip of my nose, my cheeks, my eyes. "I'm your protector," he said, guiding me backward. My knees hit the bed and we went over, his powerful weight on top of me. His hard gaze rooted me in place.

I couldn't move if I wanted to.

Dimitri claimed to be my protector, but he never actually, officially . . . oh heavens. He slid a hand down the front of my leather pants and found my very core. Pleasure spiraled down my spine. I almost shot off the bed, and he somehow used the opportunity to leave my pants in a pile somewhere. I had no idea what happened to my underwear. He pressed against me as I gripped his shoulders, trying to stop his—yow—roaming mouth from finding mine so I could at least try to have some kind of conversation. This was important.

It was hard to concentrate, impossible to do anything but feel.

I gasped before giving in and tasting the saltiness of his shoulder, his collarbone, the curve of his neck. I braced my forehead against his shoulder. "I don't want you protecting me if it means, if it means . . ."

He shoved hard into me, and I nearly combusted. I felt every inch of him as he moved inside me. God, I'd missed him. I didn't know what I would have done if he hadn't come back.

He took my mouth in a rough kiss, his entire body

pushing me, driving us to a place we'd never been before. I gripped him tight, holding him, reveling in him. With a shout, he drove us both to the edge and over, the pleasure coming in wave after glorious wave.

# CHAPTER ELEVEN

Dimitri rolled over, nestling me in the crook of his arm. His fingers wound through my hair in a way that would have been soothing if things hadn't been so . . . different.

He felt positively toasty under my cheek. I ran a finger along one of the cuts on his chest. It had healed amazingly fast. If I hadn't seen the gash for myself earlier, I never would have believed it. "How?" I asked.

"My people heal quicker than most. It's a gift," he said, trailing his fingers through my hair, "one that I've been especially grateful for since I met you."

"Well look at that, a griffin comedian." I kept it light, knowing that I couldn't order him away from here. No, I had to come up with a better idea.

I shivered and snuggled closer, trying to steal some of his warmth. My body felt like I'd gone skinny dipping with the polar bears. I closed my eyes and invoked the girlfriend privilege, planting my icy feet in the warm spot between his calves. Oh yes . . . his heat seared my frozen toes.

"Dang, Lizzie!" Dimitri yanked back, and I took the opportunity to snuggle in up to my knees.

"Don't even try it." I savored the feel of his legs

wrapped around mine. "I'm on you like an Appalachian tick."

His chest rumbled. "I can see that." He wrapped himself around me in a huge Dimitri blanket.

Ahh . . . good thing he'd surrendered because, frankly, I didn't feel like moving much.

He ran his fingers down my spine. "So is frostbite the price of love these days?"

"Something tells me you've got plenty of heat to spare." I planted a soft kiss above his nipple.

The cuts had healed into a series of angry red slashes. I hated that. For once, I wished for a bit of peace with this man—without soul-sucking demons to battle or creatures trying to tear holes in us.

I traced one down the side of his abdomen and he inhaled sharply. "Now that it's impossible for us to move," I said, trying for some humor before I completely ruined the moment, "tell me. Honestly. What's happening to you?"

No excuses. No kissing and pretending to forget. Something terrible was eating him alive, even as we lay in his bed.

Dimitri didn't move, but I felt his muscles harden.

His voice was rough. "I can handle it."

"Oh really?" I fought a shiver as I dug myself out of his embrace. He looked sinfully raw and downright frightening as he lay in the tangled sheets. This wasn't my powerful yet gentle Dimitri. No. He was turning into something else entirely.

"Level with me, Dimitri. I know something is corrupting you. Now tell me how bad it is."

He brought his eyes to mine, and I almost fell off

the bed when I saw the flecks of red. "Oh heaven, I pushed you further, didn't I?"

H-e-double-hockey-sticks.

The she-demons were feeding off his lust. Mine too.

Goose bumps erupted up and down my body and I had to keep my teeth from chattering. He'd—they'd—stolen my heat, my energy. I'd given it willingly, not realizing the tight hold they had on him. They'd turned him into some kind of a conductor.

I opened my mind and felt them, like a pounding at the door, as they stole from him.

I scrambled for the nearest article of clothing and came up with my black leather pants. I held them in front of me. "You have to get out of this city. Now." I didn't know if it would lessen the hold they had on him. Heck, for all I knew, it was too late for that. But we had to try. I wasn't willing to risk the alternative.

He had the nerve to stare me down. "I'm taking a hit," he said, bringing himself up like a giant cat accepting a challenge. "But it's nothing I can't handle."

God, I was tired. Still, I forced myself to look at his defiant face. "Your eyes are yellow."

He tugged the pants away. I pulled them back, well, at least to my belly button.

Dimitri traced a finger over my stomach, his touch decidedly chilly. "You think I'm going to leave you alone in this city with twenty-five succubi on the loose?"

I resisted the urge to tell him that he had, indeed, left me alone when he took off for Vegas without me. To most women, having a boyfriend help them meant he'd act as a one-man apartment mover, or if she was really lucky, a mechanic. I had to get the guy who'd put his soul on the line.

"How did you know there were so many?" I asked. I hadn't told him.

His eyes trailed down the column of my throat, down to my naked breasts and back up again. "Let's just say I was able to connect with an individual who shares our dislike of demons."

I stiffened. It couldn't be someone from the Department of Intramagical Procedures. "Who?" I asked, crossing my arms over my breasts.

How did he even know where to go?

"There's a hunter," he said, his words cold.

Not Sid's hunter. I rubbed at my arms in a vain attempt to keep them from going numb. "A DIP officer warned us about a rogue hunter. Where did you see him?"

Dimitri didn't answer for a moment. The muscle in his jaw flexed before he said, "He found me. And he'll probably try to find me again. I wasn't able to finish the job."

"You mean you wanted to kill him?" I couldn't believe he'd be that shortsighted.

If there were more of us, we might be able to fix what had gone wrong. At the very least, I'd like to meet the guy. I'd be willing to help if it meant getting Phil back and Dimitri gone from this place.

Dimitri looked like he wanted to punch the headboard. "You don't understand, Lizzie. He's not a slayer like you. He's . . . a *thing*." He ran his hands through his hair. With a shock, I noticed it had begun to gray. "This hunter is more of a creature than a man."

Fine. I rubbed my temples. *Focus*. I couldn't hope to help Dimitri without all the facts. "What is a hunter anyway?"

Dimitri seemed to know I was up to something. Still he answered, reluctantly. "Hunters kill demons, but they aren't born to it, like slayers. They're chosen. And with each kill, they lose a part of their humanity. The one I met tonight is no better than the demons he slaughters."

I found that difficult to believe. Anything or anybody willing to slay a demon got a gold star in my book. "How can you make a blanket statement like that? How do you know that hunters—"

"I've met my share of them, Lizzie." He drank me in like a cat contemplating a particularly tasty snack. "I learned about this one years ago when I was looking for a slayer—you."

Of course. Back when Dimitri would have done anything to kill the demon who'd attacked his family. Now he'd shifted that loyalty to me.

"You attacked him, didn't you?" The old Dimitri would have tried negotiation first. I wasn't so sure about this new man in front of me.

He snarled at the memory. "Actually, he went after me. He seems to think I'm bad for the neighborhood."

The truth of it shocked me to the core. "He knows the succubi are feeding off you."

It drove me nuts that he felt he had to be here—defenseless and alone—for me, when facing the hunter was probably the one thing I could have done right tonight. I was a demon slayer, and curse it all, I might not know the ins and outs of the magical world, or who did what, but I knew how to throw a switch star.

This was another area where I could—and would— take charge.

He eyed me suspiciously.

"Why are you looking at me like that?" I demanded.

Dimitri secured a small, ornate box from the table next to the bed. It reminded me of an antique snuffbox. "Stay away from the hunter," he said, his back to me as he clicked the box open.

He rubbed an ointment along the scratches on his neck, down the angry red slashes on his chest. My throat went dry as I watched his fingers glide lower, over muscle and skin.

I forced myself to look away.

"We lost Phil," I told him.

I explained how we'd had him and how Serena had stolen him back right from under us.

"We need to do something," I told him. "Figure out their plans, even if it means forming an alliance with this hunter."

"No." He shoved the box back onto the dresser. "I know how much you want to act immediately, Lizzie," he said, choosing his words carefully.

He should. Dimitri was the king of barreling off. I'd seen him go after black souls, possessed werewolves, you name it. He brushed back a lock of my hair, and I almost felt like I was speaking to the real Dimitri, except for his possessive grip, and the roughness in his voice.

He rubbed his thumbs over my palms and I detected

some sort of oil. "Did you get this from Battina?" I asked, catching a faint hint of aloe and spice.

"It's an old family recipe. I told you I could handle this," he said, his eyes fading to amber.

They still weren't brown, and I still didn't believe him.

"You need to understand," Dimitri continued, as if he wasn't in mortal danger, "it's suicide to chase a succubus in this city, especially if she's gained an immense amount of power. We wait for them to act."

I wanted to say something snarky, given who was dishing out that particular piece of advice. But deep down, I knew he was right. I wasn't stupid. I was desperate.

Tears welled at the back of my eyes. If we'd focused on freeing Phil this afternoon . . . If we'd acted faster . . . I dropped my head, trying to collect myself.

Now I was about to fail with Dimitri. "I'm going to ask you this once, with everything I have. Please, for the love of . . . us. Leave this city."

Dimitri drew his shoulders back, like an immense Greek wall. "I can't," he said, resigned.

"I don't want to lose you," I pleaded. Surely, he had to see the logic.

He took my hands, warming them. "I can do some things that other griffins can't," he said. "I'm pure-blooded, and from a royal line. That gives me extra strength."

I wanted to believe.

"You do realize I belong to a clan with some standing."

"But I thought your clan died out." I cringed as I said it. Like he needed to be reminded he and his two sisters were all that remained of their family.

"When I realized what we'd be facing here in Vegas, I pledged myself to the Domonis clan in Rhodes. They have numbers, and the power of an old family," he said. "We lend each other our strength."

"Is that what they get from you too?"

"When I have it to give. They also get my loyalty and my bloodline. I've been too busy to start a family of my own." He fingers caressed my arm, leaving goose bumps in their wake. "Now, I'm ready. Well, as soon as we finish here."

I wasn't sure I wanted to talk about the future, not with what was happening in the here and now. "You're being corrupted, Dimitri. I can see it." It was more than the yellow eyes; he'd *fed* off me. When I thought of how pale he'd looked before our lovemaking and how robust he was afterward . . .

Dimitri's fingers found the sensitive nook behind my ear. A trickle of warmth threaded through me and at that moment, I couldn't think of a better place to be than in his arms. He grinned, his eyes crinkling at the corners as he pulled me toward him.

Like a dash of cold water, I realized what I was doing and drew back. Whatever he was using to treat himself seemed to be holding off the succubi for now, but if the she-demons were feeing off his arousal, we didn't need to make it worse.

He watched me, as if he knew. "I don't have much," he said, stretching like a cat against me. "Except my pure griffin blood." His thumbs traced circles along my spine. "But that will be enough."

I let him fold me into his arms. I found an unmolested part of his chest and rested my cheek there as we lay back down. It seemed like he'd generated a measure of strength from my closeness, at least that's what I told myself as he leaned close and nibbled my neck, my earlobe. Mmm . . . I felt myself go limp then delightfully stiff with anticipation as his fingers trailed through my hair, found my scalp and pulled me toward him for a scorchingly perfect kiss.

"This is temporary, Lizzie. I meant it when I said I could handle it."

Bless his loyal streak, I almost believed him . . . if not for the yellow eyes.

"We're going to find a way to retrieve your uncle, and his power," he said like a promise.

I touched the edges of the raw pink wounds slicing across Dimitri's chest. "I wish I knew how," I said. "And why she needed to marry him."

"They seem to need more from him. There's something big going down," he said. "I'll bet your uncle is involved somehow."

I didn't understand how. "My uncle wouldn't cooperate with demons."

"You don't know him," Dimitri reminded me.

He would have to bring that up.

Still, I saw those marriage vows. Phil had been forced. Besides, in a way I couldn't quite explain, I felt like I did know Phil. He'd always been there for me, even if he hovered on the sidelines. He saved my life, but more than that, he'd been a part of it. And I'd make sure he'd keep being a part of it. I'd build my family, one member at a time.

"Listen, Lizzie. Whoever's behind this, they've got the nonmagical world involved too."

Holy Hades.

I wished I had the power to stop all of this. Some demon slayer—I couldn't even stop one demon without being swarmed, much less the multitudes feeding on Dimitri, or the devil that married my uncle. If I didn't figure out something fast, I had a feeling someone I cared about was going to get hurt even worse.

Overwhelmed, I closed my eyes for a moment, and woke to find him gone.

# CHAPTER TWELVE

During my short time in this magical world, I'd learned that first impressions can mean everything. They can buy the respect you need to survive or set you up for a whole lot of hurt. I dressed carefully the night I went to meet the hunter. He might be on his home turf, and he had more experience. But he had no idea what I could do to him.

Neither did I.

I scored a lavender dress in the hotel shop downstairs—shorter, silkier, brassier than anything I'd ever owned. The neckline plunged between my breasts and into a band of glittering silver beads. Some would have gone for red or black, or gothed it up. Sue me, I hadn't quite been able to give up my pastel roots.

The silk skirt lapped at my legs as I walked. I could run too. My low sandals, in glossy silver, crisscrossed my feet like my Adidas Supernova Cushion 6 trainers. I felt amazing. And I looked good too.

Pirate weaved between my legs like a cat, his tags jangling against one another. "Say, you're awfully dressed up. You sure you're going to the vet?"

My demon slayer utility belt felt cool against my hips. "You want to go to the vet with me?" I asked, securing the crystal buckle below my navel. I probably didn't need to lie when an organic doggie food bribe usually did the trick. Still, I didn't want to take any chances tonight.

Pirate sized up the mound of Paw Lickin Chicken Biscuits I'd dumped onto our bed. "You know what? I think I'll stay in for a change."

"Praised be," I said, tamping down a coil of guilt. I hated to leave him alone, but Pirate would only be a liability tonight.

The same went for Dimitri. While he could be downright lethal in a fight, he was compromised. I didn't want to get him any closer to the she-demons. Tonight would be about negotiation. Mission one—make contact with the hunter. Mission two —well, I had a feeling that with all the succubi in town, the hunter might know a way to get Uncle Phil back, body and soul.

And since negotiation required actual talking, it was best I go it alone. Judging from the marks on Dimitri last night, he hadn't exactly sat down for a cup of coffee with the man. The last thing we needed was for the two of them to go at it again. And Grandma? She had the people skills of Genghis Khan.

My hair brushed my shoulders as I gave it a final toss and a coat of finishing spray.

"Pirate, you stay here and don't open the door for anybody, okay?" I hoped no one would bother a twelve-pound Jack Russell terrier.

I kissed my dog good-bye and checked the door locks twice before I headed out.

As if locks would stop them.

The Paradise felt eerily quiet. I'd half expected to see Grandma sending out concierge Skeeps in the hallway or tracking demons down in the lobby, but she was nowhere to be found. In fact, I hadn't seen Grandma all day—or Dimitri.

I took a deep breath as I stepped out into the warm desert night. Groups of tourists, some dressed for the evening, some still in shorts, streamed past. Traffic jammed The Strip, and I could detect a faint trace of sulfur in the air. Something was going down.

Okay. I smoothed my dress. I could handle it. Probably. Times like these, I wished there were more than three Demon Slayer Truths. *Look to the Outside. Accept the Universe. Sacrifice Yourself.* Maybe they should add, *Watch Your Back.* Because, really, that's the only thing I could do until this shadow of a threat decided to reveal itself.

When it did, it was my job to get the hunter on our side.

According to Officer Sid Fuzzlebump, the hunter frequented Pure, a popular night spot at Caesar's Palace. As I walked through the tall glass doors of the club, I caught a flicker of the supernatural. It didn't even try to hide. My breath quickened and my palms began to sweat.

Pure billed itself as "two floors of decadence," which didn't even begin to cover it. Blue and green lights splashed over a backdrop of white, ivory, cream and silver. Toned, expensively perfumed twenty-somethings graced lush, oversized beds and flitted between towering columns and flowing white curtains. A hip-hop mix thumped with a heavy bass dance beat. Bodies bumped and ground against each other, both on and off the dance floor. I opened my mind and let my senses spread like invisible fingers throughout the opulent space.

How far would I be willing to go to get my friends out of Vegas? With any luck, I wouldn't have to find out.

The hunter wasn't obvious among the partyers on the main level and immense terrace above. It didn't mean he wasn't here. As I made my way through the crowd on the main level, two polished businessman-types toasted me while hunkering over a low, candle-strewn table. I straightened my spine and felt my skin flush. I should be offended. I *wanted* to be. But, frankly, I found the attention as flattering as it was shocking. I'd never been the kind of girl to draw stares. Of course, I'd never been to a place like this, either.

I found myself inexplicably lured to the long, curving bar, backlit with frosted white glass. Odd, because I didn't really drink. If anything, I should make a lap of the bar until I found my quarry, or at least determined the best place to hold to the shadows and wait. But something was about to happen here.

Fighting the urge to glance behind me, I squeezed in next to an ordinary looking man wearing a gray dress shirt and cuff links shaped like old-fashioned water faucets. The one near me said, "cold." I'd bet the other side said, "hot." I resisted the urge to compliment him on them. Who knew what constituted flirting? Not me.

Lights from the dance floor echoed off the white and chrome bar—green, white, blue—they pulsed to the beat of the never-ending dance track.

The bartender—who wasn't quite human—rattled a martini shaker, his eyes fixed on a point above the flowing curtains covering the back exit. He topped out at around seven feet, and if I wasn't mistaken,

seemed to be of Hawaiian or Polynesian descent. I
followed his gaze, and when I didn't detect anything
strange, used his distraction as an opportunity to focus on the odd slant of his ears, and was that a five
o'clock shadow . . . on his forehead? I couldn't quite
tell in the dim light of the club. He felt *smoky*, not
demonic. Not exactly friendly, either.

He caught me watching, and I managed a smile.
Eyes narrowing, he *thunked* a Long Island Iced Tea
down in front of the hot/cold man and bypassed me
for a patron at the other end of the bar. Just as well. I
wasn't here to drink.

The party girl on the other side of me squealed at
something her date had said, nudging her bare tanned
back against me. I was about to put some space between us when the man on my other side stiffened.

A pale, bony woman in a shimmering silver gown
trailed her arm across his shoulders and glided into
place on the other side of him. Gauzy hair wisped
about her face and her entire body seemed to glow
around the edges. Her features were as frighteningly
regular as a plastic doll's. Seduction hung heavy in
the air, along with unmistakable, infectious evil.

Succubus. I reached for my switch stars and felt them
warm against my hand. Every instinct I had screamed
at me to bury one in her chest. And I would—if she attacked. Problem was, if I struck, I'd be announcing my
presence to every demon in Vegas. That's the trouble
with slayer powers—they're like a bomb going off.

Add that to the two demons approaching outside,
and one in the parking garage next door. I didn't
want to reveal myself unless I had to.

The man groaned, arching like a cat, as she fed off

the briefest contact. What would she do when she really got going?

*Remember why you're here.*

I'd come to find the hunter, not pick a fight with the she-demons of Vegas. One wrong move in this crowd and we'd have a lot of dead humans as well.

The energy of the room surged, like static before a storm. My nerves tingled and my stomach flip-flopped. Almost as if time stood still, I watched her hand on his shoulder. Only this time, it wasn't plasticky or uniform at all. Yellowed talons hissed and curled from an appendage that was more claw than anything. Tendons and muscles worked under the emaciated skin.

She was a devil who feasted on men. A cunningly masked locust. My throat tightened as I watched the air around her stir and shimmer even more brightly than before. Her pale body flushed with life. Her shapeless silver gown wound into a sleek black minidress, hugging her suddenly voluptuous curves. Thick brown hair tangled down her back, bouncing and curling the way hair always does in commercials but never in real life. Her nose was pert, her lips lush and full as she cast a seductive smile.

The man about choked on his cocktail. "Excuse me for saying," he said, his breath husky, "but you are about the most beautiful woman I've ever seen."

I didn't doubt it. She'd tapped into his mind, rifled through his fantasies.

She threw her head back and laughed. My fingers clambered for my switch stars once more, positively itchy.

I didn't want to give up my identity or what I'd

come here tonight to do. But I wasn't going to let her keep feeding on him, either. Where was the frickin' hunter?

Her perfectly manicured hand lingered on the man's forearm. "I could eat you up," she purred fetchingly.

No doubt she could.

*Hell's bells.* I was the only one around who could stop this. She hadn't given me a second glance, which was ideal really. I'm not that great at hiding my emotions.

I could feel my teeth clench, the rage boiling inside. I hated her and everything she was about. What she wanted to do to the man at the bar, what her kind had done to my uncle. I wanted this one dead.

Before I did something stupid yet supremely satisfying, I felt the hunter. I hadn't even realized how tightly I'd drawn my shoulders until I released them. He was close. I could see him in my mind's eye. He drew me with the kind of magnetic pull that was completely unnatural and at the same time, felt right—like finding a kindred soul.

He approached her from behind, eyes on me the whole time. If it were possible for a man to glow, he did. He radiated power, from the gold of his honey-blond hair down to the ease with which he handled a switch star. He carried himself like a Navy Seal, his angled features betraying a hint of trouble.

He'd be an interesting one to deal with.

And let's just say he didn't look like the type who would screw around. No talk, all action—which was perfectly fine with me. He dug a red switch star from his belt. The blades spun like a chop saw the minute he hooked his fingers into the otherworldly metal.

Without so much as a flicker of emotion, he slammed it into her back.

She blinked, stunned. But she didn't die.

My jaw dropped as the hunter cupped her heart-shaped face and drew her mouth to his.

"Hey, wait—" the man in front of me stammered as the hunter drank from her in an all-consuming kiss.

Without missing a beat, the hunter grabbed a fist full of crisp gray dress shirt and shoved the man away. I couldn't hear what mister hot/cold said next. The crush of conversations and beat of the club music drowned out everything but "asshole," before the world's luckiest man disappeared into the crowd.

But I could hardly take my eyes off the succubus and the hunter. She groaned and thrust herself forward as she willingly gave herself to him. He dug his fingers into her hair and took her deeper, each kiss harder, darker than the last. He embraced her as her beauty faded. Her flowing brown hair thinned until it was once again white and willowy. Her skin shriveled and shrank back from her talons. She sank four long claws into the hunter's shoulder as she moaned into his mouth.

No mistake—he was somehow feeding off *her*.

He kissed her, devoured her, ground her body against his. She issued mews of pleasure, twisting in his arms, coiling against him, willingly giving herself. He used her like a lover, arms around her and driving himself against her. It was the most erotic, disturbing, addictive surrender I'd ever witnessed. My breath quickened and I felt myself go wet. I wanted to be her, even as he consumed her.

Her talons tore into his shirt as she struggled to

pull herself closer to him, to take more, give more. A living, breathing, skeleton of a *thing,* she gave him everything she had. And still he kept taking, until there was almost nothing left.

A wisp of the creature she'd once been, the succubus clung to her executioner, barely more than a living shell. She pressed closer, still desiring him. And then, with a long echoing groan and a gasp, she collapsed upon herself, her body crumbling into a fine powder.

Only then did he release her, her ashes flittering away on an invisible breeze as a papery thin black dress pooled on the floor. She was dead. And he was . . . a monster.

Shocked, I raised my eyes to find the hunter watching me.

Moisture glistened on his lower lip, making his hard features arrestingly sensual. His amber eyes held an almost dazed quality, one of indulgence and—if I read him right—satisfaction.

And the demons outside didn't move. *They didn't know.*

He dipped his head slightly, in a courtly gesture of greeting and leaned uncomfortably close. My fingers trembled against my switch stars as the beat of the music anchored me to the here and now. I breathed in the light, spicy scent of him, mixed with the sulfur of the demon.

"I wasn't expecting one so early," he said, his voice husky from the kiss. "Thanks for distracting her."

Early? I drew back. It was nearing midnight. And as far as what he'd done . . . "What are you?"

His mouth spread into a toothy Matt Damon grin,

which would have completely disarmed me if I hadn't known exactly what he was capable of. He held out a hand, palm up. "You must be Lizzie."

"Who are you?"

"Call me Max," he said, his warm hand closing on my arm. "Come with me, and I'll tell you everything."

A tempting offer, if I had any reason to trust him. My demon slayer essence seemed to recognize him on a certain, uncomfortable level. The part of me that had itched for a fight realized he was on my side. Still, something about him wasn't entirely right. And even after that display, I still didn't know everything a hunter could do. He hadn't exactly been friendly with Dimitri last night.

"Actually," I said, careful to maintain eye contact. "I have a few questions first."

The man had some explaining to do. He'd just drunk a succubus like a milk shake.

He tilted his head, sizing me up. "Either way, I suggest we leave immediately."

"More succubi?" I asked.

"There's that," he said, indicating over my left shoulder, "And it seems you've brought trouble with you."

I turned to see Grandma arguing with Ant Eater near the entrance.

God bless America.

The last thing we needed would be for Grandma or the Red Skulls to get hurt.

"Come with me," he insisted, wrapping his arm around my shoulders as he drew me through the crowd toward the back, muscles taut, every bit the soldier under his tailored blue club shirt.

"Yeah right." I barely went *to* bars, much less left bars with strange men.

"We're kindred souls, Lizzie. Don't bother denying it."

I could and I would. We might both kill demons, but the similarities ended there. I caught a glimpse of his chest through one of the rips the succubus had torn in his shirt. Eerie white scratches laced his body, glowing faintly in the darkened club.

Impossible. That creature would have ripped me to pieces.

His lips curled into a sideways, entirely too intimate, smile. "You can strip-search me if it makes you feel better."

Somehow, I thought that could be just as lethal as his kiss of death.

The man could literally consume minions of the devil. It didn't mean he was on my team, but it didn't give him a reason to kill me, either.

I took stock of him. The small bend on the bridge of his nose, the hard set to his jaw, the way his hair curled slightly from the heat of the club. There was an old demon slayer truth, *Accept the Universe.* Right now, it seemed the universe was directing me outside with this enigma of a hunter.

I offered him a handshake, ignoring the way his chest rumbled against my back. He could be amused all he wanted.

The hunter took my hand with unexpected, yet soothing force. "Lizzie Brown," I said, introducing myself.

"Max Devereux." He didn't bother to hide his satisfaction, or his interest.

"You want me?" I asked him. The games ended here.

His arm tightened slightly against my shoulders. "Yes." He said, his amber eyes bordering on predatory.

"You won't get me if you don't play one hundred percent straight from now on. And you might not even get me then."

He barked out a surprised, delighted laugh. "We'll see about that."

On the way out to his car, I sent a quick text to Grandma. *Met the hunter. Name is Max. Back soon.* She'd thwomp me for leaving with him, but I had to trust my gut. Besides, I'd been in worse places than the front seat of Max's black Mercedes.

I only hoped Dimitri would understand. I didn't have a boatload of experience with men, but the ones I'd dated hadn't been nearly as cool and unemotional as they liked to believe. Dimitri had to know I was doing this for him, for us. As soon as his ears stopped smoking, he would.

Max slid into the driver's seat, pulling the door closed with a silencing *ka-chunk*. I breathed in leather and spice and suddenly Max seemed much larger than he had before. He turned the key on a premium smooth-riding engine, light years away from the heart-pounding motorcycles I'd grown to appreciate. Despite myself, I longed for my fierce, kick-butt griffin boyfriend.

"Why did you attack Dimitri?" I asked as Max braced an arm on the seat behind me and pulled out.

The leather rumbled as his fingers tightened. "Is he your lover?"

"That's none of your business," I snapped.

"Because if he is, you've got a problem," he said, cold creeping into his voice.

Max's warning hung in the air as he pulled out of the garage and into the teeming traffic on The Strip. I wasn't about to start questioning this hunter about my boyfriend. He could either elaborate or not. I wasn't going to beg.

He kept his eyes on the road, the lights of The Strip flicked over his face. Finally, he said, "Dimitri Kallinikos claims to be a griffin, noble no less. But he's not."

"What?" I asked, not entirely understanding.

Max shot a long look out of the corner of his eye, sizing me up. "Dimitri is *not* entirely griffin. He has some slayer in him. Of course, he denies it."

My body froze into a thick, heavy lump of dread right there in the passenger's seat.

Hadn't I known there'd be consequences?

I mashed my head back against the seat. I'd tried not to think about it since it had happened. Cripes, it had only been a week, but I couldn't get the sight of Dimitri's blood on my hands, or the gaping hole in his chest out of my mind. He fought so hard for me. I couldn't let him die. I did what I had to do.

"How do you know he has slayer?" I asked.

My only other witness had been Grandma. She'd knelt beside me when I used part of my essence to save Dimitri's life. Before I did it, she'd warned me nothing comes for free. At the time, I hadn't cared.

"I can feel it in him," Max said, tilting his head as if he could read my secret simply by looking at me. "I'm sure it's there. Just as I'm sure he'll never be one of us."

No. Guilt crashed down on me in wave after suffocating wave. Of course Dimitri denied it. He didn't know. His entire identity and future was wrapped in his heritage, the purity of his griffin ancestry.

He'd bet his soul on it.

I had to get him out of here. Tonight. Once I told him what I'd done, he'd probably want to leave.

The entire time I'd known him, he'd been working to get back to Greece, to fulfill his destiny as a noble griffin.

In one step, I'd taken that away from him.

At the time, it seemed like a taste of my power would only serve to strengthen him. I hadn't counted on the fact that it might open him up to a kind of danger he had no protection against.

Max's hands slid over the steering wheel, almost in a caress. His collar shifted, revealing a silver chain around his neck.

"I'm surprised you didn't sense the griffin's slaying power, however minor." Max said. " You knew me."

Did I ever.

But of course I wouldn't be able to feel Dimitri's slayer essence. I didn't sense myself. And that was what he had inside of him, a small part of my energy, a taste of my power—an indelible stain on the very thing that made him who he was.

*Forgive me, Dimitri.*

"He's a liability," Max stated. "He could have been a help if he were of pure griffin blood, like he claims. But his blood is tainted. Granted, it's slayer blood, but not enough to make him useful. He'll suck your energy dry trying to regain his strength."

"You mean like you did to that succubus?"

A wicked laugh rumbled from his throat. "I don't want or crave their essence. He wants yours, and he'll take it."

The memory of it chilled me to the core. "How can you know he'd just take it?"

Max locked me into a smoldering gaze. "Who wouldn't?"

We drove for a long time until Max finally stopped the car along the side of an abandoned prison thirty miles outside of Henderson. Gray metal guard towers flanked rusted fences. Barbed wire coiled along the tops, sagging in spots. Weeds littered the ground and sprouted between the concrete basketball courts in the yard. A dented sign read *Southeast Nevada State Women's Minimal Security Correctional Center.* I wouldn't want to recite that each time I answered the phone. And I wasn't about to get out of the car, not until Max the hunter put my mind to rest about a few things.

I crossed my arms in front of me. "You think I'm too stupid to live?"

He seemed almost surprised. "Where did that come from?"

Oh please. "Let's see. Is it the dark, abandoned prison? Or the fact you could be a raving lunatic?" One who eats women. Okay, evil she-demons. But still . . .

He considered the question. "You know I'm a hunter," he said, eyeing me thoughtfully. "I've left you your weapons. My reaction time would have been pathetic if you'd decided to switch-star me on Highway 95." He leaned back, crossing his arms over his chest, matching my stance. "You seem to be mated to a raging beast who could have killed me last night."

A smile tickled the sides of my lips. Go Dimitri.

Max seemed less than amused. "And, Lizzie," he said, abandoning pretext and leaning forward, his words clipped and biting, "if you don't screw up and get yourself killed, you're my secret weapon against an invasion of succubi the likes of which I've never seen."

Ice trickled through my veins. "What do you mean invasion?"

I almost didn't want him to answer. Because deep down, a part of me had already known.

"Come on," he said, "I'll show you."

*Excerpt from* The Dangerous Book for Demon Slayers:
*Demon Slayer: In our hands, switch stars kill demons.*
*Demon Hunter: A different breed of demon-fighting warrior. Hunters have the strength to throw switch stars, but only to stun or wound. To make the kill requires them to give up a part of themselves to the demons. Beware of the darkness that enables a hunter to choose this type of killing.*

# CHAPTER THIRTEEN

I could feel the demons the minute we slipped past a cut in the fence, near where we hid the car. There was no mistaking the pungent stench of sulfur in the night air. Along with it, the hint of rot, decay—of utter wrong in a place that hadn't been quite right to begin with.

They waited. For what, I could only guess.

Being in the middle of the desert at night reminded me of the quiet after a storm. Back home in Atlanta, crickets, frogs and all sorts of nocturnal whatnots screamed until dawn. I'd always taken it for granted. Night = noisy. That was when I hardly believed in the devil, much less met one.

The oppressive stillness was unsettling on a fundamental level. I couldn't figure out why until my mind trickled back to the last time the silence of a place had swallowed me whole.

I'd been with Dimitri in the wastelands of hell.

Just where was Max taking me?

Our dress shoes sounded like army boots as we crunched over the crumbling parking lot. Scraggly weeds scratched at my ankles and large cracks tore at my heels. Signs reserving spots for VIPs and visitors lolled drunkenly. The building itself hunkered like a large, dark beast, stark against the endless desert behind it.

I wished we were alone, that I didn't feel something watching us from behind the darkened windows.

Reaching out with my mind, I tried to locate the diciest hot spots, or heck, anything that felt like attacking. I almost preferred a straight-out fight to sneaking around waiting for something bad to happen.

The worst of the malevolence rested low in the building. And it was very, very angry.

"What in the world happened here?" I asked, fighting to keep my voice above a whisper.

"I came," Max said, flatly.

Sometimes, a half answer is worse than no answer at all.

He led me behind a row of dead bushes at the edge of the parking lot and past an old prison cemetery on the side of the building. The chill of the desert sent goose bumps skittering up my skin. I hadn't planned on exploring a demonic, abandoned penitentiary tonight or I would have worn something more than my purple silk dress.

Max had talked about an invasion of succubi. Had the battle already begun?

My throat caught at a blur of movement in one of the windows ahead of us. A dazzling red orb hovered behind the chain-linked safety glass.

"Max. Look."

He followed the direction of my outstretched finger, alarmingly unconcerned. "That's not one of ours."

I stiffened. "Ours?"

He arched a brow. "You *are* a demon slayer, right?"

Bad question. My reply hitched in my throat. It was just as well. It took me a moment to realize his attempt at a joke. Let him figure out later that I probably couldn't kick his ass.

Max clicked open the padlock on a side entrance and led me into a large industrial kitchen. I inhaled stale air, mixed with the last of the fresh as he eased the door closed. Darkness consumed us, save for the scarlet light of an orb as it hovered over the chef's serving station.

The thing practically pulsed with energy. "Is that the same one?" I asked.

I stood in the dark and listened as Max locked us in. "Don't waste your energy. Unless they attack." He handed me a Mini Maglite. "Shine it down, away from the windows."

Annoyed, and more than a little scared, I flipped on my light. The beam, surprisingly strong, illuminated the black safety mat in front of me, as well as the giant ladles, serving spoons and tongs hanging over the metal counters on each side of us.

My heart fluttered as the orb approached me low, like a mountain lion stalking its prey. I hadn't even realized I stopped breathing until I started again with a gasp. It flared and circled around behind me, a glowing ball of malice off my left shoulder.

*Be strong.*

"*Look to the Outside,*" I said to myself, trying to find comfort in my Demon Slayer Truths. "*Accept the*

*Universe.*" Okay, we could skip the last one—*Sacrifice Yourself.*

"Be strong," I repeated out loud.

Because whether I liked it or not, my white knight was AWOL. I was the only one who could rescue me. And it was not the time to let Max know I was on a learner's permit.

"This way," Max said, not even bothering to make sure I followed.

His brisk, even stride forced me to jog a half step behind as we left the kitchen for a neglected service corridor. The orb matched my pace. I'd ignore it unless it attacked, which was easier said than done. It hovered at the edge of my vision, a constant threat.

Our flashlights cast milky circles on the cement-block walls. I was hyperaware of every cell in my body as my heels clacked in a steady rhythm against the linoleum of the endless passageway. It was almost as if something waited for us to get closer, to cut ourselves off completely before it made itself known.

"You've got to be kidding," I said, when my light found a gaping stairwell, a scant few steps head. It led straight for the mass I'd felt.

Max ignored me, rumbling down into the darkness.

I've never been overly religious, but I made the sign of the cross anyway as I paused at the top. Now was not the time to give in to claustrophobia. Sulfur tingled my nose, along with the unmistakable rot in the air. Each step down into the dark abyss felt like sinking farther and farther into black water. Our lights barely penetrated the pitch dark of the place as we took the first stairway, the second, the third. The orb, if possible, seemed to glow brighter.

"It's a good repellent," Max said, shattering the silence, nearly causing me to fall down the last six steps.

"What?" I asked, grasping for the banister. "The flashlight?" If so, I wanted a bigger one.

"The iron," he said, as if I already knew.

"Are we talking about demons?" I asked, reaching the concrete floor of the prison basement.

Max flipped on the lights, blinding me with their brightness. "How much did you have to drink at that club, Lizzie?"

"Geez, nothing!" I said, shielding my eyes, willing for them to adjust faster. I blinked several times while Max stood waiting, impatience written across his angled features.

"What would we be discussing if it *wasn't* demons?" He demanded.

Evidently nothing, which was peachy with me.

"Okay," I said, giving my eyes a final rub, and the orb another check. It hovered off my right shoulder, eerily alive against the stained concrete walls. They'd been aqua once and still were in some places. In others, large chunks of paint peeled away like dead skin on the floor. A massive network of pipes loomed overhead. "Start from the top."

Max scowled. Thank goodness he assumed my ignorance in steel making rather than in demon slaying, because he said, "I'm talking about the steel in this place—the bars, the doors, the grates, the holding cells. Steel is made from iron."

"And iron repels succubi." I tried to make a statement, rather than ask.

"That I can guarantee," he said, shooting me a look that told me he'd been starting to wonder.

Join the club.

"This way," he said, leading me through what had been the kitchen laundry. The machines had been torn out of the walls long ago, leaving shadows of bare concrete and rusted pipes thrusting from the walls. "The older steel down here has an unusually low carbon count," Max said over his shoulder. "It gives us an even higher concentration of iron. Believe me, we need it."

Iron repelled succubi. Nice to know. If we got out of here, I was going to order Uncle Phil a pair of iron underpants. Double thick.

I watched Max's wide back, the sliced shirt flowing against his muscles as he moved. Max could write *The Dangerous Book for Demon Slayers* with his eyes closed. Of course, we'd have to rename it.

Burying the urge to ask more, I followed him through the labyrinth. Too bad I needed him to think I was badder than I was. For now at least,

But I couldn't resist one giant presumption, based on the thick silver cross he wore. "And succubi are attracted to silver."

"No. Platinum."

"So that's a platinum cross?"

He stopped.

"You have holes in your shirt," I reminded him.

His suspicion faded, but it didn't leave entirely. "I find it's easier when they come to me," he said tightly.

"Do they?" I asked, unable to imagine what a horrible life that would be.

"Sometimes," he replied.

Max led me into another hallway, then stopped in front of a set of massive steel doors. In fact, I realized as I took in the whole of the place, the cramped hallway consisted of nothing but door upon door, at least twenty, down to a dead end. The overhead pipes didn't even reach this far into the underbelly of the prison.

"The hole," he explained. "It was put out of commission long before they ever modernized the place. Lucky for me," he said with a little too much relish. "Each of these babies is a perfect steel box."

The wards in this place were amazing. I didn't even feel them until I touched the door nearest me. It stung like dry ice.

"Is this where the invasion starts?" I asked.

Max laid his hand, palm down against the door, hissing at the pain, welcoming it. "This is where it ends."

Yeah, well I liked things spelled out better than that. "What do you want?"

He straightened like a Marine, his intensity admirable and frightening at the same time. "I need both you and your twin."

"I don't have a twin," I answered.

"Damn it, slayer," he snapped. "This is no time to bargain. It is your obligation, your destiny to destroy these creatures. If not, you're going to see a slaughter the likes of which you can't imagine. And if you think you're safe because you don't come from around here, think again. These demons will spread like the plague. Rest assured, if you don't give your blood and guts to stop it, I'll kill you myself."

With a roar, he yanked the door clear open.

I didn't even have time for a *holy Sheboygan*. Claws and teeth extended, the succubus screeched for me. I ducked and flung a switch star, catching her in the throat as icy lips descended onto mine. She exploded into a cloud of gray ash, but not before I felt her begin to tease out my essence, or was it my soul?

I rolled, crunching my shoulder into the wall as I grabbed another switch star, ready to throw. When I realized no more demons were coming for me, I leapt to my feet.

Nothing else lived and breathed in the corridor, except a smug-looking Max. "I thought so," he said.

Adrenaline coursed through me. "What the hell are you doing?" I demanded. I wanted to scream, punch the wall, throttle him.

"I had to make sure you were who I thought you were," he said simply.

Oh. Sure. Righty-o. "And if I wasn't?" Or if I'd had a bad day? Or if my fingers had been too sweaty? Or if I'd *sneezed* at the wrong time?

"Then you'd be dead." He crossed his arms over his chest. "This is war, Lizzie. And I'm playing to win."

I wanted to scream as I shoved my switch star into my belt while keeping an eye on him.

"That was my most powerful prisoner." He strode purposefully over the ashes scattered on the concrete floor between us. "You're good," he remarked, as if we'd just played a round of golf.

"You're an asshole."

"Maybe, but I'm still alive."

My hacked-off state amused the man. Evidently, he'd been hanging out with she-demons for too long. Whatever he wanted from me, he was going to have to ask real friggin' nice from now on.

"Are you set?" he asked.

Suspicion rolled over me. "For what?" I barked, hitching my final star.

"I've got more holding cells. Seventeen more demons. Want to go again or do you want to tell me about your twin?"

Oh for the love of Pete. "You can't let it go, can you?"

He stared at me, dead serious. "This is war, Lizzie."

"Fine," I shouted. If we didn't need him in this world, I'd switch-star him myself.

I blew out a breath. *Chill out. Forget that he launched a soul-stealing demon at your head.*

It was the first time I'd felt the urge to punch another human being. It would feel good. I knew it. But it wasn't me. None of this was me. What did I do in preschool when I needed to calm down? I counted to ten.

"What are you doing?" He demanded.

"I'm counting to ten!" I screamed.

"Oh." A smile quirked on his lips. "Well, that seems to be working."

I ignored him and launched into the truth. Screw him if he didn't believe it. "I wasn't born to be a demon slayer," I began.

"But you are the exalted—"

"Shut up and let me finish!" Criminy. No wonder this guy had to date she-demons.

I took a calming breath. "Every three generations, my family produces twin slayers," I explained.

"Of course. You and . . ." he said.

"Me and nobody. Try my mom and my aunt," I corrected. "And while my mom's amazing family brought her up, loved her, flew instructors in from all over the world to teach her everything she needed to know, she spent the whole time figuring out a way to beat the rap."

"I've never heard of that."

"Well, now you have," I said, with a tenacious hold on my temper. "My Aunt Celia died like a heroine while my mom passed her powers to me, dumped me off to be adopted and thought it would be the end of our line. Well," I said, my anger filtering to my mom, "until the next poor saps a few generations later, which would actually be her great-granddaughters, not that she cared."

Max watched me intently. "It must have been quite a shock as a child to learn that this, we, existed."

Try last month. But I wasn't about to tell him that.

"And you have no twin," he said slowly.

I hoped it was finally sinking in. "That's what I've been trying to tell you," I said, none too charitably. "Now you mind telling me something?" I rubbed at the shoulder I'd jammed into the wall. "What in sweet creation are you doing down here? You don't seem like the type to take prisoners. Why are you letting these things live?"

He sized me up, as if deciding how much to tell me. Considering the heaping helping of demon surprise he'd served back there, he'd better lay out the facts.

"When I was young, I was more rash."

I had a girlfriend back in college who used to take forever to get to the point, but this guy took the cake. "Abridged version, please," I said, planting my back against the wall. No way were these things going to get the jump on me again.

Max considered. "Maybe we should go someplace

more comfortable," he said. "Come on. My quarters are right through here."

I couldn't have been more shocked if a demon flew out another door. "You *live* with them?"

He didn't answer, leading me instead to an old guard's station turned bedroom. At least that's what I assumed from the cot and stack of Campbell's chicken noodle soup cans. The man existed like a monk. His narrow military-issue camping cot nudged against the far wall. Underneath, a steel lockbox. Other than that, I doubted anything else in the fading office belonged to Max. He'd better have an apartment somewhere.

The cot crackled under him as he took a seat. I preferred the old aluminum desk in the corner. I planted my butt on a stack of papers, back to the wall, and waited for him to speak first.

"I joined the fight when I was eighteen," he said, threading his fingers together. "He wouldn't take me earlier."

"Who?"

"My trainer," he said smoothly, with reverence, "my mentor."

Great. He had a friend. "Will he be here tonight?"

"No." Max stood and walked the short distance between his cot and a map on the wall. "They killed him years ago," he said, absently studying the map. Clusters of red and green pins dotted the map like a macabre Christmas display.

"Are those kills?" I asked.

He nodded. "And captures. We fought together."

What sort of creature was this mentor? "He trained you to do this?"

Max shot me a look that could have hung me up on the wall. "I didn't need training in order to kill."

I felt myself tense. His admission shocked me at first. I didn't understand how anyone could kill without remorse. Regret was a requirement. You were a monster if you wanted to annihilate another living thing.

Until a horrible realization sprouted deep inside me. I didn't regret him killing the demon at Pure. It was one less supernatural locust. Come to think of it, I didn't regret the fifth-level demon I killed last week or the unholy monster in the hallway outside. If I wasn't any better than Max, what did that make me?

"Why don't you kill them?" I asked.

"I can't," he stated simply. "There are too many."

He hesitated, almost imperceptibly, but I caught it. "What else?"

We locked eyes. Max, deciding if it was worth the risk to tell me. Me, wondering how much worse it could get. But I wasn't about to go in without all the facts. Never again.

"Tell me or I walk out of here," I said. He'd searched me out. He needed me. I'd use it. Heck, it was the only thing I had.

He drew a red switch star, slower than before. Still, I took it as a threat. I whipped out one of my own, the blades casting pink against the florescent lights of our dubious retreat.

Max smirked. "I could kill you faster than you'd see it coming."

"Want to try?" I shot back. Damn. I was starting to sound like Grandma.

He sheathed his star. I kept mine out.

"I can't kill them," he stated. "Not with stars, anyway. I'm a half slayer. A hunter. I can stun them, but to kill them, I have to consume them."

I found myself blinking uncontrollably, trying to process, "What are you?"

He seemed surprised. "Don't you know? I'm a cambion."

Max said it as if I should understand—which meant I had to let him in on a dirty secret of my own. "I have no idea what that means."

He frowned. "You're kidding me, right? I never picked you for an elitist."

I wanted to cringe. But explaining would cost me more than I was willing to give. "Are you going to enlighten me or what?"

He suddenly seemed much older. "My father was human," he began. "My mother was one of them. She ate him."

"Oh," was all I could think to say.

He bristled. "I've taken out my share. My slayer killed more."

Holy h-e-double-hockey-sticks. "Where are they all coming from?"

"That's what I want to know," Max said.

He warmed when talking about his mission, which must in fact have been his life's work. "We've never had this many. They're going to pull more in before it's over." He watched me. "Something big is going down. Right before it happens, I think they're going to try to break out their prisoners."

"Then what?" I croaked.

A predatory smile lit upon his mouth. "Well, slayer. Then all hell breaks loose."

I couldn't imagine what one succubus could have done in Pure, much less an army unleashed on Vegas.

For the first time, I wished I had a twin—or more power. I didn't know if what I had would be enough.

Max paced, all business once again. "They're killing people, and sucking up an unprecedented amount of energy. I think they're using it to open up a portal, a one-way ticket to hell and back. Problem is, it's been impossible to locate."

He seemed to look to me for ideas. Lovely. Last time, I'd gone to hell, I'd had to jump off the back end of an enchanted riverboat.

"I don't know how two of us can take on twenty-five demons." It was impossible.

"I don't care." He ground the words between his teeth. "I'll take out as many as I can until I'm dead. But I can't stop this alone. I've gone without a slayer for almost sixty years, but now I *need* a slayer."

Great. Immortal servitude. Or if he was mortal, he wasn't like anybody I'd ever known. "What happened to your other slayer?" I asked, not really wanting to know.

His gaze wandered past me, remembering. "She slipped."

"Oh." My stomach fluttered, but I forced myself to ask more. "And her twin?"

"They turned her."

My veins iced over. "What do you mean?"

He searched me for some sign of comprehension. "You really don't know anything, do you, Lizzie?"

"Not as much as I'd like," I admitted in the most colossal understatement of all time. "I came here trying to get rid of one succubus." Oh, for the days when I thought there was only one.

"You're going to have to fight with me, Lizzie."

"We can't kill them all," I insisted.

Max stood, the desk screeching backward. "I'll give you a day to think about it."

My life suddenly seemed like a minor battle in the middle of a great big war.

# CHAPTER FOURTEEN

Max's sleek black Mercedes roared into the circle drive of the Paradise Hotel. He paused long enough for me to step out, a shiver jolting through me as the cool desert air touched my skin. I barely had my door closed before he zoomed off into the night.

The lights from The Strip bounced off the X30's tinted windows, unable to reach the man inside, as Max disappeared into the endless stream of traffic on Las Vegas Avenue. He'd never pretended to be a gentleman. He was a soldier in the middle of a great big war. And now I was involved too.

A startled bellhop rushed to greet me. "Are you all right, miss?"

Which was code for *you look like hell*. Fitting, since I'd indeed caught a glimpse of it tonight. I smoothed my dress, wrinkled and torn from my encounter with the demon. "Sure," I lied. "Everything will be fine once I get to my room."

I wished I believed that.

The bellhop didn't buy it, either. But he allowed me my fantasy, escorting me to the entrance and opening the smaller glass door next to the massive, revolving one. The unexpected gesture made me pause. "Thanks," I told him. "You're sweet," I added impulsively. I don't know why I wanted him to know, except that seeing the darkness always made me want to look for the light.

Even at three thirty in the morning, the Paradise Hotel lobby seemed brighter, the slot machines louder, the patrons more boisterous than I'd seen them before. Of course compared to Max's prison, Frankenstein's lab would have felt cozy.

The wards at the entrance practically sizzled with energy. Battina and Jan had been busy. I reached out with my mind to see what kinds of creatures I could detect. Several unknowns scattered throughout. I'd have to get better at sensing, along with everything else.

If Max was right and the demons were planning something big, I wondered how on earth my gentle fairy godfather could be involved.

At the twelfth-floor maintenance entryway, I slipped my key card out of my black utility belt and quicker than you can say, *home, sweet, hotel room,* stepped into the lapping waters of our hallway. My shadow stretched over the glistening water.

It would feel good to hug my little doggie. I hoped he hadn't gorged himself too bad on Paw Lickin Chicken. I even looked forward to dealing with Dimitri and Grandma. Sure, they'd be ticked that I left with Max. No question it'd been worth it. Max's demon war would affect us all. They had to see it.

My thoughts lingered on the ageless half-demon vigilante and his Spartan devotion to the cause. I didn't know how Max did it, alone every day. Come to think of it, he wasn't alone anymore. He had me.

What a terrible thought.

The hallway smelled like pizza again. I hoped someone on the floor just really liked pizza, because if Pirate had learned how to order room service, my meager savings could go from stretched to nonexistent in the space of a couple of dozen hotel platters.

My hand had barely touched the knob of my door when it came crashing in on its own. Dimitri stood in the entryway. His eyes sliced into me, dissecting every scrape, bruise and broken nail I'd suffered tonight.

"What the hell happened to you?" he demanded.

He was on me before I could answer. Devouring me in a superheated, melting kiss that chilled me to the core. It quickly grew harder, possessive. His fingers slid up my shoulders and neck, into my hair, gripping me and forcing me to understand exactly how worried he'd been.

I felt myself weaken as my energy flowed toward him. I pushed him away before I melted into his kiss.

"Are you hurt?" he asked against my lips, his caresses turning to inspection as he frowned at the growing bruises on my arms. His touch was light, but his eyes hardened as he scanned the remains of my dress. My body didn't quite get the message. Pleasure seeped through me every place his fingers traveled . . . and even a few places where they didn't. Call it denial at its most delicious. Was it that much of a sin to want this escape? Who wouldn't want to forget Max, his demons and everything else that had happened tonight?

One of Dimitri's superlarge hands rested on my waist, while the other traced a particularly nasty scrape that disappeared into the lilac silk of my bodice. It would have been the ultimate distraction, only his eyes glowed yellow again.

"Lizzie!" Pirate jumped up and down against my legs. "You hear me, Lizzie?"

His claws caught a cut on my leg I didn't even know was there until, "Ow!"

Pirate intensified the assault. "I don't think you hear me because you're not saying anything and I'm your dog and I'm right here. Lizzie!"

Good. Yes. Think about the dog—*and not Dimitri, who is being corrupted right in front of your eyes.*

"Baby dog!" I broke away and reached down for my Jack Russell terrier.

Pirate's spindly legs wriggled as fast as his tail. "I was starting to think you'd never come back," he said, digging his wet nose into the crook of my elbow.

"Yes, well." He also thought that when I walked out to the mailbox without him.

Pirate could sniff, lick and talk at the same time. "And Grandma," he said, "I don't know where she went."

My body froze.

"She and Ant Eater are working on something," Dimitri said.

"Oh no." I shuddered to think. "They aren't chasing Serena, are they?" I was the only one who could defeat her, and frankly, they'd be more of a hindrance than a help.

"Don't worry," Dimitri said. "Battina and Jan have them tracking down ingredients for extra wards. Something about stinkbugs and more turtle knees."

"Fine," I said, clutching my dog to my chest. "Excuse me." I edged past him and deposited Pirate onto the nearest bed.

"Now that you're back, we have some things to discuss," Dimitri said to my back. The *alone* was implied.

"Yeah, well me first," I said. "Let's move." His room would be better than mine, especially if Grandma showed up.

"Oh, now you know I can keep a secret," Pirate protested as Dimitri clicked the door shut behind us.

"Let's go," I said, splashing backward down the hall, waving Dimitri on.

Before I could turn around, Dimitri lit upon me like I was on fire. "What is this?" He seized my right hand, turning it over. Gone was the insistent touch of a lover. In its place, a hardened griffin warrior whose power I was only beginning to understand.

He held out my right hand and there, in the center of my palm, pink slashes swirled across my unbroken skin. I squinted at them in the dim lights of the hallway. They looked like the wounds Max inflicted on Dimitri. They were about the only thing on my body that didn't hurt. In fact, I didn't know what had happened.

Had Max marked me?

I flexed my palm, stretching the marks out over my skin. He couldn't have marked me without my knowledge. Could he? It could have been something I'd touched—the banister leading down to the basement, my switch stars, the steel door that held back an ancient demon.

Three parts of a whole swirled, in almost a floral pattern. Squat sides together, lines reaching out. I didn't understand the significance at first, until Dimitri traced each symbol that marked my palm—6-6-6.

I stared in horror at the fluid numbers etched over my palm. I fought the urge to rub them against my stained dress, to keep rubbing until there was nothing left. If I thought it had a chance of working, I would have done it.

A sudden realization made me go brittle inside. What if it wasn't Max?

*They killed one slayer and turned the other.*

Voice unsteady, I asked the question I feared the most. "What does it mean?"

I didn't like Dimitri's somber expression one bit, but I knew I could count on him to lay it out for me. "It seems you've made a deal with the devil."

My heart thumped hard, threatening to take over my rib cage. "That's impossible," I gasped. "I didn't agree to anything."

Dimitri cut me off. "Evil comes whether we invite it or not. What do you want, Lizzie? Are you really looking for things to be fair? A demon isn't going to wait for an engraved invitation to strike. You of all people should know that. Don't kid yourself about the hunter, either. He's out to use you."

"Max is on our side," I insisted.

Dimitri gave me a hard look. "So now he's Max?"

"Yes, that's his name." I wanted to say Max didn't mark me, either. But I couldn't go that far. I just didn't know.

No question about it—something had happened to me down there. I couldn't change it, but I could do my very best to fight it.

Dimitri looked like he wanted to smash something.

"Open your eyes, woman. And do it fast, because I'm not going to stand around and watch you destroy yourself."

"Look who's talking. You need to leave this city. Now!" This wasn't the way I'd wanted to tell him, but . . . "I have a confession to make." My insides churned at the thought. "The night we went to hell and you were really hurt"—I searched his face—"remember?"

Of course he remembered. I was stalling, racking my brain for a better way to say it. But there was no way to say this right. "You were going to die. I gave you part of my demon slayer essence to save you."

Dimitri looked like I'd hit him with a brick.

"That's not all," I said quickly. "It tainted you. It opened you up. Whatever protection you think you have—you don't. I'm sorry, Dimitri." I reached for him. "I'm so sorry."

He backed away, shock etched across his features.

"I didn't tell you because, well, I didn't know how. I didn't want you to feel obligated to me. I never thought in my wildest dreams this could happen."

Dimitri's yellow eyes focused on a spot on the wall behind me. "I knew something was wrong," he said roughly, almost to himself. "I felt it."

"There's nothing we can do. And you certainly can't protect me like this. If you stay, you're only making them stronger. Let it go. Leave." Then softer, I said, "They've won this round."

He stiffened, eyes darkening. "Not if I have anything to do with it."

Oh no, no, no. He wasn't going to deny this. "You're feeding them!"

My voice echoed down the empty corridor. Now I knew why it was dim. The concierge posts stood empty.

His nostrils flared, his body tight with resolve. "I'm also resisting them." He loomed over me. "And doing a damned good job of it. Better than I should be given these . . ." He couldn't even say it. "Circumstances."

"You need to leave," I said.

He gave me a predatory smile. "Point taken."

Stubborn, stubborn man. He might think he could control his own destiny, but he couldn't deny one basic truth about the fight ahead. "Fine. Whether you stay or go, we're not going to beat this thing without Max." Facts were facts.

"You don't know what the hell he is."

"Max can kill demons," I said. "We need him."

Dimitri closed his fist as if he wanted to punch something. "He is a demon," Dimitri said, grinding out each word.

"Half demon."

His mouth twisted into a mockery of a smile. "Now you're splitting hairs."

"And you're lumping him in with the devil."

His temper burned. "He's a vigilante, Lizzie."

"Fine, so he's not a slayer." He killed for revenge. It left the demons just as dead. "And how he kills them . . ." Disgusting wasn't the word. I'd seen him consume a she-demon. I'd touched his steel holding cells with my own hand. "But you have to admit, he's killed more than I ever have."

If possible, Dimitri's rage intensified. "Can't you feel him turning?"

I stood, rooted in place.

He thrust his hand out, gripping my shoulder, his fingers tight with fury. "Every demon Max consumes takes away a small part of his humanity. Until there won't be anything left."

"What about you?" I demanded.

"I'll survive."

"This is not a choice."

"He'll turn."

It took me a moment to hear him. Maybe I didn't want to understand. "You mean he'll become one of them?" I gasped.

What was the male version of a succubus? "An incubus?" I wouldn't wish it on my worst enemy.

Dimitri gave me a cold look. "I don't know what he'll become, but I don't want you to be around to find out. We need to fight our own part of this war and leave Max to fight his. In the meantime, I'm on you like a second skin. If he shows up again, he'll have to answer to me."

"Oh yeah, because that's what demon slayers do. We hide from the demons while our boyfriends fight our battles for us."

"You know that's not what I meant."

"You can't protect me from the entire world, Dimitri. I don't want you to." I'd walked into tonight determined to take my place as a demon slayer. Max had taught me more in one evening than Grandma had since we'd set foot in Vegas. And he'd launched a demon at me. And, yes, I'd been marked.

The war was on and I wasn't ever going to become a true demon slayer without facing down creatures like the ones I'd battled tonight.

Every urge from my old life would have had me

clinging to Dimitri. That's why I knew I couldn't. It was like the winter I'd wanted to learn to ice-skate. I'd been so scared of falling that I kept to the wall of the indoor rink, never risking a trip onto the seemingly endless stretch of ice, knowing for sure that I'd fall. And, yes, I didn't fall that winter. But I didn't skate, either. I had to get off the wall.

"I'm doing this," I told him.

"I'm making sure you survive."

"What are you going to do? Lock me up like a terrier?"

"I heard that," Pirate's voice echoed from the other side of the wall.

Dimitri let out a string of curses I wouldn't say in front of a roomful of biker witches, much less our entire hotel floor, who was no doubt listening.

"Stuff it," I said, stomping down the hall toward his room. If he wouldn't get out of the hallway, I would.

I yanked up the straps of my ruined dress, venturing a glance at my marked palm. Times like this, I really missed my old life.

Last month, nightclubs were nightclubs, concierges were human and the demons were the name of the local high school football team. Now my shape-shifting griffin boyfriend couldn't seem to get along with my biker-witch Grandma, much less a half human/half demon potential ally, who as far as I could see was key to helping us stop an invasion of succubi that could not only kill my Uncle Phil and "turn" me, but could also go all biblical on the good citizens of Las Vegas, Nevada.

And right when I was working up a really good

rant, I reached Dimitri's room and realized I didn't have a key. His shadow fell over me as he popped open the door.

We were barely in the room before Dimitri slammed the door closed behind us.

"First of all," was all I managed before he pinned me to the wall, his body hard against mine as he assaulted me with his mouth. The man did amazing things with his tongue, his teeth. Yum. I ground against him. Pushed him harder. I heard him groan. Or was that me?

He pulled back, his lips almost on mine. I tried to close the gap, just for a moment. The temptation was too overwhelming. It wouldn't cost much, I told myself.

But he resisted. "I'm not stupid," he said. "I know what you have to do here. But it doesn't mean I have to like it, and it doesn't mean you need to go riding off with assholes like Max. He's half demon, Lizzie. You remember demons, don't you?"

Like I could forget.

"Here's the deal," I said, ready to lay it out as plainly as I could.

I told Dimitri about my night with Max, how I watched him suck the life out of the she-demon at Pure. I told him about Max's abandoned mental hospital/prison and the succubi Max held captive there.

Dimitri had to get it. I watched his face for signs of understanding. "Vegas is on the edge," I said. "This is the gathering place. You said it yourself. Something big is about to go down. Uncle Phil is involved, and now I am too. We only have one choice in this. One. And that's whose side we're going to be on."

Dimitri gave nothing away. "Not his."

"Oh, come on."

"He's sucking out their immortal essences, Lizzie. He's no better than they are."

"Yes, but he's doing it to destroy a demon." At a huge sacrifice to himself. I might not agree with how he did it, but it didn't make the demons any less dead.

Dimitri's jaw tightened.

"Fine," I said. "We'll agree to disagree." It seemed like we'd been doing that far too often lately. "The only thing I can't figure out is how my Uncle Phil fits into any of this."

Dimitri considered it, his expression darkening. "If the succubi are planning a war, fairies could be incredibly useful.

That's right. Grandma said the fairies could anticipate events, fly undetected, even change the near future.

"But Uncle Phil's only half fairy."

"Exactly. He's half human. They can get to him." He took my hand, heading for the door "Come on."

*Excerpt from* The Dangerous Book for Demon Slayers:
*Fairies: a species of magical creature that will drive you insane if you let them.*

# CHAPTER FIFTEEN

We jammed our Harleys into gear and drove straight to McCarran International Airport.

"Let me do the talking," Dimitri said, as we left our bikes in short-term parking.

It sounded good to me, considering I didn't quite understand who I'd be talking to, anyway. I had a feeling I'd be adding another chapter to my demon slayer handbook.

"The fairies in Vegas have to stay on the down low," Dimitri continued, taking my hand as we walked. "Did you wonder why the DIP office sent you a fairy?"

"Because he's good at going undetected?"

Dimitri nodded. "Also because he's expendable."

"Ouch."

"In a lot of places, fairies are considered second-class citizens. Vegas is no exception. They don't allow fairies anywhere near casinos or gaming halls. They're not even permitted inside the airport here. Management is convinced they'll make a break for the slot machines." He rubbed a thumb along a sensitive spot near my wrist and I had to force myself to stay on track.

I leaned into him as we walked. "What and influence the near future?" The magical world had much bigger problems than a few gambling wee folk.

"Gambling is big money here. And it wouldn't just be the fairies who win big. If a person's will is strong enough, they can compel a fairy to do their bidding—in big ways and in small."

No wonder Sid Fuzzlebump was so defensive.

We jogged across two lanes of traffic to the taxi stand outside the Arrivals gate. "They used to burn fairies as witches in the Middle Ages," Dimitri said. "Hold up. Dispatch said he'd be here soon." He found us a spot next to the taxi line. Dimitri watched traffic as he continued his explanation. "These days, ninety-nine percent of the population would never recognize a fairy. I saw one in Tulsa once, working as a TV weatherman. But as a race, they have trouble assimilating. A lot of the premier athletes, Wall Street types, successful literary agents you see are only a small part fairy. They don't even know they're influencing the future."

I hated to state the obvious, but . . . "It seems like fairies could do a lot of good."

"Pure fairies aren't interested in making their mark in the human world," Dimitri said, "and most magical places ban them."

"That seems kind of harsh." Good thing Uncle Phil was only part fairy. Still, his mom must have had it rough.

"I don't make up the rules," Dimitri replied. "In any case, expect the fairies you meet to be on guard. Don't take it personally."

"But if they're not allowed inside the airport, where—?"

"There!" Dimitri lunged forward into traffic, taking me with him.

An aquamarine Gossamer Cab veered away from us, jamming into a mass of taxis right before an airport limousine blocked our path. We sprinted past a honking BMW and a Ford F-150 exhaling hot engine air. We dashed alongside the limo and when I thought we'd make it around, we almost missed the cab again as the light ahead turned green and traffic surged. Dimitri yanked the door open and I dove in, with him right behind.

Sid Fuzzlebump, DIP officer and cab driver, glared at us through the rearview mirror. "Get out of the cab. I'm off duty."

Dimitri slammed the door closed behind him. "Like you didn't see this coming."

"Contrary to popular belief, I don't know everything. Now scram."

"We need to talk." Dimitri said. "It's not like the DIP offices are going to send us another fairy."

Sid threw a stubby hand over the seat and glared over his shoulder at us. "The DIP offices are a little busy trying to verify your count. I was the laughingstock of Temp Area Three when I turned in your esteemed findings." Horns blared behind us. He pounded on his horn in response and made an obscene gesture out the window with a certain stubby finger.

The fairy cursed under his breath. He hit the gas and made a hard left, stopping at the curb as traffic whizzed past. "I did my job. I met you once. Now beat it."

"Did you see anything unusual on your cab route?" I asked. "You said you'd check." I looked him straight in the eye, willing him to answer me, to help us.

"I don't want to talk about it," Sid said. "And stop trying to compel me. It's annoying."

"Fair enough," I said, almost throwing up my marked right hand, catching myself at the last moment. "But we need your help. Phil Whirley is my fairy godfather."

His eyes narrowed. "No kidding. I think I saw your dance recital tape. Nice to meet you. Now vamoose."

"You're the most obnoxious fairy I've ever met," I said, digging into my utility belt. Let him think I'd met more than one.

"And yet you're still here," he sniped.

"Okay, Sid. Let's bargain," Dimitri said. "What will it take for you to help us?"

"Look, you two," the fairy said, the bubblegum air in the car thickening, growing even sweeter. "I'm not talking with you, I'm not going anywhere with you and I'm not driving another inch. I've got enough going on without running a charity for displaced demon slayers. Now scram."

"We need your help," I said, holding up my cell phone. "What is the DIP not telling us? Why would demons want my uncle? Are they going after any more fairies?"

"You want me to bash you over the head with that thing?" He took a swipe for my phone.

I yanked it back and hit the button for a ring tone I should have erased after last Christmas. A chorus of bells blared through the cab. Fairies hated bells.

Dimitri looked like he wanted to kiss me.

"Gaaa!" The cabbie threw his hands over his ears. "Stop it! Shut it off!"

I hit the volume until it maxed out at ten.

Sid cringed. "We'll talk. Did you hear me?" he yelled, "We'll talk!"

I snapped the phone shut. "It's a deal."

"Yeah, well goodie, goodie gumdrops," Sid muttered, flooring it.

Sid the fairy hit every green light as we sped straight east down Highway 160.

"So?" I asked.

Sid ground his fingers around the wheel. "Yes, okay? The demons have been going after fairies for the past few years. They haven't been able to catch a full-blood. We don't keep track of the rest."

The cab's radio crackled and Sid picked it up. "Fuzzlebump here."

Sid took much longer than he needed to talk to dispatch. Yeah, well the fairy could stall all he wanted. We weren't getting out of this cab without some answers.

I flopped back onto the seat. "Why taxis?" I asked Dimitri. "Why not highway construction or farming or anything else you can do outside of town?"

"Fairies like to stick to the same routes their ancestors traveled," Dimitri said. "This way, they can draw on the strength of their community while they work their magic. They know which traffic spots to avoid, they can keep lights green longer, steer out of accidents. Fairies can tell by looking who'll tip them, who will have the higher fares."

And who would be trouble.

Sid cranked up the theme song to *American Bandstand,* a dance tune guaranteed to get into my head worse than any demon.

"The thing is," I said, leaning over the front seat, catching a strong whiff of bubblegum. It wouldn't hurt to have Sid on our side, or at least understand where we were coming from. "Last month, when I thought of fairies, I pictured Tinkerbell."

He raised his bushy brows.

"Now I picture my fairy godfather. He saved my life, and I'm going to save his."

Sid huffed, his ears reddening.

"My uncle's name is Phil Whirley. He's half human."

Sid's bushy brows lowered. "Then he's not very powerful."

"Whether that's true or not," I said, refusing to get into fairy politics, "a succubus has him."

The pudgy fairy squirmed in his seat. "Look, I'm sorry to hear about your loss, but let's not drag everybody else into this, okay?"

"He's not lost." I hoped. "She married him. We watched it happen. There's something she wants bad enough to keep him alive. But she controls him, body and soul. Any idea why she'd do that?"

He rubbed his lips together while considering the question. Finally, he said, "Well you're right about one thing. By marrying him, she took control. As far as why? I have no idea. If your uncle is only half fairy, he can't do much about the future other than give someone a lot of luck." Sid made a right turn onto Wayne Newton Boulevard. "Whatever she wants him for, it isn't fairy magic. He's not powerful enough."

*Focus.* "If they don't want him for his magic," I said, more sharply than I'd intended, "what in the world—"

The fairy stiffened. "Switch your ring tone."

It took me a moment to understand. "On my phone?" I asked. My phone wasn't ringing.

I dug it out of my utility belt and found the ringer switch. "Sure." I turned off the fairy bells.

"Good. Now answer this—after you try to save your uncle, why do you give a rip about a bunch of fairies? And no games. I'll know if you're lying."

"I'm in it to stop the she-demons," I said, "once and for all."

"You would have to say that."

The phone in my right hand chirped. I glanced down at the Caller ID.

Grandma.

"Answer it, hot stuff," Sid said, lurching the cab into a U-turn.

I grabbed the seat in front of me and held on. "Are you influencing the future?"

"Oh yeah, I'm conjuring up all kinds of goodies," he said, an eye on my ringing phone. "Now answer the damned phone."

With dread pulsing in my temples, I flipped open the phone.

"Lizzie!" Ant Eater's voice sounded hollow, and about a million miles away. "Get back here! We're under attack!"

Not the demons. They couldn't break through the wards.

"Incoming!" she hollered before the line went dead

I dashed down the ordinary twelfth floor and thrust open the door to the stairwell. My demon slayer senses told me there were three of them waiting up there. Three. *Could I even handle that many?* I had no idea. I just hoped the witches had made it out all right. And poor little Pirate.

*Don't think about it.*

My boots pounded on the concrete stairs to the maintenance closet that led to thirteen. I shoved my keycard at the door, hit it wrong and broke the thing in half. Criminy!

Dimitri wedged his into the slot.

The air in this hallway used to be stale and metallic. Now the only thing I could smell was the sulfur stench of demons.

I ducked past Dimitri and threw open the closet door, switch stars ready.

*Where were they?*

The waters of the magical hallway churned with a murky froth, like the ocean after a hurricane. They'd gone from crystal clear to dishwater gray. A dead fish floated past, tangled in seaweed. I stepped in and pitched forward when the waters of the hallway swallowed me to the knees.

"What the . . . ?" I stumbled three feet and braced my hands on the opposite wall. The water had gone from tropical to downright chilly. Before, it had lapped at my toes, but left them dry. Now, I was wet. And cold.

Goose bumps skittered down my legs.

The sulfur in the air made my eyes water. I could actually taste it in the back of my throat.

I fought back a wave of nausea.

Half the chandelier lights had been ripped from their sockets. Every Skeep post down the long corridor stood empty. It was like a bomb had gone off on the thirteenth floor. The air sizzled with energy, and yet the silence was deafening.

Like all hell had broken loose.

Dimitri braced his hands on each side of the closet doorway. I'd never seen him so resolute, or so terrifyingly vulnerable. I could almost see them suck him dry.

Well, not if I had anything to say about it. I waded back through the frigid water, grabbed his key card, and slammed the door before he knew what I was doing.

"Lizzie!" He pounded on the door.

I ignored him. He had to trust me on this one.

Who was I kidding? I had to trust myself.

I could feel them stalking me.

Shadowy forms floated beneath the surface of the water in the hallway. Despite the chill, sweat pooled under my arms and on my palms. I wiped my switch star hand on my shirt and began wading toward Battina's room full of wards.

No way the witches would have gone down without a fight. I had to believe they'd made it out or—my breath caught in my throat.

Grandma floated faceup in the murky water, her dirty hair tangled across her forehead.

"Oh no." Shock slammed through me.

Grandma's mouth slacked open, and a thick rusty ooze bubbled from her forehead. Oh geez. I touched it gently. Had to know if it was blood or magic or . . . I would have plopped down from relief if I hadn't been so scared—possum goo. Protective magic. Thank God.

Her skin felt cold and clammy, her neck worse as I felt for a pulse. It was weak, but there.

Grabbing her around the shoulders, I lifted her out of the water with more strength than I knew I had. Ice-cold water sloshed down my body.

I reached up for the handle and flung open the Exit door. Dimitri, the jerk, had had been trying to jimmy the lock with my broken key card. "Emergency! Take her." I unloaded Grandma onto him, swiped half the broken card and slammed the door again, ignoring his cursing from the other side. No way they'd make it out of this hall alive in a fight. Heck, I wasn't so sure even I'd make it out.

A high-pitched whistle sounded, and before I could think about it, a demon dropped out of a chandelier. It screeched, claws outstretched. I nailed it with a switch star, just in time to see two more coming from behind. A sulfuric wind threw me face-first into the water, my eyes stinging with salt water. No way I could recover in time to switch-star them. I dove straight down, forcing my arms to pump as hard as I could, fighting the numbing cold.

I could feel the mass of demons in Vegas, like an army of locusts. I could sense their hunger, their need to suck the living energy out of everything they encountered. Maybe a city like Las Vegas could handle a few, but not this many. It was like they were using Grandma, Ant Eater, the energy of the witches to open a gateway. They were feeding, taking and growing stronger and more menacing with every passing minute. I felt them like a weight in the very pit of my stomach.

The dark mark throbbed against my palm. It recognized them, and it wanted them. Yeah, well so did I.

# CHAPTER SIXTEEN

My hair tangled around my face and my lungs burned. The dirty water heaved with broken bits of seaweed and remnants of paradise. Bubbles forced their way up through the underwater nightmare, but I knew better than to give in to the desire to break for the surface. It churned above me, surrounded by the pure white walls of the hallway and the slick black shadows of not one, but two demons landing on the surface. Yellow talons attached to black leathery legs broke through the water right on top of me. I couldn't let them corner me. But I couldn't throw switch stars though the water, could I?

I said a quick prayer and zinged one for the demon right above me. The thing shattered into a million flecks of light. Yes!

Lungs ready to explode, I broke through to the surface. I scrambled out of the depths like I was climbing out of a pool, though I could make it out only to my knees. The salt water stung my eyes and dripped down my lips. I gave them a quick wipe and crouched, shaking as the air-conditioning of the hallway hit me like an arctic wind. "You found your slayer!" I screamed down the deserted hallway.

Switch star in hand, I sloshed down the corridor. "Come out, come out wherever you are."

I could feel the last one siphoning the energy from the floor. It didn't even need to be in devil form. These things could exist anywhere.

"Come on, girlie. Let's see what you've got."

She rushed me from behind. I turned at the last second, switch star out, ready to throw. She slammed right into it, burning me with countless pinpricks of energy. The impact seized me like an electric charge. I closed my eyes against the glare as the impact punched me backward into the murky water.

The ocean swallowed me whole. My face, arms, chest shocked and useless. Salt water flooded my mouth and I choked. Terror gripped me as my arms refused to move.

Sweet switch stars. I couldn't survive a triple demon attack only to drown in the aftermath. I forced my legs to move. Nothing. My arms. Nothing.

I held my breath, salt water going up my nose. If I choked, I'd breathe in more water. It was the only thing I could control.

Holy mother, I was sinking fast. My left side caught a sharp coral reef and I winced at the impact. Dark blood—my blood—clouded around the wound, reaching with gauzy tendrils until it faded into the suffocating waters. The murkiness consumed the streaming light of the surface until it took too much energy to bother to look up at it.

I closed my eyes. Numb. And I thought of the dark mark.

Maybe I couldn't move my hand, but I could feel the

The Dangerous Book for Demon Slayers 167

power of the mark on my palm. I called out to it, invited it to flow through me. This mark had been given to me for a reason.

My cheek hit the soft, sandy bottom and my hair streamed around my face. I kept my eyes closed tight and focused on the mark. Flooded with a cool calm, I let the power of the mark wash over me like the water that was killing me. I felt it snake through my fingers, burn through the veins of my arm. It pricked into my chest, into the very core of me. I floated in the mire and let it come.

*Give me the power to save them and to save myself. Give me the power to make a difference.*

The pain ebbed and for a moment, I thought I was dying. It wasn't as unpleasant as I'd imagined—almost a way out of an impossible situation.

At least I still had my soul.

Suddenly, my arms and legs crackled to life. They tingled as if they'd been asleep. I pumped my way to the surface and burst through. I spit water and inhaled sharply, ready to choke as I scrambled for the safety of a wall. I couldn't stop shaking. I was half standing, hands braced against the white swirling wallpaper when I realized I was breathing normally.

"Son of a gun," I murmured, feeling a raw burning in the back of my throat, the only indication that I'd been practically breathing salt water.

The door to the outside rattled on its hinges.

Correction, it was mostly off its hinges as Dimitri cursed up a storm on the other side.

"Hold up!" I called.

I glanced up and down the deserted corridor. The hallway felt clear. For now.

Legs tingling, I tested each step on my way to let Dimitri into the hallway. Grandma had looked terrible when I handed her over to him. Fingers numb, I felt my face and inspected my skin. My arms looked sunburned, the water at my knees sizzled, and my dark mark positively glowed. I touched it to the door lock and heard a sharp intake of breath on the other side.

*I did what I had to do.*

The situation had gone from bad to completely terrifying. Still, I didn't regret using the dark mark. Dimitri may not like it, but this was the supernatural gift I needed to help us survive hell. I'd be a fool not to use it.

I'd barely turned the lock when Dimitri exploded into the murky hall, running straight into me and sending up a wave of water.

"Lizzie." He gripped my shoulders like he wanted to pick me up and drag me back to Greece with him.

"How's Grandma?"

"She woke up right when everything went quiet with you. What happened?"

She woke up when the demons died. There'd be more. "We have to get out of here." I looked past him and saw Grandma braced against Sid.

Her mouth sagged and dark circles ringed both eyes. "They'd been hitting the wards all day. Typical. Like a raptor testing for a weak spot. I don't know how they found one."

I nodded. "Can you walk?"

We sloshed our way down the hallway reviving

witches, most of them still in their rooms. They'd all suffered severe energy drain, but at least they were alive. Dimitri kicked in doors in a way that was both scary and efficient. After being held back by the dead bolt in the hall, he was enjoying himself a little too much.

White streaked his hair. We had to put a stop to this, before I lost him entirely. If he'd been whole, a dead bolt wouldn't have held him back. He'd have shifted in the maintenance closet and burst into the hallway, a huge utterly majestic griffin. The only reason he didn't do it today, I feared, was because he couldn't.

He was fading. It wasn't just his eyes anymore or the white in his hair. I could see his magic dull along with the emerald he'd given me. His protective necklace had morphed into body armor when I needed it, tied me to a tree when I didn't and had even offered butt protection during my foray through Uncle Phil's living room window. Now, twice when I'd been under demon attack, it had remained utterly still. I fingered the teardrop-shaped stone that used to be warmed by Dimitri's magic. It still tied him to me. And I felt, *I knew,* that it still protected me. Still, it was a painful reminder of what had happened to him—to us—as it lay cool and lifeless around my neck.

Because I couldn't stand to watch him a second longer, and well, because Pirate needed me, I sloshed down the hallway to my room.

"Hey, doobie." I listened for Pirate's clawing as I slid Grandma's key card into the door. "Pirate?" I opened the door to a disaster. The television had exploded, along with the light sockets and every other electrical gadget in the place. And worse—no Pirate.

Panic flooding through me as I searched the remains of our room. He wasn't under the bed, in the bathroom, or behind the drapes. My chest tightened as I tried to think of other places he'd hide during a storm.

Tears burned the backs of my eyes. What good was it to sense every demon from here to Hoover Dam if I couldn't find the one little guy who depended on me to protect him?

"Lizzie."

Dimitri-the-door-basher stood in the entryway, cradling Pirate. Blood seeped from my pup's left leg, his coat stood on end and his ears dangled lifelessly.

"Oh my god. Is he . . . ?" I took his scruffy body in my arms.

"No," Dimitri said quickly. "He's fine. He's just beat."

I buried my face in his wiry neck and felt his heartbeat against my palm. Relief whooshed through me. Through the cold, matted fur, I could feel an undercurrent of warm, doggie heat.

As if he knew what I was thinking, Pirate curled into me and buried his wet nose in the crook of my elbow.

Mmm . . . wet dog. *My* wet dog. "I'm gonna get you out of here. I promise."

In fact, we had to get everyone out. Pronto.

"What's the latest on the witches?" I asked Dimitri.

"All stunned but alive. Seems like you interrupted the succubi before they could finish."

Or they'd attacked the witches in order to trap me. Sure, I hadn't announced my presence in town, but I had slaughtered one of their sisters last night in the basement of the old prison.

The war was on.

I was suddenly glad to have the dark mark. It might have been the thing that kept me alive tonight. Still, I wasn't about to let Pirate and the Red Skulls get caught up in another round. "Let's get everyone out of here. Now."

"No." Dimitri stopped me with cool, steady hands on my arms. "The Red Skulls are already on top of it."

"You're kidding." I never thought I'd see the day when the Red Skulls had a plan.

The tiny lines around his eyes crinkled as he tugged me toward him. "Come here, sweetheart."

My insides melted at the idea of letting him hold me. I could use a little comfort right now, to close my eyes, sink into his arms and let someone take care of me for a change.

I forced myself to stiffen and pull away, ignoring the hurt that flashed across his strong features. He might have been the one for me, but not now. Just because I wanted him, didn't mean I could have him. I couldn't let him drain me or feed the demons that had their claws in him.

"We don't have time," I said gently. "So tell me. What's the plan?"

His features hardened, making him impossible to read. "Battina and Ant Eater are working on a new ward," he said. "It won't hold forever. In fact, they'll drain it even faster once they realize they'll need to send more than three demons to finish us off. But it'll do until we decide where we can go."

My first instinct was to get the heck out of Dodge. Dimitri hadn't been the first one to feel what it was like to sink down into the hallway. Something had turned the warm water into a dark ocean. Freezing droplets still clung to my skin.

I wanted to argue, but curse Dimitri, he was right. There was nowhere we could go that the she-demons couldn't follow. Our best bet would be to create our own safe place here until we could figure out what to do.

"You sure Battina and Ant Eater are up to it?" I hadn't gotten a look at either one of them, but if they'd gotten hit half as bad as Grandma, I didn't want to count on them.

"I heard that, Miss Permit." Ant Eater's voice, weak but still annoying, echoed from the hall.

Okay, so maybe she was feeling better. "You're welcome," I answered. "You know, for me saving your life."

Ant Eater leaned her head inside the door. Her gold tooth sparkled, but her eyes had lost their hellfire. She'd wrapped her arms around half a dozen recycled pickle jars. Inside, the greenish brownish sludge took on a life of its own.

One side of her curly hair was mashed to her head. "Yeah, well you could have gotten here before those twits gave me the magical hangover of the century." She grinned, despite herself.

"Anything I can do?" I asked, eyeing the sludge.

"Stick to demon slaying," she said, smashing a jar at my feet and taking great delight in watching me jump back.

"Lovely," I said, wrinkling my nose at the slime oozing across the carpet. It smelled like moldy basement and feet.

"A G-bomb a day keeps the demons away," she said, standing next to me, surveying her work. "Just make sure you keep it wet and out of the sun. Also, try not to look directly at it."

"Sure," I said. "Is it a ward?"

"It's not an air freshener." She clapped me on the back.

"Are you sure this is going to work?" I didn't think I could handle another demon attack right now. We'd barely survived the last one.

"For a while," she said. "It's not like we ever used to fight 'em. We'd spell and run. Battina and I keep a stash of emergency wards. Otherwise, you're never going to get enough turtle knees on such short notice."

"Sure," I said. I was all about planning.

I found Grandma hunched on the bed nearest the door to our room, the phone to her ear. I was about to ask her what she was doing when I caught an unusual sight out the thirteenth-floor window.

Gargoyles circled the top of the Luxor, screeching and pounding their leathery wings. Even the smaller ones were about the size of a German shepherd. I dragged the curtains shut. I couldn't take any more weirdness.

"I need as many rollaway beds as you can find," Grandma ordered into the phone.

She nodded at my upshot eyebrows and did a curlicue with her finger. "Wards are safer in these three rooms."

I plucked the receiver from her ear and slammed

it down. "We can't stay. In fact, I need you to think. Where is a safe place for you and the witches?"

"Lizzie Brown, what has gotten into you?"

"*Into me?*" I'd saved her life. I'd rescued the whole coven.

Never mind the fact that I seemed incapable of saving the one man I might actually love. I could hear myself growing angrier with each and every word. "You have to get out of here. These succubi don't want you. They want me." And I had a feeling they'd follow me until I fought them—all twenty-two of them.

Make that twenty-four. Damn. They must have used the witches' power to draw two more out of hell. I could never destroy them all—not at this rate.

Grandma stiffened. "What I meant, sport, is how did you kill the phone?"

I stared down at the crumpled heap of plastic on the nightstand. Sure enough, I'd slammed the receiver down *into* the phone. A rivet of shock ran through me. The beige plastic split open like I'd run over it with my Harley.

"Dimitri says you wasted three demons." She glared at me, her body sagging but her mind as alert as ever. "You're not trained to kill that many."

I wasn't? "Well, that's just great!"

"What the hell happened to you?"

What indeed? I clutched my marked palm against my skirt.

Her eyes narrowed. "We came here because we're in this together."

Not when "together" meant floating unconscious in the hallway. "I just about got killed tonight trying to save your butts. You're not helping. You need to leave. Don't even tell me where you're going."

If I couldn't protect them by being with them, I'd do the next best thing—get them as far away from here as possible.

"News flash. You need the coven."

"That might be true." I'd certainly needed them in the past. But it wasn't about what I wanted. It was about knowing in my gut what was right and what was wrong—and then doing something about it.

She flung the broken phone on the floor. "This after we protected you, we trained you, we accepted you as one of our own."

"Some training," I scoffed. "When were you going to teach me to kill three?"

"When you were ready!"

"Yeah, well I think I'm ready."

"You can't handle everything!"

"Yes, I can." The dark mark burned into my skin. "I killed the fifth-level demon that chased you around the country for thirty years. I killed one last night. Three today."

She let out a string of curses that would have burned my adoptive mom's ears clean off. "You can't do this alone. You probably don't even know how you killed three just now."

A sudden fear snaked down my back. She was right. I had nothing going for me but my instincts and my God-given skills. Grandma hadn't shown me what to do during a multiple demon attack. She'd never told me that Max, a half demon, half human could even exist, and she certainly hadn't shared how to keep from being marked by a demon. "You didn't teach me jack."

Her face blazed red. "You think I can teach you a lifetime of lessons in two weeks? People want to be lawyers, they spend three years in law school. You want to be a vet, you go to eight years of medical school. You skip thirty years of demon slayer training and you want to learn it in two weeks, half of which we spent on the run from a fifth-level demon and the rest we spent trying to get here to save Phil's sorry ass. There's no easy way. I taught you what you needed to know to survive."

Well, it wasn't enough. The only thing I did know was that I wasn't going to be responsible for the coven getting wiped out.

"I'm the only one who can slay a succubus. So I'm staying and you're going."

"You need me," she said, biting off every word.

"No, I don't," I retorted, sad, angry and very much alone.

If I could have slammed a door in knee-deep water, I would have. Instead, I slogged down the hallway, avoiding dead fish. I rubbed at the 6-6-6 that had etched itself deep into my palm, the edges burned black.

Someone splashed up behind me. It wasn't a demon, so it could have been Mary Poppins for all I cared. I had to think.

"Hold up!" Sid hollered.

I'd forgotten he was even there. Still, I kept walking, despite a string of fairy curses.

"Excuse me? Hey, lady. I'm risking a crab up the pants, so you need to park your ass and listen."

I sighed. "What, Sid?" I turned around to find him

struggling to shake a tangled string of seaweed from his fingers. He was shorter than I was, and the water reached halfway up his thighs. His brown trousers held a pocket of air that made him look even rounder.

"I should be asking you the same thing," he said. "What happened here? We've never seen succubi attack like this, and they don't usually go for females. What'd you do?"

"Nothing," I said. "Obviously, the witches had something they wanted." Like life energy. I shivered despite myself. "Sid, we need to get the survivors out of here. Does the DIP have a place they can stay?"

He furrowed his brows. "Maybe." He wiped his hand off on his sleeve and pulled his phone from the pocket of his tan striped shirt. "They don't normally like to get involved, but I think they're going to have to make an exception here." He dialed in a text message. "Call me a softie, but a full-scale slaughter won't look good on my performance review. Besides"—he gave me a quick once over—"you're about to have bigger problems."

That's right. Fairies could predict the near future. "So what's going to happen?" I asked, a bit too breathlessly.

"Demons. What else?" he said, far too flippantly for my taste.

"Soon?" I asked.

"Soon enough. Me and the Red Skulls are making it out. You, I'm not so sure about." He shrugged at my utter shock. "You can't do anything about it. Except you'd damned well better ask for help when you need it. *Capiche?*"

Not help from the witches, I hoped. I couldn't risk

them like that. "Tell me everything I need to know," I said.

"I just did." He tapped something else into his phone. "Geez. See, this is why I don't tell people things. They ask for details that I don't have." He took a closer look at a message on his phone. "Says here we've been able to confirm your report, at least so far as there's some weird shit going on."

"Hallelujah."

Sid wrestled a handkerchief out of his back pocket, found a dry spot, and used it to mop his head.

He shot me a disdainful glare as he dug something out of the pocket of his loose brown dress pants. "I'm going to regret this, but . . ." He held a small vial of glitter. The clear contents churned and sparkled with energy. "Fairy dust," he explained, "Mine. Just don't go summoning me during any demon attacks or I'll kill you myself."

"Wow," I said, "thanks." I had a feeling this didn't happen every day.

The fairy scowled. "Yeah, well if you screw up, I'm allowed my quid pro quo. You know, restitution. And I will take you up on that."

"I shudder to think," I responded. As for the fairy dust, I held it up watching it cluster thick in places where my fingers touched the vial.

But it wasn't the fairy I was worried about.

*Excerpt from* The Dangerous Book for Demon Slayers:
*Gargoyles are a good measure of the evil threat in an
area—both demonic and otherwise. These horned creatures resemble giant bats and are attracted to the nega-
tive energies. Gargoyles will eat any evil that wanders
too close. It's good in the short term, but a bad sign over-
all. Too many gargoyles in one spot means they've found
a place to feast—and to breed.*

# CHAPTER SEVENTEEN

Wouldn't you know it, Sid and the DIP actually came
through. Less than an hour later, he'd found accom-
modations outside of the city for all two dozen of the
Red Skulls. Grandma lay on her bed, resting up while
the rest of the witches packed.

"You mind if I ride with Bob?" Pirate asked. "He
found me a special helmet in one of the gift shops. It
has racing stripes!"

"Go ahead." I scratched him between the ears. I'd be
glad when they were safely on the road out of town.

I was about to check on the witches when the door
to our hotel room flung open. Pirate and I both jumped
an inch.

Witches crowded the corridor outside as Max
hitched himself out of the knee-deep water in the
hallway and strode into the room like he did it every
day.

He looked like the devil himself, in black leather
pants and a red club shirt. Hell and seduction seemed
to press around him. How did he even find us?

"I need you," Max said, his eyes flicking over me. Naturally. "Well, take a number."

I had my own problems to solve. As soon as I marshaled the witches and Dimitri out of Vegas, my biggest challenge involved a giant war with two dozen succubi.

Max stood rod-straight. If he was affected by the scene around him, he gave no indication. He took me in, inch by inch, settling on the darkened emerald at my throat. "You're flinging slayer energy up and down The Strip. Cut it out. We're leaving now. I've word that a succubus will be at Coo Coo Lounge. Get your switch stars."

Something had happened to him. I could feel it like a black hole at the very core of him. "What's wrong with you?"

He gave a predatory grin. "I'm mourning the one that got away."

I'd never seen a cambion turn, but he felt close. I stole a glance at Grandma. She seemed to be thinking the same thing. And it worried the snot out of me that she wasn't even saying it.

"You need to leave," I said to Max. I didn't want him around anyone when he went over the edge. Besides, he was going about this the wrong way. Picking the demons off one by one would likely get me killed and push him over to the dark side. And it wouldn't do any good if they kept bringing more in. It'd be like attacking a roach infestation by stomping just the ones you see. Only these roaches were huge and evil and wanted to kill us. We had to attack them at their source.

"Slayer . . ." Max warned.

I crossed my arms over my chest. "There are too many of them, Max. What good is it going to do to kill one?"

Max raised a brow. "Want to tell that to the family of the man she kills?"

"Damn it." I reached for my switch stars, despising him for saying the one thing that would get me off track. Whatever life we saved was as important to somebody as Grandma or Uncle Phil or my own adoptive family was to me. "I'll go." I raised a finger in warning. "If you let me do the killing."

Grandma looked ready to punch somebody.

"You'd better be gone by the time I get back," I warned.

Max and I shoved past the witches in the hallway. "What, Lizzie?" Frieda protested. "Are you working for him now? We need you. And besides, your Uncle Phil needs you. His soul's in trouble and you're gonna run off? Don't let that devil on wheels use you."

I pinned her to the wall with a glare. "He stands up to his enemies. I know you can respect that." I raised my voice to be heard loud and clear. "I'm leaving, so you guys need to clear out. Now."

"What? Are you just shoving us aside?" she demanded.

"When you're a liability?" I said to her, and the group, "yes."

That got me some attention and a few middle fingers.

Like they weren't used to being on the run.

"You're making about as much sense as tits on a

tree," Frieda snapped over the jeers of the rest of the bikers. "Well, you can kiss my go-to-hell. Leave. It'll serve you right if we get attacked again."

Max's eyes flared. "You need to get the griffin out of Vegas."

As if I hadn't thought of that.

"This attack didn't come because of Dimitri," I said, keeping him moving. "The succubi know I'm in Vegas. The coven is a perfect target. They can get to me and steal energy from the witches to bring more demons in."

Max stopped cold.

Dimitri had just made it back to the thirteenth floor. Despite his weakened state, my honorable griffin had been schlepping luggage for the battered witches. His shock at seeing Max quickly morphed to disgust.

Max's face hardened. "There's your energy leak."

"Dimitri is leaving too," I said, hoping I was right.

Dimitri stepped around me, blocking Max. "Not with him around." He shoved Max into the wall.

Max scowled. "You are the reason for all of this!" No question he was a killer. I had no doubt he'd attack anyone who got in his way.

Dimitri's hair had gone white, and he'd grown leaner, bolder than I'd ever seen him. "I'm not the one keeping them in my basement."

"Enough." I stepped between them. "The question is what we do about it."

"Attack," Max growled as he stormed past me.

"Wait!" He couldn't mean . . . I tried to see it from Max's warped sense of justice. If the griffin is feeding them, giving them power . . . *Kill the griffin.*

Max leapt at Dimitri, sending them both flying down the hallway and into—

"The wards!" Ant Eater hollered, as goo splattered and Dimitri's head hit the far wall with a resounding crack.

"Not good." Grandma yanked me by the arm. "We're leaving. Now."

She had to be kidding. "I'm not going to leave Dimitri and Max to be ravaged by the she-demons."

Dimitri held Max's head underwater as Max brought his fist straight into Dimitri's gut. "Let him go!" I screamed. Dimitri slammed against the wall, bounced off and drove straight back at Max. "Stop!" It was like watching two dogs fight. I had to stop them, but I couldn't jump in the middle without getting bit. Hard.

"Go!" I told Grandma.

"Aw, hell. But the wards—" Fear burned in her eyes.

"That's why you need to go!" I said, herding the Red Skulls down the corridor. I could feel the demons circling, looking for a way in. For the second time that evening, I shoved Grandma through the doorway. The witches might like to talk smack, but they were smart enough to get out of the way of a demon. One by one, they rushed for the door.

Meanwhile Dimitri and Max had worked their way closer to the flickering wards. "Dimitri! Stop!" If I could only get Dimitri and Max out of here before the succubi broke through.

Dimitri had to listen. "Dimitri!"

I made a dash for them, not knowing what I'd do when I got there, but sure I had to stop this somehow.

"Hold it!" A bullet exploded the ceiling above my head.

I spun around and couldn't believe what I saw. "Sid?"

His pudgy face shone with sweat, and he aimed a small silver revolver straight at me. "Back up now or I'll bust a cap in that sweet ass. Come on. All three of you."

"What are you doing, Sid?" I said, as calm as I could manage with my heart hammering in my throat.

"Back up." Sid thrust the revolver to my chest and yanked me against him. Fairy dust rained down around us, and I nearly choked on the stench of stale bubble-gum. No question, Sid was stressed. Good.

Dimitri rushed for Sid, Max on his heels. Sid tried to drag me into an open doorway as an explosion rattled the far end of the floor. Heat seared me down to my underwear.

"Duck!" Sid hollered as the far wall burst into silver flames. I crouched, my elbows in the water, my hands flung over my head as sparks burned fist-size holes in the ceiling above. A soaring inferno devoured six Skeep posts and a potted fern at the end of the hall. I shielded my eyes against the intense glare until it exhausted itself. The flames licked away the last of the Skeep posts and fizzled out.

"You knew—" I began. Wait, of course he knew the end of the hallway would explode. And, my stomach flip-flopped, he said the demons were coming.

"Ward failure," Sid muttered, shoving away from me. "Looks like Battina cast a backup system. Smart lady. That means you got about two minutes." He stuffed his gun down the back of his pants and used his sleeve to wipe the fairy dust from his forehead. "I already told you I'm making it out of here alive."

The thin ward belched smoke and super-energized air. The hallway felt like the desert at noon, and with each step I caught a jolt of static electricity. Lovely, considering we stood in knee-deep water.

"Lizzie! Get back!" Dimitri ordered.

I pitched myself against the wall, not even hearing the piercing shriek of the switch star until it buried itself in the wall to my left.

Max was still going to attack?

I'd switch-star him myself if we didn't need him.

Blood poured from Max's temple and tangled in his golden hair as he sloshed down the hallway. His eyes glowed red like a demon's. "You're feeding the devil himself," he said, his face stiff with concentration. "You need to die."

Max the brave, the unstoppable, the lone vigilante lunged for the man I loved.

We had to immobilize him and get him out of here. No way we could face what was coming, even with Max.

Dimitri thrust out a fist and caught him by the throat. Max slammed into the water. He shot to his feet, but Dimitri caught him in midair, hurtling him down again. Shock ricocheted through me. How strong was Dimitri? Even after he'd been drained.

Max had bested demons. He was half damned himself.

"Stop, Max!" I ordered. "Think! We need to leave now!"

His jaw set in a snarl. "First things first." He glared at Dimitri, hate burning in his eyes. "You are a scourge, a plague." Max breathed heavily, water dripping off him.

Max attacked again. Dimitri spun sideways and grabbed the last switch star from Max's belt. He held it down at his side, as the red blades began to churn. I gasped. I knew Dimitri had slayer in him. I'd put it there myself. Still, it was an entirely new thing to see the blades churning like they would for me.

Max had to know it was over.

He didn't. Max launched himself at Dimitri and they toppled sideways, the switch star burying itself in Max's side.

"No!" I choked.

Steam hissed from the wound. Thick blood surged like a pot boiling over, searing the star, melting it as if it had been dipped in acid. Max's eyes widened. He let out a choked gurgle before collapsing headlong into the water. Blood bubbled to the surface.

I cringed at the smell of it, like singed copper mingled with the overwhelming scent of sulfur. At the same time, I refused to believe it. He had to be only half dead, half . . . holy heck. I rushed to Max's side. His blood sizzled at my skin.

"Max!" I dug through a wad of seaweed, felt for a pulse, trying to ignore my own blood rushing through my ears.

My limbs weakened and my insides churned. Bent on my own misery, I practically fell sideways when a wave of energy slammed into me. It surged through me, filling me to the core. My strength surged, along with my determination, and an immense desire to kick butt. My demon slayer mojo had never kicked in so strong before. Then I knew.

Max was dead.

His captured demons rejoiced in an immense wave of power. It pounded in a heady, almost addicting rhythm. I reached out blindly, bracing myself against the wall as the force of seventeen starving demons threw me off balance. I yanked my hands back and braced them on my hips. It took immense concentration to stay that way. I felt the demons' strength growing, expanding. They fled Max's prison, ready to devour Vegas and their newfound freedom.

Dimitri's eyes shot from yellow to orange to red. His skin paled and his muscles withered. We had nearly twice as many demons free in Vegas and they were draining him, killing him right before my very eyes.

Demons pounded on the wards until the magic gave way. My demon slayer instincts screamed for me to run headlong into the fray, face the new succubi threat, drive them out as I slogged through the wasteland of Max's demon blood.

Too bad they had me outnumbered by about forty to one.

Energy rolled down the hall like a wind. I forced myself to stand tall.

As if giving life to my greatest fear, succubi shrieked through the charred holes in the ceiling. Wave after wave, they roiled upon each other until all I could see was black, leathery bodies. The stench of sulfur made it almost impossible to breathe. They surged, red eyes burning with hunger.

Max was dead. Dimitri was dying and I'd be next.

"Sid!" He wanted to be a badass fairy, well, here was his chance. "Sid!" I forced every bit of will, every bit of strength and desperation I had into that one word. "Sid!"

For a moment, the world seemed to slow. I tried to call out again, but couldn't. And an instant later, I knew why. Time began to slowly rewind itself. The weight lifted from my body. I shifted backward to Dimitri, back to Max's body, backward until Max and Dimitri fought to the death.

Sid's voice echoed in my ears. "Told you that you needed my help. Brace yourself. I'm not too good on landings."

With a pop and a sickening heave, time lurched forward once again.

Dimitri thrust out a fist and caught Max by the throat. Max slammed into the water. He shot to his feet, but Dimitri caught him in midair, hurtling him down again.

"You are a scourge, a plague." Max breathed heavily, water dripping off him.

"He'll kill you!" I yelled, directing every bit of will I had at the hunter.

Max, the suicidal jerk, ignored me.

"Dimitri will kill you!"

Max's mouth quirked at the corner. "Impossible."

"He's part slayer, Sherlock. And answer me this—if you die, what happens to the starving demons you're holding?"

Max touched his side, almost as if he remembered.

I took advantage of the break to squeeze in between them. I laid my palm flat against Dimitri's chest and tried to work him backward. He didn't budge.

"If you don't stop now, Dimitri, you're going to kill him. His demons will eat you alive."

And then they'll come for me.

Dimitri's eyes—brown, still brown thank goodness—seemed to remember.

"So both of you. Step back!" I ordered, voice cracking. To my amazement, they did.

"Dimitri," I said to the impossibly handsome, thick-skulled, entirely too focused griffin on my right, "listen to me. You have part slayer in you. Push it and Max dies." Dimitri stared at Max, his eyes widening slightly.

Max barked out a laugh. "It's not enough."

I wanted to wring his thick neck. "Think hard. Remember. You know it is."

Max unsheathed his last switch star.

"Do it and you die, Max."

Max's face, tight with concentration, gave nothing away. "Yes, well I don't care."

I didn't doubt that for a second. On some level, I think Max wanted to die. "That's all fine and dandy, but I'm not fighting seventeen extra demons just so you can take the easy way out."

Max could do whatever he wanted—after we stopped the succubi, saved Dimitri and Phil, and kept me from, well, I didn't know what the dark mark was doing to me.

I glanced at the wards. Battina had done a good job. Barring an attack from Max's seventeen starving demons, I think we had a minute.

I exhaled. "You are dangerous," I said to them both.

Dimitri didn't move. Only the pounding pulse at his neck gave him away.

Max first. I walked up to the scowling angel of vengeance. He wasn't afraid to die, and I certainly didn't want to be around when he turned. "I thought I could work with you, but I can't. Get out of here. Now."

He stared at me, his face a mockery. I'd done my best to explain to him what was happening and frankly, there was nothing else I could do.

"You won't make it without me," he said.

"It's just too much." I'd barely kept him and Dimitri from killing each other. I didn't want to risk round two.

His red eyes blazed with fury. "Suit yourself, slayer." Max took a backward look at the thinning ward and left us.

I wanted to exhale, but not yet.

Dimitri wrapped an arm around my shoulder and tugged me to him. "Well, that was—"

"I'm not done," I said, turning to my lover, my protector, my friend. "You are a danger—to yourself and to me. You're feeding them and you don't seem to care. You might not have been able to see what could have happened to you just now, but I did."

*Forgive me, Dimitri.*

I couldn't believe I was about to do this, but I didn't have a choice. I'd asked him to leave with the witches and he'd refused. I told him the danger he was in and he didn't listen. He'd run me out of options, save one.

My throat felt tight. "I don't think we should see each other anymore."

Dimitri looked like I'd punched him in the stomach. He glared at me, shock and betrayal plain on his face. "I don't believe it."

Tears welled in my eyes. Dimitri was my first real boyfriend. I was hoping he'd be the first man to tell me he loved me. Despite the witches and the demons and everything that had happened. But that wasn't going to happen—not now.

He'd changed. And the only way he'd leave is if I left him.

Dimitri touched me on the back of my neck. His hands cooled my skin, even as we felt the presence build. "Lizzie, I love you." The dark veil lifted and for the first time since we'd gotten here, I could see his true emotions. He stood expectantly, his feelings bare, waiting for me to accept the amazing gift he offered.

Warmth rumbled my spine, threatening to explode. "You love me?" I asked like a complete fool. The practical side of me knew I had to bury it, think instead of a way to get him out of there. The soft side of me wanted to hear it again. Nobody had ever said it to me before, except for my preschoolers. And they said the same thing about Elmo.

Dimitri loved me.

I closed the distance between us, allowing myself a whisper of a kiss on his roughened cheek. It took everything I had to pull away. "If you love me, then leave."

He paused for a brief moment, searching my face. Whatever was written there, it made him nod.

"Good-bye, Lizzie." He kissed me softly on the forehead.

Shoulders back, he strode down the hallway and out of my life.

My heart seized as I watched him go. How could this happen to us? He was the first man to really know me, to believe in me. He was the first to tell me he loved me. I willed myself to stand tall when I'd rather curl into a ball and cry.

It had to be this way, no matter how much it hurt.

I touched my fingers to the ancient emerald Dimitri had given me, his promise that he'd always be with me. I held the dead stone to my chin and let the tears come.

# CHAPTER EIGHTEEN

I made my way to the twelfth-floor elevators as hotel workers rushed down the cookie-cutter hallway. Several of them carried bundles wrapped in black velvet. Weapons, I assumed from the glints of silver peeking from underneath.

Yeah, well I just hoped they brought their wards. We'd saved Max and prevented his seventeen demons from escaping. Now if they could hold the rest away from the hotel at least, well, I might have a minute to think.

No telling where Sid had gone after he wound back time. I wondered if it was me calling him or if he'd stuck around because he knew his city needed his help. Either way, I wasn't one to take a second chance lightly.

Trying to look inconspicuous in my soaked dress and switch stars, I ducked into an empty elevator as a half dozen bellhops unloaded a massive iron urn from the elevator next to me. I jabbed the lobby button until the heavy doors thunked closed.

Patrons crowded the casino downstairs, gambling and drinking as more hotel staff rushed for the magical thirteenth floor.

I spotted Pirate next to the Keno parlor eating

peanuts from an abandoned buffet plate. "Lizzie!" Pirate forgot his meal and dashed across the pink- and green-swirled carpet.

"What are you doing?" I scanned the casino lobby. "Are the witches here?"

"Nope," he said, snuggling into my arms. "I escaped."

I sank into a pink casino chair with him.

"So," Pirate said, "tell me about the fight. You kick some butt?" He closed his eyes as I rubbed his head. "I tried to get up there, but they don't make elevators with dogs in mind."

"I don't want to talk about it."

I was relieved, grateful that we'd prevented a tragedy. Yet I'd never felt so alone. There'd be no help from the Red Skulls or Dimitri. I knew I had to let them go, but at the same time, I didn't know what to do next. The demons were still coming. They'd slowed, but they certainly hadn't stopped.

The dark mark burned against my palm. It had given me the power to survive—so far—but now what? Was I here, alive, only to watch the demons take Las Vegas?

"Aw, well that's nice," Pirate said, roaring out a wide doggie yawn as he settled in next to me. "Let's go upstairs and get a nap."

Bless Pirate. "The thing is," I began, trying to figure out how to explain the last twenty-four hours. I was starting to feel like Jack Bauer. The thirteenth floor was destroyed, the demons wanted the Red Skulls and we had to get out of here ourselves. I needed to figure out my next step, yet one thought tugged at me.

Dimitri loved me.

On some level, I think I knew. I'd certainly craved it. But it was an entirely different thing to have him say it. I loved him too. And it wasn't because he was strong, loyal and all together devastating in the sack. He was the first man who made me feel like I wanted to be more than Lizzie the superorganized, Lizzie the good girl. True, he hadn't been himself lately. But I had to think there might be some hope for us yet.

My gut twisted with how I'd let him down. He'd blown into Vegas, thinking he had the power to fight off the succubi. I'd taken that away from him. I'd saved him, but I'd also lied about it. In my defense, we'd just gotten back from the second layer of hell, so I hadn't exactly been thinking straight. Besides, we'd known each other for less than two weeks. I've never been the type to jump into things. It had been too early. I wasn't sure. I didn't know how he'd feel about me—or the fact that he could no longer claim his pure griffin heritage—once he'd had a chance to think.

Fear skittered through me. If we didn't play this thing right, I might never see him again.

"No," I said. "It ends here." I launched myself off the chair.

"Hey, now," Pirate said, slipping sideways into the spot I'd vacated.

If it was up to me, then fine. I'd figure out how this whole thing started, exactly why—out of all the half fairies—Serena chose Phil. I had to think it was something more sinister than mere chance. Whatever it was, I'd use it to fry the demons.

"We have to think," I told Pirate. "What does Phil have that could possibly give him any power?" We hadn't seen anything in his house to indicate he was particularly magical. I tried to recall anything out of the ordinary among the wedding brochures, shrine to my retainer and lunch receipts. He didn't have a strong fairy heritage. What then?"

"Oh, gee, Lizzie. I don't—"

Blood rushed to my head as it hit me. It *was* about power, and then some.

I rushed to the concierge desk. "Skeep! I need a Skeep!"

# CHAPTER NINETEEN

Eight Skeeps rushed straight for me. "Meko!" I called out to the orange ball of fire. "I have an important mission for you, okay? I need you to find someone who knows the Hoover Dam. Fast."

Meko zipped away.

Shoot. I hadn't mentioned I needed someone close by. I wasn't too eager to stick around with everyone rushing to the emergency on thirteen. Eventually, they were going to start looking around for survivors . . . or someone to blame.

According to Grandma, Skeeps tended to be literal. I sure hoped fast meant close, and while we were getting specific—connected. I needed to see some things for myself and I doubted Hoover Dam officials were going to let just anybody in. Uncle Phil worked at one of the biggest power-generating plants in the nation.

I tossed my keys to a second Skeep. "Listen, can you send someone to retrieve two Harleys parked at the airport, section L-8?"

"Immediately!" He and my keys disappeared with a large pop.

Twenty seconds later, Meko reappeared.

"My apologies!" he gushed. "I would have been back

sooner, but my aura tends to stick." He shook himself like a wet dog. "I have your expert."

Son of a gun. It had taken me longer to brush the peanut crumbs off Pirate's back. How they got there was still a mystery.

"Ezra," Meko dipped into a row of slot machines against the wall. "We have a guest who needs you."

A ghostly head emerged from the Lucky 7-7-7 machine. He had sandy red hair and a dusting of freckles along his nose and cheeks. "If I can have a minute to compose myself," he said, cringing.

"Hey," I said, trying to imagine his head without the polished slot handle sticking out of it, "you're one of the doormen, aren't you?"

"I'm a bellhop," he corrected.

"Sure," I said, nodding. I recognized him from when Max had taken me to see the demon prison. It had been a tough night and I'd been impressed with how sweet the bellhop had been. He'd looked real enough to me, well, before he'd poked his head through the slot machine.

The phantom bellhop glided out of the Lucky 7 and hovered a few inches off the floor.

"Hiya, Ezra!" Pirate rushed in, paws out, mouth open, wet doggie nose and tongue at the ready and ended up leaping straight through the ghost.

"You two know each other?" Impossible. I'd only met Ezra once.

The ghost's shoulders slumped.

"Oh yeah," Pirate said, winding in, around and through Ezra's ankles. "He's been teaching me how to play Scrabble!"

I stared at my dog. "You can't spell."

"Not with that attitude." Pirate plopped his rear onto the carpet.

Fantastic. Pirate had been having people over. "Is this true?" I asked the ghost, already knowing the answer. Pirate could make friends with a garden gnome.

"Aw, Lizzie. Don't get him in trouble. I asked," Pirate said. "Just like when Meko took me to Jodi Maroni's Sausage Kingdom."

"How?" What had Pirate been doing while I was away? Couldn't he stay put like a regular dog?

"Easy," Pirate said, his tail thumping against the floor. "He's a Skeep and I called him and he said, 'How can I serve you?' and I said I'd give anything for a bratwurst."

Meko glowed with pride.

At least Ezra knew he'd overstepped his bounds. "I'm very sorry," the ghost said. "I don't normally visit guests in their rooms. I know it's a breach of protocol, But his essence called out to me."

"Um, hum," Pirate said. "I've got one of them special essences."

He had an essence all right. Wet dog. "We're going to discuss this later," I said, more than a little annoyed.

The ghost glanced at my hand and visibly paled. His eyes rested on my devil's mark.

Was he afraid of me? Okay, yeah, I'd been feeling edgy since I sent Dimitri and the witches away, and the ghost knew he'd been out of line sneaking into my room.

Pirate nudged a cold nose under my hand. "Dang, Lizzie."

The 6-6-6 glowed with an eerie red light. I clamped it against my thigh, ignoring the sizzle that shot down my leg.

Ezra opened his mouth and then closed it, his body flickering.

"Don't you dare fade on me." If I had to be the problem solver for every witch, fairy and leprechaun within a fifty-mile radius, he could at least give me the facts. "I'm looking for an expert on Hoover Dam. Is that you?"

Ezra ducked his head and smiled. "Yes, ma'am. I worked as an engineer on Boulder Dam."

"Sure. Why not?" I said, trying to wrap my mind around the ghost currently scratching the spot on Pirate's neck that made him thump his back leg. I thought I was the only one who knew about that.

"You can call it Hoover if you like, but it'll always be Boulder Dam to me," the ghost said.

Frankly, I didn't care what they called it. "We'll need your brains and also somebody who knows what's going on at the dam right now."

"I'll take you to see Joe Lipswitch."

That surprised me. "You know someone who works there?"

Ezra scoffed. "Joe lives and breathes that place. Spends most of his time in one of the old inspection tunnels off the Nevada spillway. I keep telling him he needs to get out more, but he's a stubborn one." Ezra shook his head sadly. "We'll have to go to him."

The realization crept over me. "Joe's dead, isn't he?"

"High scaling was dangerous work. Lots of guys got hit by falling rocks or those forty-pound jackhammers they had to have lowered down to them. Joe says it happened so quick, he didn't feel a thing."

"And Joe's the best we have?" I glanced at Meko.

The orb dipped. "Ma'am, it is my job to bring you the best sources, information, snack foods, panty hose or anything else you require. I can assist you with restaurant reservations, tickets to the hottest shows on The Strip and plenty of—"

"Of course, Mcko." I hated to cut the poor thing off, but we were in the middle of a crisis here. "I should have known you'd have it covered."

Meko glowed.

Why couldn't I meet a normal person with good information? Someone who wasn't a biker witch, eighty years dead or a half demon? Someone who hadn't been wandering the bowels of Hoover Dam since its construction. A real source like any other normal frickin' woman-on-a-mission would have?

"Field trip!" Pirate declared, launching himself off the chair and rushing for the door. He turned in a circle and sat. "You know you're going to need a ghost sniffer along. We canines have a sixth sense about us."

I hated to admit it, but . . . "You're right. We could use you." I certainly wasn't going to leave him alone.

It would be nice to have someone along who wasn't creeped out by the devil's mark on my hand. I adjusted my switch stars and slid my new hotel key card into an empty slot on my utility belt.

"Lighten up, Lizzie," Pirate said, practically dancing in place. "It's not like Joe's gonna marry a demon or start a big succubi invasion or give you a devil's mark or—"

"No, of course not," I said, before Pirate could

cheer me up any more. For all I knew, Joe could be far worse.

Joe Lipswich lived in one of the tunnels used to inspect the dam during the half a century it took for the concrete to cure. Naturally, Joe's residence had to be sixty feet below the towering edge of Hoover Dam. Since he wouldn't come to us, we went to him, via the two o'clock Deluxe Hoover Dam Tour.

"Did it start yet?" Pirate's nose tickled me from where I'd hidden him in an oversized purse. I'd bought the thing at the Paradise Hotel gift shop. Made of woven straw, it made everywhere it touched itchy.

"Hush," I said, arranging the purse flap over Pirate's prying nostrils. There were no dogs allowed on the tour—or anywhere on the dam for that matter. Pirate shifted inside my purse.

Voices tended to carry in the sparse lobby below the observation deck. Our tour group was small, less than twenty of us in all. I tried not to fidget as the tourists checked their cameras and flipped through their guide books. I wished we'd had more of a crowd. It would make it easier for me to disappear into one of the inspection tunnels. I flipped through the guide book, one eye on Ezra. Luckily, no one seemed to be looking for a ghost squeezed behind the bronze statue dedicated to the men who built Hoover Dam.

People liked to see what they wanted to see.

Still, I motioned for Ezra to tuck in his elbows.

At last our guide introduced himself and led us into an immense elevator.

"Hoover Dam was begun in 1931 and dedicated by President Franklin Roosevelt in 1935," the guide said as the elevator dropped seventy feet into the concrete bowls of the dam. It made my stomach dip to think of being surrounded by six million tons of concrete, steel and darkness.

We exited into a tunnel that grew narrower as we went. And where was Ezra? I craned my neck to see behind doors and into dark corners. I looked behind fellow tourists and even past a "restricted" door. Maybe I did like it better when he had his elbows sticking out.

We saw intake valves and turbines before our deluxe guide led us through round tunnels smelling of concrete and old steel. The passageways were barely taller than I was, their light bulbs dangling above us, casting shadows and daring me to depart down a lonely dark tunnel.

A soft voice touched behind my ear, nearly scaring me out of my gourd. "It's time," he whispered.

I whipped around to find Ezra poking his head out of the top of the tunnel. "Where have you been?" I hissed.

He nudged his head back to a particularly dark artery we'd passed. "Follow me."

I glanced at our guide up front, showing my fellow tourists the chalk inspection marks left behind in the 1930s and '40s. When he turned his back to us, I slipped into the side tunnel.

My heart echoed in my chest. I couldn't believe I was doing this. The light quickly vanished, and I had to reach out to the cold walls of the tunnel to guide myself. Ezra glowed faintly ahead. It was a strange feeling, this deliberate breaking of the rules. I didn't even like to walk on other people's lawns, much less cut out on a tour group at a major national landmark. A lot of the things I'd had to do in the last few weeks, I'd done because they were forced upon me. I'd had no choice, or at least that's what I'd told myself. But now I had a choice. And I was still doing it. I think sometimes when you change, the last person who knows about it is you.

Ezra halted and I had to make a quick stop myself to keep from barreling straight through him. "Joe does like to wander," he said with an apologetic glance over his shoulder. "Fortunately, he's not going too far."

Yeah, well those two might have all the time in the world, but I didn't.

"You ready, babe?" I dug Pirate, warm and snuggly, out of the bag.

"Hee-yah. I was born ready!" Pirate's nails scratched at the concrete as I eased him down next to me. He took the curve of the tunnel NASCAR-style.

Pirate took a quick left, with Ezra and I right behind. I cringed as the soles of my sandals hit a hollow metal grate. "Hold up, everybody." My voice echoed down the round passageways. "How sturdy is this?"

"It's hard to say," Ezra said. "But I've seen inspectors in here."

"What? In 1952?" I said, fighting a twinge of panic. I could see it now. Lizzie Brown, survivor of multiple demon attacks, taken out by a tunnel. This Joe person had better be worth it.

"Come on, Lizzie." Pirate took off, his tags jingling. "Follow me. I can take the pressure. I was bred to take the heat."

I pried my hand off the wall. The eerie red light revealed a metal grate with nothing underneath. The emptiness under my feet seemed to stretch into oblivion.

We took a series of twists and turns, more than I wanted to think about. Still, I tracked them like my life depended on it—which it would if Pirate lost his way.

Near the end of a shaft that I swear curved unnaturally to the left, Pirate hitched up on his back legs. "Hey! Nice hat."

Ezra let out a whoop. "Joe, you clown!" He clapped at a glowing, yellow orb. "I've got visitors for you."

The orb lengthened and grew into a lanky construction worker in dusty 1930s-style overalls. His white shirt stretched around muscular arms streaked with dust and sweat. He wore a crude-looking hat covered in what looked to be black goo.

He lifted his head and grinned as if he hadn't seen a woman in years. Joe had a rawboned, friendly face, with a hooked, Roman nose and a dimple at the chin. "Well, dang, aren't you a sight?" he said, eyeing me a bit too appreciatively.

"Joe," Ezra said, embarrassed. "She's about seventy years too late."

Joe shook his head, as if to clear it. "My apologies, ma'am. It gets lonely down here. Add that to the fact that nobody can see me, hear me, talk to me. 'Cept Ezra here. And Mad Mertle, who jumped in '62."

"And Farsworth," Ezra added.

Joe rubbed his hand against his chin. "Nah. He gave up. Went to the light." His eyes searched as if we were outside instead of in a narrow tunnel deep in the dam.

"Aw, now that's too bad," Ezra murmured.

"I was hoping you could answer a few questions for me," I said to Joe. "I have an uncle who works here. Phil Whirley. I'm not sure what he does, but whatever it is, he's got demons after him."

Joe winced at the mention of demons. "Used to be I could go years without even smelling one. Now I have to work to avoid them."

"At the dam?" Now we were getting somewhere.

"How much do you like your uncle?" Joe asked.

"What do you mean?" I asked slowly.

Pirate wound his stubby little body around my legs. "Enough that she got the devil's mark," he said.

Joe's gaze swept over my body and rested on my glowing palm. "So I see." The muscles in his jaw worked. "In that case, you'd better act fast. Your man is sabotaging the dam's turbine timing system."

A shiver ran through me. "Not Phil." He wouldn't.

Ezra shot me an apologetic glance. "You said he married a she-demon."

"I said?" I hadn't told Ezra anything. "You've been telling him our business?" I asked Pirate.

He shot me an innocent doggie look. "Oh, this and that. In between high-stakes, winner-take-all Scrabble trash talk."

Ezra cleared his throat. "It's unnatural, a succubus marrying a half fairy. She probably hooked the human side of him, but with her ability to enhance people's powers, I'm willing to bet your uncle could do some serious damage."

Oh frig. I hadn't thought about the succubus giving *Phil* power.

Joe nodded. "He's got something going on. I've seen

it myself. Now I'm no engineer, but I've been around long enough to know Phil Whirley's working on a massive power outage. This place lights up a good chunk of the West Coast."

We still didn't have all the facts. "Why would the demons want Phil to knock out the lights?"

"Beats me," Joe replied. "But it gets their rocks off. Word is the succubi have been hacking the power system out West for decades. They're the ones responsible for most of the rolling blackouts. And the 2003 blackout that hit the East Coast."

"Okay," I said. It still didn't make sense. "I hate to think what could happen to Uncle Phil after they're done with him." Their needing him was probably the only thing keeping him alive.

"You'd better figure it out quick," Joe said. "The way he's been running it, the turbine timing system could blow."

"Soon?" I gaped. We needed time on this.

"It could have gone today. As it stands, he's got another shift tomorrow," Joe said.

"Tomorrow?" I braced my hands on the sides of the tunnel. It was too soon. I couldn't fix this by tomorrow. Even if I could get to the DIP office before six o' clock, they'd be so tangled up in their bureaucratic hoo-ha, they'd wait for an actual demon invasion to step up. And the nonmagical authorities weren't going to believe me, at least not in time to get an inspection crew in here tomorrow. And what could I possibly say to convince them?

*Hey, I've come to tell you that two ghosts warned me that a half fairy is tinkering with the Hoover Dam to the point where we'll lose power. It's all part of a demonic plan to trigger Armageddon when the lights are out.*

"It's too soon," I said.

"The West Coast will be the first to go, right after some kind of concert," Joe said, hovering close enough for me to smell the dampness on him. "I heard him talking with his lady friend on the phone."

Joe looked immensely sorry as he shrugged.

I had to figure out how they planned to bring the demons in. I had to shut off their power source, if you will. The problem was, Phil held the answers and he was brain-warped.

Serena had been clear. I could still feel her rage. *Leave us alone, demon slayer, and I'll only kill him when I'm finished. Push me and I'll take his soul.*

My stomach dipped when I realized it wasn't even a matter of rescuing his soul anymore. *Sacrifice one for the many.* I just wish I wasn't the one who had to make that choice.

Well, I refused let her win. I braced a hand on my switch stars and asked the ghost, "How good are you at getting into places most of us can't?"

He nodded thoughtfully. "I can hold my own."

"If we can find Phil . . ." I began.

Joe grinned. "They'll be at Club Viva." He said, "Phil's been talking about it all day."

"Okay," I said, letting out a breath I'd barely realized I was holding. "Let's go save the world."

*Excerpt from* The Dangerous Book for Demon Slayers: *Meeting a ghost reminds me of the time I bought my gold Saturn. I thought it was unique, until I had one and started noticing every gold Saturn on the road. I'd assumed the first ghosts I met were the only ones I'd see for awhile. Then I opened my eyes and found them everywhere. Fortunately, most people don't bother looking for them. Perhaps if they did, the McDonald's drive-thru wouldn't be so popular. Some drive-up customers seem to notice the slight chill in the air. But they never seem to notice the ghosts filching one or two of their french fries.*

# CHAPTER TWENTY

I've never been good at sneaking. I hate spying. I don't even like playing Secret Santa. So why, oh why did I think it was a good idea to spy on my Uncle Phil and the demon who'd stolen his mind? Simple—lack of options.

The demons were putting their plan into motion sooner rather than later. I'd sent Dimitri away, Grandma, Max, anyone who could help me. It was time to see what Ezra and I could do. It had better be enough.

Meko had retrieved my things from the trashed thirteenth floor and we'd stopped by the lobby-level executive's lounge so I could shower. Afterward, I changed into a black leather skirt and a black corset top so clingy it would have given me hives a few months ago. Ezra found a Gucci shopping bag for Pirate, who protested heartily. I didn't blame him one bit. But we all had a price to pay.

Traffic whizzed past on the road out front of the club. It wasn't even nine o'clock at night, far too early for the Las Vegas club scene. Most folks were probably still on their way to dinner.

"What do you know about the devil's mark?" I asked Ezra as I cut the engine on my Harley and backed it into a dark, weed-strewn corner right outside the exit of Club Viva.

The ghost seemed startled by the question. "You mean you don't? Oh," he said, trying to be smooth and doing a lousy job of it. "Those who wear the devil's mark have chosen a," he chewed at his lip, "how shall I put it? An unholy alliance."

But I hadn't—

I ground my right palm into the leg of my too-tight leather skirt. I'd used the mark for good—to stop the demons, to give me the strength I needed.

Max didn't seem to think there was anything wrong with it, although he'd probably been the one to curse me with it in the first place. To say Max was morally ambiguous was like saying the Unabomber might need to get out more.

The top of Ezra's head shimmered and went transparent, along with a large chunk of his left side. "It's a brand," he said, his eyes darting back and forth as if the devil himself would leap out from behind one of the scraggly bushes lining the walk. "It's their way of recognizing one of their own. I've seen it make men do terrible things. It heightens your powers," he said, practically whispering. "You must have seen that."

I had. And I took it out on Grandma's phone. Problem was, I had trouble sorting my new powers from what had been in my demon slayer tool kit all along. When it came right down to it, I'd had my DVD player for five years and I still hadn't figured it out.

Taking extra care not to touch my doggie with the palm of my right hand, I dug Pirate out of his motor- cycle harness. "Are you saying whoever marked me can control me?" For some reason, the very idea ticked me off.

I'd had a temper lately. And freakish strength. I'd taken it to mean I was growing into my powers, chang- ing for the good.

Ezra hesitated. "I don't know."

"Fine." If nobody wanted to answer my questions, I'd do what I'd been doing for the last month—figure it out on my own. I relaxed my guard a little, let the power flow. Call it a test drive. For a moment I let my new strength surge through me, mmm . . . heady and alive.

Ezra shrank back. "Um, oh my. Please don't do that."

"What?" I said, grinning at my belt, watching my switch stars spin on their own.

He cleared his throat hesitantly. "Some believe the mark fosters the evil within."

Anger surged through me. My pulse pounded in my ears. "I didn't choose this." My voice rumbled in a way it never had before and, dang it, I had to suppress a chuckle when Ezra flinched. Yeah, well the days of Lizzie the doormat had passed.

Pirate dipped his ears forward and whined at my feet. Oh for the love of Pete. "Aren't you supposed to be my fearless dog?" Rage surged inside me and boiled over when Pirate, *my Pirate,* backed away.

"Why would I choose this?" I demanded advancing as Ezra scuttled backward. "I dare you to tell me."

Ezra went completely transparent, his words floating on the warm night air. "I don't know."

Pirate made a mad dash for the alley behind the club. He'd always had a nervous bladder. Yeah, that's it. He's not terrified of *me*.

I felt the anger drain out of me. I'd never even been able to summon fear from the squirrels that ate my tomato bushes every year. How had things gotten this messed up?

With a flick of the wrist, my switch stars churned to a stop and an empty feeling settled over me.

Ezra's voice floated from somewhere above. "If you please, excuse me while I investigate the situation inside."

My throat had closed. "Sure," I said, unwilling to attempt more.

*If you please?*

*That's what you get for scaring the poo out of him.*

I leaned against my Harley and ripped a snippet off one of the scraggly bushes that brushed my bare legs.

I was the pleaser. Disturbingly so. I tore the flat leaves off the wiry branch and tossed them to the ground. Up till a month ago, I was the girl who put her cans and bottles through the dishwasher before they hit the recycle bin.

I tossed another leaf to the ground. I'd like to think I'd turned into a badass, but I knew better. Unholy powers or not, I'd write an entire encyclopedia on demon slaying if it helped me understand exactly what I needed to do in the magical world. Even now, I certainly wasn't skulking in shadows for my health.

"Pirate?" I ventured into the pool of light at the entrance to the narrow road. A collar jingled somewhere in the darkness. "Stick close." I tossed the remains of the branch I'd been tearing and took a second look when it jangled on the pavement. It wasn't a branch. Shock trickled through me. I'd been tearing barbed wire that had leaves tangled in it.

I inspected my hands, stomach tickling because I already knew what I'd find—not a scratch on them. Damn it.

*Focus on what you can control,* which didn't seem to be much at the moment.

Before long, the back door clicked open. Ezra's head popped out of the brick wall nearby. "This way. Quickly."

"Pirate!" I held open the Gucci bag and he scampered in without so much as a high-pitched doggie whine. It was exactly what I wanted—and it wasn't. I felt like a stranger in my own skin. My dog of six years was afraid of me.

At the same time, I was more powerful than I'd ever been. And I'd need every bit of strength in the battle ahead. The third demon slayer Truth bubbled to the top of my mind. *Sacrifice yourself.*

I rubbed at the tears burning the back of my eyes. I hoped it would be worth it.

The bag rustled as Pirate situated himself. You'd think with everyone and their brother craving my powers, I wouldn't feel so alone all the time.

The more I figured out, the more confused I was about what I was even doing here. Yeah, well that and fifty bucks might get me a bus ride out of town. In the meantime, I buried my emotions, drew back my shoulders and hustled for the red light illuminating the door at the back of the club.

Inside, a dark purple hallway led endlessly to the right and to the left. A hard bass beat thumped from deep inside the building. In its stillness, the hallway felt like a harbor, a final refuge before the point of no return.

A burning, twisting feeling seized my gut. There were demons in this club. I was so tired of running into demons. The sulfur burned clear over the combined stink of bleach and spilled beer.

"You smell that?" I picked up on something else. A sweetness in the air, like seduction.

My Gucci bag shifted and rattled. "Oh, Lizzie, I never thought I'd say this, but let's just go home." Pirate's nose popped out of the bag, then an ear. "I want my bed and my squeaky frog. And I want to curl up on the couch and eat popcorn and watch girlie movies. I'll even let you rent *Beaches*. Let's go home. You and me."

I wanted that too. Now, more than anything. But . . . "It's too late, Pirate."

Ezra's face appeared, his eyes seeming to scan into the wall in front of me. "Hurry." He shrank into a miniature orb. "Follow the hellhounds."

"Hell-what?" My voice caught in my throat as I made out a pair of ghostlike dogs far down the passageway. Three heads snarled from each sleek, coal black body. With long snouts and empty sockets for eyes, they almost seemed to wait for us.

With effort, I summoned my voice. "They're not guards, are they?" I asked, ready to trade Pirate for a switch star. For the first time, I was glad I had him trembling, safe in my bag.

"Whenever I've seen them before, they've been omens," Ezra said stiffly.

"Well then," I said, watching their doggie drool sizzle on the concrete floor, "I'm guessing they don't foretell bright sunshiny days." Good Lord, the paint started to bubble. Would it have been too much to ask to get a good omen once in a while?

Ezra looked at me like I'd grown a second and third head.

"They foretell events that impact all of mankind," Ezra said.

I nodded one too many times. My head hurt. I didn't want to impact all of mankind. I came here to finagle my uncle out of a bad marriage. That's all. We didn't want a she-demon in the family. Instead, I'd gotten a devil's mark, a potential showdown at the Hoover Dam and now this.

Ezra couldn't seem to tear his eyes away from the hellhounds. "Look at those teeth. Some ghosts go their entire existences without seeing one hellhound, much less two."

"Lucky you," I said, wondering how I'd save the world when I wasn't quite sure I had a handle on what was happening in this second-rate nightclub. I wondered if this is where the succubi had been luring men and killing them. It was remote enough.

The dogs seemed to be waiting for us. Sure enough, when we moved, they did too. They kept a steady pace in front of us, never even looking back, as we followed them down the left corridor. The beat of the music grew stronger and so did the sulfuric stench of demons. The final turn landed us behind a red curtain as a performer on stage crooned the first words to "Mi Amor."

*I need you. I want you. Wrap my world around you.*

The three-headed dogs turned in circles and dashed off into thin air.

"Where'd they go?" I asked, as disturbed by their disappearance as I was by seeing them in the first place.

Ezra shook his head. "Not good," he said, almost to himself.

I glanced toward the stage curtain. The singer belted out a set of lyrics I knew all too well.

*Take me. Please me. You know you need me.*

Ricardo Zarro, the King of Love? I couldn't believe it. I'd seen Ricardo Zarro performing "Mi Amor" on *The Tonight Show* last week. The man was famous for singing the kind of songs that put people in the mood. He lived at the top of the Billboard charts. And he looked quite striking in person, like a young Elvis.

But why would he sing in such a dinky club?

As quickly as I dared, I inched over to stage right and pulled back the side curtain. He'd tucked a yellow silk club shirt into buttery leather pants that (I'd be willing to bet) had never seen the hard seat of a hog. Zarro twitched his hips and belted out the lyrics.

*Take me. Have me. Put your arms around me.*

Sweat glistened on his brow, against the shock of black hair tossed artfully over his forehead. He grinned at the nonexistent audience, showing off a set of perfectly capped teeth.

I tried to understand exactly why he'd be performing here. Half the people in Vegas probably didn't even know about this place.

Then it hit me—privacy. The succubi were working on something.

A demonic presence floated up the empty staircase leading under the stage.

"Back!" I reached for Ezra and came up with a handful of frigid air. "This way!" I motioned to him as I darted behind a stack of black-light boxes. Sure he could go invisible. But dang it, I needed him around and it would be nice to have a clue where to find him.

Feet clomped up the staircase like the next invasion of the heavens.

"Excellent," said a scratchy voice, a demonic one. I knew it as sure as I had to fight the overwhelming urge to attack it. "And tomorrow, the crew knows when to cut the lights."

Serena cackled. *Serena?* I fought the urge to thrust my head around the side of the black-light boxes.

"We're set to take over all major network and cable stations. According to the Nielsen ratings, we'll get about thirty million viewers on the West Coast. Ricardo will handle the audience. I'll give the signal to trigger the blackout," Serena said. "Then it's up to America to take the hint."

The demon snickered, the ruby in her ear casting brilliant light. "I don't think they'll have any trouble. Zarro could put a nun in the mood. Kill the lights, and it'll be like Sodom and Gomorrah all over again. Without the donkey shit."

The footsteps halted. "Harness the power well," the demon warned. "I want the final six hundred and forty-two sisters out of hell in one glorious wave."

That would put them at six hundred sixty-six demons. I glanced at the dark mark on my hand. Not a good number.

"It shouldn't be a problem," Serena said, nails clacking against the hardwood as they began walking again. "Every freak in hell knows that once we get all our girls here, they can follow."

Sweet heavens. I couldn't fight the demons we had in Vegas now, much less the rest of hell.

I risked a peek around the boxes and nearly fell over backwards. The succubi didn't even try to look human. They loped like blackened orangutans, with rough, cracked skin hanging from their scraggly frames and cadaver-like skulls. Serena was taller than her companion, broader. Hair sprouted in wiry clumps from Serena's chin and above her clawlike hands. I'd never seen anything like her and I never wanted to again.

They had my uncle to sabotage the power systems. They had Ricardo Zarro to trigger a massive, power-inducing lovefest. Would sex be enough? Could it really beat killing? I didn't want to find out. Because if they got to six hundred sixty-six, I had a feeling their "killer prize" was Armageddon.

The creature hissed a trail of yellow sulfur.

"I hear Satan himself is monitoring our progress," the shorter one told Serena. "Promotions all around, I'm sure."

Their voices faded until the only thing I could hear was Ricardo's voice pounding out "Long, Hot Lovin'."

"Did you see that?" I whispered into thin air.

Ezra didn't answer. Bless him, he must be following the diabolical duo. I didn't envy the ghost one bit. The air felt positively electric and they'd only walked past.

I reached inside the Gucci bag and scratched Pirate's head. "What are we going to do?"

Pirate exhaled, a warm doggie sniff where he'd wedged his head into the corner of the bag. "I just want to go home."

I couldn't agree more.

As Pirate and I lurked behind the light boxes, waiting for Ezra's report, a terrible thought hit me. The demons should have sensed me.

When I'd gone to hell last week, when I'd followed Max down into the basement of the old prison a few nights ago, the demons had clamored for me. *They knew.* I couldn't think of one solid reason why they wouldn't swarm me now except—my entire body recoiled at the thought—I'd somehow blended with them.

Whoever said keep your friends close and your enemies closer was out of his mind.

"Okay then," I said, standing tall. I refused to go down cowering behind light boxes.

"Wait. Where we going?" Pirate asked, as I scooped him out of the bag.

If I was really going to do this, controlling my dog would be the least of my problems. Pirate would need to be able to move.

"We're going to figure out what the heck is wrong with me," I said, setting him down. "And we're going to learn what in Hades is going on here," I added as Ricardo Zarro hit a high note.

Pirate eyed me warily. "Ohhhh, biscuits," he said, his collar tinkling as he shook off.

"Come on," I said, looking Pirate square in the eye. "Let's show these creatures what happens when they mess with a terrier."

"That wasn't very smart of them, was it?" Pirate said, his ears pricking. "And too bad for them, I think I've got some Great Dane in me too." He snarled.

"I always suspected rottweiler," I said as we crept down the stairway and under the stage. I braced a hand against the low ceiling as I took the steep, narrow stairs. The wooden beams of the stage hung low over the cavelike room. Extra props, junk and costume racks crowded the space.

This place felt wrong. I stood at the bottom of the staircase, unwilling to go farther, the excess energy from the demons prickling my skin. No way a couple of powerful succubi had any need for anything down here. There were no other exits. I wasn't a gambler, but I'd be willing to bet we'd found their portal.

The small room under the stage reeked of sulfur. Miscellaneous stage gear crowded the place, stacked to the ceiling in some areas. We made our way past a cluster of microphone stands and around a pile of half-assembled scaffolding before I spotted the portal, shimmering among a collection of silk scarves.

No bigger than a soap bubble, the illicit pathway churned dark and menacing as a black hole.

I rubbed Pirate's head as I gathered my courage.

"Oh, Lizzie. Oh, Pup-peroni." Pirate's claws clickety clacked on the hardwood floor. "I'd eat it if I didn't think it'd try to eat me first."

"You're not doing anything, baby dog. You wait for me here."

Pirate sniffed. "You know I'll guard it for you. Shoot. That's what guard dogs do."

I braced myself. I had to see if this was our link to purgatory or hell or whatever held back the succubi. You'd think the 1936 handbook could have mentioned that. I held my breath and the bubble stretched as I stepped through.

Heat gripped me. It was ten times worse than sliding into a hot car on a hundred-degree day, but that's all I could think of as I slogged through the ovenlike tunnel.

*Steamy air scorching my lungs.*

In an instant, I'd stepped out of the portal and straight into a world of ice. My sweat gelled instantly as frigid winds buffeted me. I stood in the middle of a maze of ice, the sheer white walls towering in every direction. Creatures moved behind the opaque barriers, their claws scratching into the frost.

My heart stuttered. I'd been here before. "Welcome to the first layer of hell."

The portal spit fire and I leapt out of the way.

"It's around the corner," a voice hissed.

I ducked down the nearest passageway. Oh cripes. Last time, I hadn't even gotten my feet cold before a demon sensed me. I glanced over my shoulder. The creatures in the ice had attacked me last time. They looked like white-scaled lizards and they could bite. Hard. No way I was going through that again.

Dimitri's emerald flashed a brilliant green, and I nearly jumped with shock. "What the . . . ?" I held it away from my chest, but it had already faded to dull again.

Around the corner, a demon received her instructions.

"Assemble your team. Remain here until the portal turns blue. Then it'll be cold enough to pass."

I fought a shiver. They had entire invasion teams ready.

The portal crackled with energy, like a sadistic bug zapper that was somehow churning out superlocusts.

They had to sense me on their home turf. Unhitching a switch star, I braced for the attack of the remaining demon, hoping to heck the ice creature didn't decide to charge at the same time.

I waited, ready, until my elbow stiffened and my fingers cramped around my switch star. "What the . . . ?" I ducked my head around the corner and found the portal deserted.

How would the demon let me go? Why? I'd never heard of a demon slayer walking around in hell and nobody noticing.

Unless . . . I sheathed my switch star and stared at the 6-6-6 glowing on my palm—I somehow belonged here now.

# CHAPTER TWENTY-ONE

I was done blending. I wrapped my arms around my chest, braced myself and charged back through the portal. The heat clawed at me. This time, I didn't care. Standing it, enduring it meant I had something good in me. That meant I didn't belong in hell, even if the demons seemed to think so.

In less than a minute, I was back into the costume room and into a mess.

I could tell in an instant that the demons had left the building, yet Pirate crouched in attack mode, stranded on top of an overturned trash can, his tail quivering. The hellhounds paced back and forth in front of Pirate's makeshift island, glowering at him.

"And those grizzly bears knew there was no shame in running away," Pirate said, his nails scratching at the slick plastic, "on account of my utter fierceness."

The trash can rocked as I scooped Pirate into my arms. The creatures didn't stalk me, like they had Pirate. They darted back to the stairs—our only exit— and crouched, fangs bared, their saliva hissing as it oozed onto the floor.

"It's bad, Lizzie. Bad, I tell you." Pirate clung to me, shaking, his nails biting into my skin. "You disappeared and a minute later—zing—hellhounds. They don't talk, they don't sniff. And if you ask me, that's just creepy."

My breath hitched. "Something must have brought them back."

As if I hadn't endured enough surprises in the last five minutes, Dimitri charged down the stairs. He wore faded jeans and a clean black T-shirt, his hair still slick from a shower. "I don't believe this, Lizzie." He looked at me like this was somehow my fault.

"I told you to stay away."

"And the emerald told me differently," he said, his eyes catching the dead stone at my neck.

Lovely. It was too weak to protect me, strong enough to tell on me.

Dimitri towered at the edge of the stairs. "Exactly what have you been doing?"

"I'm surviving," I said. And I'd continue to do so because it was the only thing I *could* do at this point.

Still, in spite of his accusation and, well, everything—I was glad to see him and reassured that no matter what it cost him, it seemed Dimitri would always be there for me.

The hellhounds glared at us, their eye sockets glowing yellow. I felt my pulse speed up. Omens or not, these things smelled evil. The one on the left wheezed out a breath of frigid air as Dimitri drew way too close.

The beasts snapped and Dimitri leapt back.

Pirate tried to clamber up to my shoulders and I pulled him down. "Easy, guy."

Pirate whipped his head around. "Easy?" He snorted, peppering my shoulder with doggie snot. "You want me to take it easy? Because frankly, I don't know what there is to relax about. We got demons after us and we're trapped down in this room and you have a glowy hand and then you leave me alone with hell dogs." Pirate managed a weak bark in their direction before he nuzzled his nose under the crook of my arm. "I thought they were going to eat me whole and use my toenails for toothpicks."

Poor Pirate. He didn't deserve any of this. I rubbed him on the head and stuffed him under my other arm to free up my switch star hand. The acrid scent of demons hung heavy in the air.

We had to get past these *things*.

The hellhound on the left snarled, baring row after row of sharp yellow teeth. Dimitri thought he was being subtle, but I saw the calculated way he'd moved to their flank.

Fine. We'd deal with them together. "What do they want?" According to Ezra, these things were omens, not attack beasts.

Dimitri double-checked his weapons like a lieutenant preparing to lead his troops into battle. It had to have cost him a lot of energy to be so close to the portal, but he didn't let on. His wide chest heaved, on full alert as he positioned himself in front of the beasts. "It looks like we're altering someone's fate."

Praised be. "We can do that?"

He shot me a look that made me want to rewrite the entire book on demon slaying. "What do you think we've been doing for the past week?" He returned his full attention to the creatures. "This could mean we're getting close," he said, thinking out loud. "I'm not sure they like it."

Dimitri reached into the back of his jeans and drew out a bronze dagger. Confident and strong as he gripped the blade, he reminded me of an ancient Greek warrior. Oh Sheboygan. Now was not the time to get turned on. Shoulders back, his focus never wavering, he strode directly for the hellhounds.

The creatures roared and hissed, their spittle dripping from rows and rows of yellow teeth. They were going to be on him like Sunday dinner. I flipped the trash can upright and stuffed Pirate inside, despite his protests. I couldn't fight with a dog in my hands. Then, switch stars at the ready, I followed Dimitri's lead.

He was almost on them, graceful as an athlete and intense as a gladiator, watching them as if he were trying to anticipate which mouth full of teeth would attack first. Keeping my breathing even and my concentration tight, I had his back. Then one of the hellhound heads drooped its ears and dipped toward the floor. Then another, and another, and, "What the heck?" The beasts curled and whimpered at Dimitri's feet.

Son of a gun, Dimitri's eyes glowed orange. He'd better know what he was doing. Dimitri's full attention remained on the creatures he'd somehow conquered. His nostrils flared. "Go," he ordered. "Now."

I retrieved Pirate and hurried for the stairs, hoping like anything Dimitri would be along shortly.

We sent Ezra ahead to make sure our escape route was clear, then hustled back down the purple hallway that led to the back exit of the club.

Pirate craned his neck backward as we put some distance between us and the hellhounds. "I changed my mind. I don't think you're evil," he said, as if he'd finally decided for himself. "But I'm not so sure about Dimitri."

"Thanks," I said, refusing to look back again.

Pirate squirmed out of my arms and took up the point position, his toenails clacking on the cement floors as he zipped back and forth in front of us, nose to the floor.

Halfway down, Dimitri joined us. He looked like he'd been wrestling the things. At least his eyes were yellow again. Oh geez.

"There's no way to get rid of the hell dogs, is there?"

Dimitri guided me in front of him. "No," he said, his breathing rough.

Because we didn't have enough problems.

"What happened in there?" I asked Ezra as he zipped overhead. "Did you see my uncle?" The other ghost said he'd be there tonight. "He's short, round—"

"Smells like a Cinnabon store," Pirate said.

"I'm sorry." Ezra's eyes traveled from Dimitri's bronze dagger to the powerful shoulders showing through his torn black shirt. "He left with a dark-haired woman while you were downstairs. You shouldn't have tempted the hellhounds."

"Thanks for the tip."

"Phil is the common denominator in all of this," Dimitri said, shoving open the back door. "I'm sorry, Lizzie, but we're going to have to do some things differently."

Shocked, I stared up at him.

Was he really going to sacrifice my fairy godfather?

I scooped up my doggie and held him close. "You know what Serena said. She's going to kill Phil. But if we go after him, she'll also take his soul." I couldn't risk that. I couldn't make that decision about someone else's eternal damnation.

Dimitri reached for me. His eyes hung with what? Regret?

I ducked away and tore down the back steps of the club.

"We have to stop this. I wish there was another way, Lizzie, but sometimes the good of the many outweighs the good of the few. No matter how much we care about a person."

My boot crunched over a broken beer bottle. Easy for Dimitri to say. It wasn't his fairy godfather in immortal danger. I gripped Pirate so tight he yelped. "Sorry, bub," I murmured into the wiry fur of his neck. I didn't know. I just didn't know.

Ezra cleared his throat. "I don't mean to point out the obvious, but we have no information where they've taken your uncle. I'm sure the succubi are well hidden. Or do you have some ideas?"

I cringed. "Not where to look, but . . ." I didn't even want to think it.

Dimitri, blast him, finished what I'd been too reluctant to say. "We need to channel him."

A rock settled in my stomach. We weren't so good at channeling. When we'd done it in the bathroom at the Paradise, we lost Phil. The time before that, Grandma ended up in the first layer of hell. Besides, if we wanted to have any shot at living through the debacle without ending up in purgatory, hell, or floating around in a parallel dimension somewhere, we needed the very people I'd been trying to distance from all of this.

We needed the Red Skulls.

Heaven help us.

"We sent the Red Skulls away." I cringed, tempted to borrow a dollop of strength from the mark.

Dimitri laughed out loud and I felt the knot in my stomach unravel a bit. "Do you really think they went?"

"Of course not," I replied.

Still, I didn't relish the idea of putting them in danger again.

Dimitri smiled. "Question is, how do we find them?"

Unfortunately, I knew.

We hurried down the back stairs to my bike, hidden in the shadows. For a moment, I let myself smile at the idea of Dimitri riding behind me for a change. Pirate leapt up on the flat leather seat while I dug into my pocket for our one-way ticket to the Red Skull's new hiding place.

My fingers closed around the vial of fairy dust, given to me by Sid. He said I could use it to call him if I needed him. "Anybody know how to summon a fairy?" I asked, watching the clear contents sparkle and churn inside the small glass tube.

"You'll want to be careful with that," Dimitri cautioned, pulling Pirate's harness out of the saddlebag. "Clear your mind. Use only a pinch. Dust it over a patch of open ground and focus on Sid."

"Got it." The dust felt rough, like sand between my fingers as I drew a mental picture of the short, balding fairy with the foul mouth. "Now's the time, Sid." I released the dust onto the dirt at my feet.

The earth churned and swelled. I stepped back quickly, feeling the vibrations in my toes as the small clearing buckled. Crabgrass and weeds flew as a full-sized fairy sprouted right out of the ground. Sid. And he was pissed.

"Eyow! Argh!" He tossed off chunks of earth. "Aaak!"

If I didn't know better, I'd think he was fighting off a swarm of bumblebees.

"Get it off!" He swatted at his arms, his back, his knees as each emerged from the earth.

"Hey, hey!" I inched as close as I could with him waving and flailing. "Keep it down." I hitched my thumb toward the club. "We got a possessed singer in there."

If anything, Phil raised his voice. "I swear to God, lady." He staggered up and out of the ground, kicking something out of a pant leg. It flew across the pavement and pinged on the concrete behind me.

Dimitri wasn't pleased. He retrieved the object and held it up between his thumb and pointer finger—a shard of barbed wire.

I winced.

"Open ground, Lizzie," he said as if I should have listened better, which I should have.

"Oh, wow, I'm really sorry, Sid," I said to the fairy, who was busy shaking another barb out of the other pant leg.

He shot me a dirty look. "Gee, thanks. Now the barbs in my underwear don't hurt so much. Maybe next time, you can summon me over a pile of broken glass or maybe a vat of used hypodermic needles."

"I didn't realize open ground meant—"

"Save it. What do you want?"

Dimitri towered over the fairy's squat frame. "We need you to take us to the Red Skulls."

"Already?" Sid riffled a chink of barbed wire out of

his wiry black hair, sighed heavily and dug his cell phone from his back pocket.

"What?" I asked. "You're going to call them?"

He shot me a stink eye. "Unless you want to saddle up your dog, I need transportation." He spoke with Gossamer Cab Dispatch and a cab pulled up within minutes. The door swung open and out slid a pudgy, muumuu–wearing fairy with stacked red hair and way too much blue eye shadow.

"You look like shit, Fuzzlebump." She nodded at Sid, ignoring us.

I wasn't sure how I felt about another fairy along for the ride. Luckily, I didn't have to worry long. With a loud pop, the red-haired fairy morphed into a firefly. Her empty dress floated to the ground as she fluttered off into the night.

Sid wadded up the dress and stuffed it in the backseat. He looked back over his shoulder, his round bottom holding open the cab door. "What?"

"Nothing," I muttered, heading for my bike. Dimitri, blast him, had climbed onto the front seat of my bike. Why did men always have to drive? But my heart softened when I saw he'd harnessed Pirate onto his chest. I had a thing for men who wore baby carriers, especially when this one happened to hold my dog.

"Hey, Lizzie." Pirate's legs pawed at the handlebars on my bike. "I got taller."

Hitching my leg over the rear of the bike, I settled up against Dimitri's firm backside. There were worse ways to travel. I slid my hands up under his leather jacket and around the waist of his Levis. For the first time, he felt cold. I shoved myself against him and for the first time since we'd been in Vegas, didn't feel my energy seeping away. I didn't know what had changed, but I knew it was bad.

Sid Fuzzlebump drove like a fairy possessed. He flew down Highway 95, weaving in and out of traffic with otherworldly precision. Served me right for hacking him off, although I had a feeling Sid would be no ray of sunshine in even the best circumstances.

Dimitri took to the shoulder to stay with Sid, which made for a teeth-rattling ride. It's like the man tried to hit every pothole and anthill.

We drove at butt-numbing speeds, veering off the highway and onto a series of smaller roads. Finally, we ended up on a dirt path leading to—according to the beat-up wooden sign—Rancho Verde. I'd believe it when I saw it.

The bike lurched and jarred behind Sid's aquamarine cab. And, phew, there was no escape from the massive dust cloud Sid's cab hurled at us. From the slight cotton-candy taste, I'd say he'd made it as large as he could. I closed my eyes against the grit and buried my head against Dimitri's back.

The bike jerked to a stop outside a series of rough wooden buildings. Moonshine Bart's Old West Town lay straight ahead, dark and silent. The Critter Corner Petting Zoo, lit with red and white holiday lights, veered off to the right, past a wooden bridge that looked like it belonged on a playground.

I yanked off my helmet. "Are you serious, Sid?"

The fairy leaned his head out the window, "Past the petting zoo and the Wild West restaurant."

Dimitri wrapped my hand in his. "Come on."

Pirate struggled against his doggie carrier as we

jogged past clucking chickens, the fattest pig I'd ever seen, and an armadillo. Some zoo. Off a side path, we saw light coming from a series of low-slung wooden cabins. Horses whinnied in a pasture behind them. Other than that, I couldn't see much—except a certain witch barreling toward us, her flashlight bobbing in the dark. Ant Eater. She'd tried to kick my butt on several occasions—and nearly succeeded. That was before I drew a demon attack on the coven. Not that it was my fault, but coolheaded logic was not one of Ant Eater's strong suits.

"Before you say it—" I didn't have time to deal with her WWE people skills.

She lobbed the flashlight at my head and frowned when it whistled past my ear. "What the hell do you want?"

I swallowed down my annoyance and tried to look at the bright side. At least she hadn't kicked me in the shins. "I need to see my grandma."

She looked at me like I'd told her I wanted to eat the woman. "Screw you. She's busy."

Prickles ran from my marked hand up my arm. I found it easier and easier to feel the power from the mark. Not good.

"Can you just tell Grandma we're here?" I asked, fighting the urge to rub my hand up and down my leg.

Ant Eater planted her hands on her hips, her wide face twisting into a sneer. "You got about ten seconds to run—not walk—*run* back to your bike or I'm spelling your skinny ass to West Texas before this place blows up, too."

"You listen to me," I said, my finger bouncing against something hard and fluttery. I shoved it back at Ant

Eater and she jumped sideways. That jerk had tried to sneak-spell me.

Quicker than I'd ever moved, I grabbed her hands and pinned them behind her. "Don't." I tightened my grip. "Screw. With. The demon slayer." I twisted her pinkie fingers, in case she hadn't quite gotten the point.

Ant Eater groaned. "Son of a bitch," she gasped. "Your left ball finally dropped." She flicked her head at the dirt path behind her. "Go."

I eased up and she stepped back, shaking out her hands, her eyes lingering on my devil's mark. "Third cabin from the right. Your grandma's brewing up some stealth technology in the bathtub."

I nodded. The tingling had grown worse, like my entire arm had fallen asleep. Dimitri fitted his hand into the small of my back. I could tell he sensed something was up. Bless him for letting me handle it my way. Together, we made our way toward the cabins.

"Another thing," Ant Eater hollered, still flexing her fingers. "Don't touch the door frame."

Of course not.

Since I knew better than to ask questions that I really didn't want answered, I made my way to see Grandma.

# CHAPTER TWENTY-TWO

I opened the door to a third-rate hotel room decorated in contemporary biker witch. Silver thumbtacks
bit into the brown paneling on the walls, supporting
long swaths of dental floss that crisscrossed the room
like party lights. The floss sagged with the remains of a
colorful quilt, butchered into long strips, hanging in
jagged rainbows, dripping, well, who knew what. The
place reeked of mildew and cherry Kool-Aid.

Covering my head, I ducked under the wilting jangle of sorcery and went to find Grandma.

It wasn't hard. I could hear her singing a Prince
song from the bathroom.

"Grandma?" I desperately hoped we weren't walking into a *Pretty Woman* moment.

I exchanged a glance with Dimitri. His green eyes
twinkled as he dodged a low-hanging string. Leave it
to Dimitri to be amused.

Not to mention my dog. "Pirate, stop dancing."

Grandma began humming the melody and I heard
something else—growling.

She'd better not have summoned any creatures in
there. "Grandma." I banged on the door, leaping sideways as a scalding drip caught me right in the forehead. "Son of a mother!"

"Lizzie!" Dimitri rushed for me, rubbing the acid away with his bare fingers. "Are you okay?"

"Are you?" I asked, trying to get a grip as the pain subsided into a dull throb. "I'm fine," I said, when I realized he wasn't going to stop inspecting me.

Dimitri planted a swift kiss on my forehead. "Step back." He leaned against the old brown door, ready to force it when it flew open on its own.

Grandma stood with a drafting pencil tucked behind her ear and a towel bar under her arm. Chunks of drywall clung to each curved end of the bar. She'd tied reddened quilt strips to her wrists like poor man's sweatbands and had even fashioned a homemade necklace out of the things. "You're late," she said, ushering us into the tiny bathroom with peeling cowboy wallpaper and an extra toilet bowl propped up against a 1970s yellow tub. It had to be at least ten degrees hotter in here—and muggy. I don't know why we always had to end up in the bathroom.

"Now where are my barriers?" Grandma muttered, digging through the cabinet under the sink. She peered into the bottom of a pink and brown crocheted tissue holder. "I had some dry ones . . ."

Pirate stuck his head under the sink with Grandma, while I worked my way past their protruding behinds and next to my agile, yet admittedly smushed griffin. He tried to make room for me and accidentally stepped on the furry red tail of a fox. The animal screeched and darted behind a stained wicker trash can.

"Argh." Grandma handed Dimitri the towel bar and went digging for the fox. "I need the toenails of a *happy* fox, which is hard enough because foxes hate having their toenails clipped." She bent down and wrangled the animal into her arms. "That'a boy," she cooed, stroking the fox. "Yes. You're all right, Zippy."

"Zippy?" Pirate tilted his head.

Grandma rubbed her fingers into the downy white fur under the fox's neck. "Yeah, well the gal who runs this place is a little zippity-do-dah herself. But I ain't complaining, seeing as the DIP office gave us a place to stay while we clear out some of the gargoyles."

"Gargoyles?" I instinctively checked the high corners of the bathroom. No gargoyles. Just lots of flaking paint.

"Well, yeah. You can keep a few to ward off the evil spirits, but the things breed like rabbits." Grandma scratched Zippy under his chin and he started growling again. Or, I supposed, purring. "Believe me, we're taking our time. The longer this place is shut down, the better. You know how hard it'd be to spot a demon in a Wild West town full of tourists?"

I shuddered to think.

Dimitri inspected the tub. "Mind telling me what you're brewing, Gertie?" A pale red liquid filled the lower third. In it floated tree bark, some kind of flowers and, I assumed, fox toenails. He dipped a finger into the gunk and held it up to the light, his features clouding as he took stock of Grandma's scowl.

"No time, Sherlock. We gotta get you protected." She tucked the fox under her arm and hauled an old trash can full of quilt guts from under the sink.

Dimitri frowned at her back. At least they weren't fighting.

"Mmm," Pirate scampered up on his hind legs to see inside the tub. "Smells like strawberries and leafy bits."

Dimitri removed Pirate gently, while aiming a hard stare at Grandma. "You'd better not be brewing up any Mind Bender spells in here. Even if you could generate enough firepower to bend a demon, you don't have the equipment or the proper ventilation."

"I know that." Grandma shot back. "We almost blew up Scarlet's cabin trying. That there's an invisibility spell, so the demons can't get an aura-lock on the coven."

She checked the medicine cabinet on the wall. "Well, I don't see any dry barriers. Bob must've used 'em. Wanted one for every spoke on his wheelchair." Grandma let the fox curl up on a bed of towels and motioned for us to clear out of the bathroom. "Now hurry up or I might as well paint a big target on your foreheads."

I touched her arm. The stress of the trip had gotten to her. She had dark circles under her eyes and a fatigue about her that wasn't there before. "I'm sorry for what happened at the hotel."

She shrugged. "Past is past," she said, shoving me out the door. "Truth be told, I didn't mind you showing a little backbone."

She led us into the drippy room. "Grab some barriers," Grandma plucked a handful of sodden quilt strips from a line above her head and shoved them at Dimitri. "The demons won't be able to detect you until they see you. Tie them at your pulse points, where your blood flows the hottest. Grab extras, as many as you can carry."

I hoped these things had cooled off a bit. I grabbed the end of a strip and felt like I'd dunked my fingers in a pot of liquid nitrogen. "Son of a daisy eater!" I yanked my hand back. There went my Wicked in Westchester fingernail polish, along with the first layer of skin. Holy hoo-doo. "What did you put in these things?"

Grandma's lack of reaction betrayed her as much as the flush that crept up her neck. "I used an antidemonic spell."

"Oh hell." Fighting not to cringe, I turned my palms up.

Grandma ignored the angry red burns on my fingertips as she gripped my wrist and studied my marked palm. The swirling 6-6-6 had eaten its way deep into my skin, like a heavy scar, the edges still wrinkled and pink.

"You knew about this?" she shot at Dimitri.

The muscles in his jaw worked. "Of course I knew," he said, his voice clipped. "I stayed with Lizzie."

"Tell me about the mark," I said, before this turned into a boxing match. "I'm counting on you to be straight."

Her fingers bit into mine. "You want straight?" Her blue eyes burned hot and angry. "Here's straight. What the fuck were you thinking?"

I snatched my hand away. "I didn't do this."

Grandma searched my face. "You sure?"

I held my palm over her, daring her to push me. "I think I would know if I chose to absorb demon powers or a devil's mark or whatever the frick is happening to me."

She shoved her chin forward, glaring at my upturned palm.

Grandma pursed her lips, blowing a long breath out of her nose. "I can't believe I'm saying this to my grandbaby." She shook her head, her anger draining. "I don't know how or why you did it, but facts are facts. You opened a pathway."

"There's no way to prove that," Dimitri countered. "We don't know they've tagged her."

Grandma raised a brow. "She reacted to my spell."

"I'm also invisible to demons now," I said, remembering the way they couldn't detect me when they hadn't seen me in the theater.

Grandma backed off like a doctor after a physical. She reached for a handful of Kool-Aid red quilt strips and scrubbed her hands. "When were you going to tell me about this?"

Like my favorite learn-on-the-job witch was going to tell me anything. Besides, I'd been trying to get her away from me, not involved more.

"Look, we aren't here for protection." At least I wasn't. I glanced over at Dimitri, tying strips of fabric to each of Pirate's legs. Something inside me fractured a little. I couldn't even help my dog. "We need to channel Phil."

"Ha! Is that all?" She tossed the strips onto the bed. "Can't do it. Not after what happened when we called up Bloody Mary. They can see us," she snorted, "me, anyway. It'd be suicide."

Maybe she could teach me. I wouldn't normally risk it, but we were running out of options here. "The demons are gathering because they have a portal open. They're planning a power surge tomorrow night."

Surprise brushed across her features. "You don't know that," she said, sinking onto the edge of the bed.

"Lizzie heard it herself," Dimitri said, tying a strip to Pirate's tail for extra protection. "Once they have six hundred sixty-six demons here, they'll be able to open the portal wide. All hell's going to break loose."

Dimitri shoved a handful of strips into his pocket and sat next to Grandma on the drippy bed. "Phil is the key to stopping the demons tomorrow night. We need to find him."

Her eyes widened. "And Pop said he'd never amount to anything," she said, almost to herself. " 'Course that was the day he took apart Dad's barbecue pit to make me a suit of armor. Kids can be cruel, 'cept for your Uncle Phil." Grandma gave an uncharacteristic sniff, buried in a cough.

We'd get him back. "I have the focus object," I said pulling out the bow tie we'd used in our disaster of a ceremony at the Paradise hotel.

Grandma took it, careful not to touch me. "Don't I wish we could make use of this again," she said, twirling it around her finger. "Still, you know what happened when I tried to channel Phil the last time. Serena spotted me faster than green grass through a goose."

Sure, we failed before, but that was before I had my mark. What good would my extra power be if I didn't use it? "I can do it."

"What?" Grandma and Dimitri said in unison. Oh good. They finally agreed.

It made perfect sense. "The demons can't see me." Grandma could tell me what to do. I was the only one who *could* do it.

Dimitri looked like he wanted to clamp his hand over my mouth. "It's too dangerous," he told Grandma. "We don't even understand the mark."

She nodded. "And Lizzie's not a witch."

Hello? Over here. "You let me in the coven."

Grandma looked me up and down. "You're too young," she said.

"I'm thirty."

"You don't know how," Dimitri added.

"Grandma can teach me."

"Lizzie—" Dimitri began.

Enough. "Will you two stop agreeing? We know we have to act soon or we're fried. Now is the time. Phil needs us. Dimitri, you need this."

He shot off the bed. "Don't you even think about sacrificing yourself for me."

Mistake. "Okay, what about Vegas? The West Coast? The entire planet is screwed if they get that portal all the way open. This isn't going away on its own and I—me—I have the power to stop it."

Grandma raked the quilt strips through her hands.

"You know I'm right," I said.

"Six hundred sixty-six. All coming tomorrow night." Grandma had gone completely still. "Damned if I ever thought I'd see the day." She swiped at the corners of her eyes. "Fine. We'll do it your way. But you have to do exactly what I say."

# CHAPTER TWENTY-THREE

With a grunt, Grandma launched herself off the bed and yanked open the outside door. "Frieda!" she hollered. The blonde witch rushed up in a jangle of plastic jewelry. "Get Scarlet." She glanced back at me. "Prep the Cave of Visions. Have Sidecar Bob fetch up those armadillos from last night. We're doing a channeling."

Relief surged through me, mixed with acute paralyzing fear.

How was a demon slayer on a permit supposed to stop Armageddon?

Dimitri looked as though he'd been punched in the stomach.

Grandma turned to us. "I wish I knew how to find some help for you, sport, but you're it." She checked her watch. "Ceremony starts at nine o'clock."

That gave us an hour and a half to get ready. "Is that a magic time?" I asked.

"No. That's about how long it'll take Frieda to get to Wal-Mart and back."

"Lizzie." Dimitri touched me and I pulled back. Something bad was happening to me. Back on the bike, he hadn't been able to drain me, but what if I could do it to him now?

The hurt registered in his eyes.

Grandma watched our exchange with an inscrutable expression.

Ant Eater ducked her head in the door. "Scarlet needs the skull for the cave, Frieda wants to know how many guppies you need, and—wait," she leaned her head out the door, "and if you want fancy or plain guppies, and Sidecar Bob needs Pirate to help him unwrap eighteen dozen Twinkies."

My dog hopped up like the place was on fire. "Twinkies? I can help with the Twinkies! I know all about snack cakes."

"Fine. I'll be there in a second," Grandma said. "Now you two get."

"Come on." Dimitri took my hand and led me outside.

The warm desert air felt wonderful, especially after the antidemonic stench in Grandma's cabin. I could still smell the acid of the protection strips Dimitri carried in his front pocket.

He tugged me onto a rocky trail that ran alongside the stables. Horses whinnied beyond the age-stained walls and the odor of fresh manure ran strong. Gargoyles circled in the moonlit sky, their staccato calls piercing the night.

"You need to be as powerful as you can for the channeling," Dimitri stated, as if he was telling me to eat my vegetables.

I nodded. I knew I'd need everything I had.

"If I can take from you, I can give to you."

"What?" I stammered. No way was I going to be like the succubi draining him, even if we could find a way for it to work.

"I'm a griffin. We are protectors. What good am I if I can't protect what's mine?"

I wasn't going to debate the "mine" part, just the obvious point. "I'm not taking anything from you," I said, running a hand along the rough-hewn boards as we walked.

"Regardless of what you think of me now," Dimitri said, "I came here to help you. You need to learn how to accept it." Dimitri scanned the horizon. "And me."

"I don't know, Dimitri." He'd already risked too much.

"You created the connection when you gave me part of your essence. Now that I know it's there, I can feel it. Trust me, Lizzie. Let me redeem myself." I felt for the raw spot between us as he tugged me into his arms. "Let me save us." His voice rumbled with promise.

What do you say to a man who is willing to give everything to you?

"Yes."

The corners of his mouth tugged up, and he drew me in for a long, burning kiss. He smelled like sweat and work and rock-solid man.

I rubbed up against him and felt him stiffen.

Closing my eyes, I fought the urge to pull back.

I hated the demons for draining him, and now I was supposed to do the same? I felt my dark mark pulse. It wanted him. I did too, but not at the expense of who he was.

His lips brushed the tender spot at the back of my ear, my throat, my mouth. To think, if I failed, we might not have any of this. My kiss faded and he felt it. He drew back, a questioning look on his face.

"How will we know when to stop?" I asked.

He squeezed my hand. "I'll know," he said, his voice rough around the edges.

Hand in hand, we walked the trail, pebbles crunching under our boots.

"You don't need to do this."

Dimitri slid his arm around me as we wound down into a rocky canyon.

The dark mark pulsed with anticipation. I hoped he could trust me with his power. "You don't know what could happen if we try this." I slid my marked palm away from his. "I'm evil. Or at least I'm turning evil. I don't know." None of this made any sense.

He tipped my chin up. "Is that what you really think?"

I didn't know anymore. It certainly hadn't been good for Max's last slayer.

Dimitri regarded me with a mix of amusement and chagrin. "I'm not going to lie to you. The devil's mark is usually a bad sign."

"Thanks," I said, breaking his gaze. What kind of person was I to need a little support here?

"Hey," he said, forcing my eyes back up. "Answer me this: Have you done anything evil since the mark? Anything the old Lizzie would regret?"

Things had certainly been different, but not anything Satan would get excited about.

And the way he looked at me . . . let's just say I never thought it would be possible, before I met Dimitri. He simmered with all of the things he'd like to do to me and that I probably shouldn't have enjoyed . . . but I would.

His mouth quirked. "I think the mark is your way

of drawing closer to the danger than any of us would dare. It's in your nature to give, Lizzie. Even when you don't realize it. It can be your great weakness, or your strength. We'll see."

"And you think?" I asked, hoping there was a glimmer of the old Dimitri left, the man who believed in me more than I could have ever hoped.

"I know," he said, kissing the tip of my nose, "you're stronger than this."

I caught his mouth and kissed him long and deep, this man who knew I was good. I knew there was good left in him too. "Are you ready?" I whispered.

"Always," he said, slipping his hand into my marked palm.

"Evil is a choice. Drawing yourself close to the darkness, well, that's what you do, Lizzie. True, you're a demon slayer. But I've never heard of any other slayer looking at things quite the way you do."

"Great, I'm unique." My whole life I'd been training to fit in, and the one place I might actually belong, I learn I'm different from them too.

Dimitri smiled at that. I tried to return it. I scarcely deserved the man.

I leaned up against a flat rock, sheltered by a red rock overhang. The night was silent except for the sound of our footsteps. "I'm sorry I lied to you."

"About what?" he asked, arms tense as he leaned next to me, facing the expanse of the canyon.

"After hell. I didn't want you to know I saved you because I didn't know what I felt about my life, about you, about anything. I couldn't commit."

He kept his eyes on the canyon ahead. "And now?"

Well, of course it would be different now. If he'd still have me.

"What? You're not mad? I infused you with enough of my essence to save your life and screw up your griffin heritage and that's it?" He had to be angry, because frankly, I was angry. It was stupid and wrong and even though I'd save his life all over again I'd at least give him the courtesy of telling him what I did. I'd trust him enough to level with him. "I left you open for a succubi attack. I should have been honest sooner, and that's my mistake. But don't sit here and pretend you're not upset at all about this. At least respect me enough to tell me what you're thinking."

"So now I'm the one who screwed up?"

"I don't want to pussyfoot around this." Not if he was going to risk everything for me.

I'd lived my whole life being nice, doing the right things, saying the right things—even if they weren't true. Well, not anymore. Sometimes, you gotta love somebody enough to tell them the ugly bald truth.

"You really want to get into this right now?" he asked.

Oh, I knew I'd be in the Cave of Visions in the next hour or so. I'd be in the crosshairs with all of my strength, and now, all of his. I knew I should probably spend my last moments with him making red-hot griffin love instead of poking him with a verbal fork, but this was more important.

He was more important.

He let out a jagged laugh, heavy with regret. "You want to know the truth? I'm actually okay with the fact that you didn't tell me right away. I know I was pressuring you to leave things behind and head to Greece with me." He dug a hand through his dark hair, making it spike awkwardly. "That's why I didn't tell you I loved you. I knew it would scare the hell out of you." He braced his hands on his knees, as if he wasn't quite ready to say what came next. "I know you hate what I do to protect you, Lizzie." His face was unreadable in the moonlight, the set of his jaw intense. "And you're not sure what I'm about to give you. But at some point, you have to relax a little, let go enough to accept the gift."

The truth of it hit me hard. I couldn't accept him or the Red Skulls or anybody. I'd wanted to do this on my own from the very start. Look where it had gotten me.

A little lizard scurried over a large rock to our left, noticed us and took off in the other direction.

"What did you see when I fought with Max?" he asked.

"I saw what happened when he died." I told him about Sid the fairy and how he'd reversed time. "Like him or not, Max's power is the only thing slowing them down. For now. If the demons reach six hundred sixty-six, or succeed in whatever they have planned tomorrow night, I'm afraid Max won't matter anymore."

"Neither will we."

The cool desert air settled around my bare arms as I tried to remain stoic, resolved. I had one more question and it was worse than the fifth layer of hell.

"Those things I asked you before," I said, throat dry. "I needed to know you'd be honest, because I need the truth about one more thing." I willed myself to say what I'd feared since the minute we set foot in Vegas. "When are you going to decide it's too much?"

His brows knitted. "I don't understand."

"This," I said, holding up my marked palm. "When are you going to figure out that it's too hard? Face it. I'm a pain in the butt. I mean, you love me, but you also get my crazy grandmother, a bunch of loud-mouthed biker witches, demons that want to have you for lunch and a channeling that might not be too different from the last ceremony that sent us straight to hell."

He actually smiled.

Joker. I planted my hands against his chest and pushed. "You're officially mad."

I took a drop-dead gorgeous griffin, and I broke him.

He cradled both of my hands in his. "I'm supposed to—" he lifted my chin. "Here, look at me." He edged us into a bright patch of moonlight. Damn the man. He couldn't have looked more sincere. "I'm supposed to give up the only woman I've ever loved, over a few complications?"

Well, when he put it that way . . .

"I'm not talking about giving up your Sunday golf game to go have brunch with my parents." Did griffins even play golf? And what would my uptight, society parents have to say about me dating a shape-shifter?

His thumbs traced circles on the tops of my palms. "Ah yes, demons instead of brunch. But love isn't about what's easy. I think you would have had an easier time if you'd denied your demon slayer calling, stayed home in Atlanta to teach preschool."

True. No matter how much I disliked growing up in

a family where fitting in and looking good somehow made you a better person—I had to admit, it would have been easier to stay with what I knew, even if it wasn't what I loved.

Dimitri's thumbs caressed the hollows of my wrists. "I love you because love to me is about finding the person you want to be with." He drew me in, kissed me. "And being there no matter what."

"Through hell and back?"

"Through demons and in-laws."

He drew my marked hand to his lips and kissed me, right there on the palm. Tears singed the back of my eyes as he caressed the marks.

"Don't look so surprised."

I couldn't help it. He loved me, demon mark and all.

"Now I figure," he said, kissing his way down my neck. "We've got about a half hour before anyone comes looking for us. And I have lots of energy."

Mmm, happy pings shook me to the core. "What shall we do?"

He used his incredible griffin strength to rip my leather skirt clean up the middle, and then he showed me.

# CHAPTER TWENTY-FOUR

He tackled me against the cool rock and kissed me thoroughly. His fingers roaming—oh yes, please—everywhere. They pushed up under my breasts, teased my nipples, circling them, plucking them, sending heat coursing through me until he did the whole thing over again with his tongue.

"E-yow," I said, nearly banging my head against the rock. "If you're trying to take my mind off things, it's totally working."

"Not well enough." He slipped a hand down between my legs, stroking me, spreading me until the only thing I could think about was his fingers and where, oh where, they'd go next. His tongue tortured my nipples while he dipped one finger, then two inside me. I moved with him as his thumb rubbed, teased. Oh wow.

I felt his power surge, pure and white. He didn't stop. Even when I tried to pull him to me, he kept rubbing, kissing like he couldn't get enough. I didn't know how long it went on, only I'm not the patient woman I thought I was. It had been too long. We'd been through too much. And I could feel him, hard and ready, against my thigh.

So close.

I wound my fingers into his hair and kissed him hard on the mouth. He pulled me closer, his erection pressed firmly against me. Slowly—ohh, eee—so slowly he ran himself along my slick flesh.

Over and over.

I traced a hard, flat nipple with my finger. "Dimitri." He had to know this was cruel and unusual punishment.

And still he rubbed against me, showing me every inch of him, letting loose an avalanche of sensation. My entire body shook with the need to have him. Inside me. Now.

Mmm, the things this man taught me.

I twined my arms around his super-heated back, nibbled on his ear. "I want you."

He chuckled against my neck and flipped me over. "I know."

Splayed over the flat rock, I reached back and found the slippery tip of him. He groaned as I circled once, twice. He gripped my hand, slammed it against his brick wall of a thigh and drove straight into me.

He filled me to the hilt and I heard myself whimper with the sheer joy of it.

I opened myself to him and felt him fill me up with his strength, his power, himself.

"Trapped between a rock and a hard Dimitri. It feels soo good." He proceeded to pound into me. He snaked his hands down my backbone, as if he could pull me deeper, push me harder. "There, there, there. Right there!" I dropped my head forward. He'd found the sweet spot. Lord in heaven above.

He gripped my hips and focused on that one spot. Filled it, ground against it, worked it until I was quite sure my legs weren't holding me up anymore. He was. And he pinned me, pushed me until I came in a blind rush of sensation like I'd never felt before. It swamped me, ripped through me. Sweet griffins, it was almost like floating.

Dimitri collapsed warm and steady against my back. We lay there for a few minutes, spent. At least I was. Dimitri probably had a wicked case of blue balls.

"Hold on," I said, trying to see if my knees still worked. I rolled out from under him and lay splayed for a second on the rock. Coolness seeped through me. Seemed like we'd really warmed up our section of rock. Dimitri, heavy-lidded with his streaked hair irreparably mussed, shot me a smart-aleck smile.

I lifted a finger to tell him to wait. "I'm going to— ohh." A late orgasmic ping zipped through me from my sweet spot down to my curling toes.

"Are you all right?" he asked, quite amused for a man in pain.

I nodded, not trusting my voice—or the pings. "Are you?"

He nodded weakly.

"I'm going to take care of you," I finally croaked.

He laughed and coaxed me into his arms. "Oh, that's what you were moaning about over there? Well, in that case, you already did."

"I didn't notice."

"You were busy."

"No kidding," I said against his sweat-slicked chest. Not minding, for once, that I didn't have a complete grasp of the facts, or anything else for that matter.

He'd given me everything of himself that he could, despite the cost. I'd make sure it was worth it.

I curled up warm against him, trying not to think about what we had to face—the channeling ceremony, and worse, the demons tomorrow night. Now I'd robbed this beautiful man of his energy and strength, the very things he'd need to defend himself if I failed.

Dimitri's mouth found my shoulder, the crook of my collarbone. I'd about closed my eyes when he yanked his mouth away and coldness flooded the places he'd just kissed.

A blue light shot out over the ridge and I fought the urge to burrow into Dimitri's arms and never leave. "Please tell me it's the Red Skulls."

Dimitri rubbed my back, as if trying to keep away the chill. "It is." He kissed me on the forehead. "It's time."

# CHAPTER TWENTY-FIVE

"Hup, hup!" Grandma ambushed us as we rounded the horse stables. "Don't tell the Red Skulls about Armageddon."

Yeah. No problem. It could be our little secret.

Her gray hair tangled in a cloud of Ziploc bags packed with spinning, twirling spells. "Move your keister, Lizzie. You think the Cave of Visions is open all hours like the Taco Bell drive-thru?"

Oh please. I'd been summoning my strength. And sacrificing my new-ish leather skirt. I wound my fingers a little more tightly into Dimitri's grip.

"Nice outfit." Grandma waggled her brows at the tunic I'd made out of Dimitri's black T-shirt. Yeah, well lucky for me, the man needed plenty of material.

I'd told myself I wouldn't get embarrassed, but the heat crept up my neck and I found myself blushing a dozen shades of scarlet. "I don't want to hear it." Not from my Grandmother. Not from anybody.

Where were those dark obnoxious powers when I needed them?

"Frieda!" she hollered over her shoulder, the cabins ablaze with light behind her. "Lizzie needs some underwear!" She turned back to me. "And make it snappy.

No grandbaby of mine is going to channel with her whatnots flapping in the breeze."

A devilish grin played across Dimitri's features. I dropped his hand and inched my fingers up his sensitive rib cage, enjoying his sharp inhale. *Don't mess with me, babe*. I wound my fingers through his hair, ignoring the way the sweat from our encounter made it curl at the ends, and dragged his luscious noggin down to my level. I ran my thumbs along his cheekbones. "Next time you rip my skirt clean up the middle, I'm going to do the same to your drawers." He was so darned kissable, until his strong jaw twitched into a smirk.

He nipped my lips, sending a ripple of pleasure straight to the part of me that, hm, felt well loved. "That a promise?"

"She needs clothes too!" Grandma added, for the listening pleasure of anyone within a fifty-mile radius.

Oh for the love of Pete. "Can't you at least try to keep a secret?"

Grandma paused in the middle of coaxing a glittering spell from one of the bags at her neck. "Why?"

Like I could explain the concept of privacy to a woman who spent Saturday nights tossing fart spells at her friends.

Well I refused to be embarrassed. Or at least I wasn't going to admit it.

A flashlight broke through the moonlight, bobbing as Frieda crunched across the rocky soil, waving a pair of pink leather pants. I'd borrowed clothes from the blonde witch before. Being a demon slayer tended to be hard on the wardrobe.

I could smell Frieda's cigarettes before I could even get a clear look at the pants. "Grabbed my lucky ones!" She dragged me behind the rough-hewn horse barn, chomping on spearmint gum. She shoved the pants in my general direction. Zippers crisscrossed the hot pink leather.

"Thanks," I said, reaching for the only pair of leather pants more obnoxious than the snakeskin ones Frieda had on.

The earthy smell of manure tickled my nose and I soon figured out why. I stood uncomfortably close to a pile of the stuff as Frieda showed me how to cram myself into her pink pants. Because they couldn't have a zipper up the front like every other pair of pants in creation.

"See?" she said, blowing the sorriest looking bubble I'd ever seen. "That there side zipper goes like a vee all around your girly parts, but you don't want to open that or, well, you'll be in for a world of hurt. You want to use the side zipper here and then attach it back to the back zipper on the butt."

My fingers fumbled with the thick leather and stiff zippers. This was worse than sudoku. Finally, I managed to make everything fit, even the matching bustier.

"Tar and feathers." Frieda pulled a ribbon of black lace from her back pocket. "I forgot the thong."

I'd noticed that. "Don't worry," I said, trying not to cringe. I'd never gone without panties. Ever. But past experience had proven that Frieda's thongs weren't much different than going commando and, frankly, I didn't want to try and get into the pants again. If the witches were ready, so was I.

She glanced up at me through rhinestone-tipped lashes as she started in on my side buckles. "Don't squinch your forehead like that. You'll get wrinkles. Besides," she said, silver hoop earrings glinting in the moonlight, "we've got your back."

"That's good to hear," I told her, easing Dimitri's black shirt over the tight bustier. I'd need all the help I could get.

She slapped the skintight leather on my hips, admiring her handiwork. "Honey, this ain't my first rodeo. Now watch the armadillos—the petting zoo ones tend to get fat and lazy. And the fish are from Wal-Mart."

Fish? "Armadillos?" I hoped Grandma wasn't expecting me to do any magic in there.

Grandma shoved her head around the edge of the barn. "You happy?" She dug at her spell necklace like it was strangling her. "One of the fish just died."

Was that bad? "What happened?"

Frieda's eyes widened as she grabbed for her anti-demon quilt bits. "Hurry."

I followed Grandma to the other side of the barn and found a small armadillo-carrying army. "I know you want to do this," Dimitri said taking my hand. "But be quick about it. This doesn't feel right."

We jogged past the cabins, through the petting zoo, toward a supply shed at the edge of the Wild West town.

"Hup, hup," Grandma tugged on my black T-shirt. "Wrong direction, slick. That's the Cave of Visions." She pointed at a life-sized covered wagon over by the old-fashioned jail. The Conestoga's wheels sizzled with an unearthly blue current. A blaze of blue smoke trailed up into the night sky and—holy cripes—pearl white snakes as long as my arm slithered in Z-shaped patterns around and under the wagon. Large, flat heads thrust from both ends of the creatures as they hissed, spewing bursts of flame at each other and anyone else who wandered too close.

Dimitri didn't look happy. "What kind of magic do you think you're doing in there?"

"What?" Grandma snapped as the witches filed past us. "Do you want to run this thing? I'm trying to give Lizzie the best shot at getting out of this in one piece."

"By calling up Cold magic?" he thundered. "No wonder you killed the fish."

I felt a tugging at my mark. Something wanted me in there.

"Cripes. You know a better way to isolate a demonic presence?"

"Yes," Dimitri snarled. "Smother the Ice Winders. I can cast a protective charm."

"Wait," I said. If hissing, coiling fire breathers were on my side, I'd take them.

But naturally, no one was listening. Grandma and Dimitri had eyes—and arguments—only for each other.

"Oh sure." Grandma threw her hands out like an Italian grandmother. "You're not giving my grand-baby half-depleted magic. Besides, it's perfectly safe as long as the demons can't see her."

Dimitri shot her a dark look as he crunched past me, inspecting the perimeter of the Cave of Visions. The witches cast long shadows in a circle around us. They moved with military precision, dozens of Red Skulls carrying blue and silver candles.

Grandma nodded to each of the Red Skulls as they lined up. "A little extra juice, in case you need it."

I'd take all the help I could get.

Dimitri returned, wrapping his arms around me as he tugged me into a long shadow cast by the roof of the wagon. There were dark circles under his eyes. "Keep your grandma busy. I'm going to cast some protection for you," he said, his breath warm against my ear. I fought the urge to sink into him and nodded instead.

"You'll be okay?" I didn't know where he found the strength.

His mouth quirked. "Told you I can handle myself."

Mmm, I ran my fingers lightly along his bare back. What I'd give for another five minutes in that valley.

"Hello?" Grandma stood next to us.

The air chilled my skin as I stepped away from Dimitri. I really wished he could have gone in there with me. But I could do this. I was the only one.

Grandma clapped me on the back. "Okay, here's the skinny. I can't go in there and show you how it works because, hey, the demons would see me. But it's actually very simple."

"It can't be," I said, as she shoved a jar of guppies into my hand. Last time Grandma tried this, she ended up in the first layer of hell.

"Fine, you're right. It's dangerous as a barrel of snakes. You happy? The point is, you follow my instructions and you're golden. So first, watch the fish. We have three fish for you to take inside."

"Two!" Bob hollered.

"Oh yeah," Grandma muttered as I watched the

guppies swim circles around the dead fish in my jar. "We spelled the fish to be kind of like those canaries they used to take down into mines. An evil spirit tries to take you, they get the fish instead."

I gripped the jar tighter. "What was just after us?"

"I don't know. But that's what got your fish. Now you have two left. The last one dies, you run like hell."

"Got it." I could do this.

"We're sealing you in with a circle. A strong one," she said as the witches moved to surrounded us. I caught Battina in the crowd, Jan, Sidecar Bob. "Also, there's a goat skull in there that your Great-aunt Evie used to use in her ceremonies. It'll help you focus your strength."

"And the armadillos?" I asked, watching Bob scatter Twinkee bits for the nobbly little things.

"Yes! Armadillo tracks. Their back paw tracks have six distinct points, almost like a pentagram. Very powerful magic. You worry about what goes on in that wagon. Light a candle. Focus on Phil and watch the fish."

"Okay." I nodded. I could do this.

"Something goes wrong, run. Try not to bring anything out of there with you." She hooked a thumb under her necklace. "I've got a mess of antidemonic spells, but without any wards in place, they're basically like tossing Pop-Tarts at a pissed-off lion."

"Don't worry, I can do this," I said. I had to do it.

Dimitri took my hand, more at ease than he had been. His eyes burned green in the moonlight. "Ready?" Seemed he'd worked his magic.

No. There were too many things to say and I didn't have any idea how to go about it.

He squeezed my hand and planted a kiss on the top of my head. "I'll see you in a few minutes."

Right. I planted one foot on the back hinge of the wagon and hoisted myself up. My palm radiated power.

Grandma handed me a lighter, a stubby red candle and the guppy jar.

Frieda scooched up next to me, her platform sandals crunching across the rocky soil. She whipped off her protection bracelet. "Deep breaths, sugar" she said, her lucky dice earrings jangling as she rubbed circles on my back. "Those fish die and you get the hell out of there."

"Hands off," Ant Eater growled from behind.

"Ease up." Frieda rubbed faster. "Her circle's open."

"What's that you said?" Ant Eater bent and lit the last candle. The air grew heavy around me as the last wick sputtered to life. And suddenly, I felt very alone.

A dribble of sweat ran down my back. I lit my candle and glanced back one more time at Dimitri, standing bare chested outside the circle of witches. He looked exhausted but happy. Poor guy had given me the shirt off his back. When he caught my eye and winked, I couldn't help but smile.

*You can do this, Lizzie.*

I'd do it for him and for all of them. With that, I ducked inside the Cave of Visions.

My sweat gelled the second I stepped inside. The interior of the wagon was freezing cold, pitch black and smelled like canvas and dirt. I placed the candle in the center of the narrow space, with the fish right next to it. Breathe. I assembled myself into a Sukasana yoga pose on the floor in front of the gnarly-looking goat skull because, well, it seemed like the thing to do.

*Sacrifice yourself.* I had to believe I was doing the right thing, or I would have been tempted to sprint out of that wagon and never come back. The hexed fish swam circles in their jar, the dead one bobbing against the side. My ankles warmed where they crossed. The rest of me shivered.

You can do this, I reminded myself.

I had to do this.

I could feel Dimitri outside. He'd woven a protective spell, like a soft wind. He'd infused it with strength, purity and wisdom. Anyone else might have also tried to mess with my free will. Dimitri, curse him, was too noble for that.

The Red Skulls chanted outside, the words washing over me as I watched the yellow flame of the candle. It danced on the blackened wick and, with a start, I realized we'd used this same candle to summon Serena at the Paradise. Scratches marred the surface from the day we'd lost Phil.

I focused on my fairy godfather, thought about the way he'd taken care of me when I didn't have anybody. And how it was my turn to take care of him now.

In my mind's eye, I saw him. The mark on my hand tingled. My breath roughened, each exhale a cloud in the rapidly freezing air. My fingers clenched.

I was Phil.

Scared. In love. And insanely jealous.

*Serena doesn't want me anymore. She only married*

*me in order to control me. And as soon as I deliver
the blackout, she'll take what she wanted and get rid
of me.*

Shock threw me out of my vision. I found myself
standing in the narrow space. My heart slammed in
my throat. Serena wanted to take something? I thought
she wanted to open up the portal. I couldn't afford to
be wrong about this.

*Focus.* I steadied myself in front of the flame, forced
myself to sit back down, resume my yoga pose. Two
of the fish floated, dead.

Holy Hades.

I closed my eyes, pulled closer. I willed my mind to
calm, my breathing to grow even. I wound my mind
through the space like swimming through cold, dark
water. The mark on my hand burned, and I used it to
draw power.

Max stood in the rotting prison under the desert.
The iron doors shook and bent. They were getting
stronger. His seventeen demons were breaking out.

I caught my breath as a blackened demon writhed
out from between the cracks in the door. I lurched for
the hunter. Max stabbed the screaming, heaving succubus with a switch star and shoved her into a pile of
writhing demons. Black blood caked his golden hair
in a halo of death and red blood ran from deep cuts
in his face.

"Get out, Max!" No way he could handle the demons behind those doors, or the bloodied ones behind him, once they regained their strength.

"Doesn't work that way," he said, squinting, his
breath coming hard. "Think, Lizzie. Your Cave of

Visions is set up for revelations, not painful truths. So you'd better figure this out soon.

"They know the end is near."

"Thanks for the pep talk," he muttered, dragging a stunned, hissing demon into an iron holding cell.

"I found the portal," I said in a rush. "They're using Ricardo Zarro and sex to drive it open enough to get six hundred and sixty-six through. We can't stop the concert. It'll be swarming with succubi. I'll bet they've got the dam guarded too."

Max shot me a look. "Figure it out. You know you're the only one who can stop this now." The iron doors around him shook and groaned.

The truth cut me like a thousand switch stars.

Max's eyes blazed. "It'll be the highway to hell. You don't want to know what's in the deeper layers. I don't, either. It'll make what I'm dealing with here look like Cirque du Soleil. It'll be a massacre."

And, I realized with a start, the dark mark wanted it.

"Lizzie," Max said, his image fading from my mind, "your last fish is dead."

My mind hurtled back to the Cave of Visions, where I sat crosslegged with a smashed pickle jar in my hand. The fish lay lifeless on the wooden floor of the wagon. I'd dropped the jar.

And nothing happened.

Joy and relief welled up inside me. I didn't need Grandma or the witches' spells. I was the only one who could stop the demons tomorrow night. I alone could save Phil, free Dimitri, destroy the portal, end this thing for good.

*Sacrifice yourself.*

Power shot through me, my body aching with the pleasure of it. The demons could try to darken the U.S., summon sexual power from the masses, eat my lover. But I could take out their entire operation. I could crush Serena.

No mistake, I could feel her, out there, waiting. A smile curled on my lips. I never had to worry about finding my power again. I had it all if I wanted it.

Strength coursed through me, surged from the dark mark into every cell of my body. I needed it like I needed my next breath. This was my secret weapon to defeat the demons. I reached out with my mind, saw Serena as she really was—a blackened shell of a creature, a living locust. I nudged her with my power, and she turned, bewildered. She couldn't even see me coming. I shoved her again, laughing at the irony of it. She could be mine. I could take her. And then, I realized, I'd have to give something back to the dark mark. This could consume me.

Oh Sheboygan.

This wasn't me.

I swallowed a lump in my throat.

This felt too good, too easy. Holy smokes, I wasn't even cold anymore. I didn't know what I'd invited in, but I did know that absolute power corrupts. There would be a price and no matter how good it felt, I couldn't keep the strength if it harmed, well, me. Who I am.

I pulled back from her, watched as she wrapped her arms around herself and searched for me. She stood in a narrow art deco hallway right below the control room of the Hoover Dam, where Phil worked to cripple the turbines. I had the information I needed now. So why couldn't I let go?

My fingernails bit into my palms as I resisted the urge to shove her once more.

This mark was wrong. I didn't need it. I didn't *want* it. I was strong enough on my own.

*Sacrifice yourself.*

I didn't need to sacrifice who I was. I needed to let go of the temptation to be something I wasn't.

I let go.

With a blaze of power that sent goose bumps up my arm, my hand absorbed the mark like it had never been there. I stared at my palm, amazed, unwilling to believe I'd actually gotten rid of it. I felt whole, grounded. Good gravy. I felt like myself again. Relief erupted in me, followed by the sheer joy of having my life back again. Dimitri was right. I could do this with the power I had.

And that's when things went to hell.

# CHAPTER TWENTY-SIX

Serena's fiery red eyes caught mine. Holy Hades—she could see me. I stared at the demon, my unmarked hand, the demon. Shock darted across her features before she grabbed me by the soul.

I tumbled through cold, wet air. Winds crashed into me from every direction. My lungs screamed as they fought to breathe. I couldn't see up, down. The whole time, Serena's fingers dug into my chest, pulled me through the freezing, churning void. I grabbed for my switch stars, but couldn't get a handle on them in the whirlwind.

Warm air smacked me in the face like a wave as I crash-landed on something cold and hard. I gasped for breath, planted my numb fingers on the slick surface and fought to get my bearings. My head swam, my neck burned and my mouth tasted like I'd been chewing tinfoil.

White boots strolled into my line of vision. "I'll give you one thing," said a voice dripping with sex. "Your family is certainly original."

Serena.

I struggled to stand, did a bad impression of a baby deer and flopped butt first back onto the floor. Yeah, well the she-demon had made a big mistake. I dug for a switch star, ready to end this debacle for good when I came up empty. My chest constricted. My utility belt was gone.

Serena shot out a laugh. "Oh please, I'm certainly not going to suck you through the eleventh dimension so you can put a switch star through my forehead."

I shoved my tangled hair aside and peered up at her. Serena had tossed my utility belt over her shoulder, a single claw looped through the buckle. The roughened black talons crackled under leathery skin. She'd hidden the rest of her demonic nature behind her petite body and Barbara Feldon good looks.

She seemed relaxed, too relaxed, for a demon standing in an art deco hallway under Hoover Dam. "Good to see you didn't blow town." She tilted her head, showing off a long neck. "When I stopped sensing you, well, let's say I was ready to send out an entire army." Her predatory smile told me she wasn't kidding.

I flexed my hand, wishing I had something to zap her with. Amazing. I'd given up the dark mark as easily as I'd gotten it. Both times had been a disaster. I planted my hands on the floor in front of me, gathering strength.

Rage churned inside me. She didn't think I could fight back. If I wanted the dark mark, I'd bet I could have it again. I could shove her, push her, destroy her. My strength surged just thinking about it.

I made a running leap for her, snagged the belt and went for my switch stars. Holy Hades! The belt was empty. I dug through the pockets. Everything was gone—even the creature who lived in the back.

Serena crushed me to the floor. I was too shocked to

scream when my left hand sunk into the pink marble. H-e-double-hockey-sticks. I grabbed for the belt with my free hand, only to watch in horror as both of my hands sank up to the wrists.

Serena's two-way phone crackled and beeped, echoing down the hall. "Hell Fire Three reporting."

"Go ahead," Serena said.

"Lover boy is blowing out the turbines. Zarro is on stage." She talked like she was reading from a to-do list, like she wasn't about to unleash hell on Earth. "Do you have the demon slayer secured?"

She grinned, showing very un-Barbara Feldon–like double row of jagged teeth. "Affirmative."

"We'll commence as soon as the turbines blow."

"Thanks, babe," Serena chirped sweetly.

"What?" I struggled to stand. The end, the concert, the demolition of the power system—that was supposed to happen tomorrow night. Even then, I didn't know how we were going to stop it, but now? I needed more time. And how could they possibly move up a complete takeover of the North American airwaves?

"You can't," I insisted. Because, they couldn't, they simply couldn't. "It's impossible to move up a concert by a day."

Her brows knit. "This is Saturday," she shoved me with her toe. "Your fault," she added, as I lunged back at her.

Hell and damnation. Had I really been hurtling through that pathway for nearly a day?

Serena sighed. "I'd have been up there twenty-one hours ago if I hadn't been busy dragging your stubborn butt through the eleventh dimension. Broke a nail too." She flexed her talons. "Oh wait," she said, as it grew back, long and sharp. "One problem down. One to go."

I struggled against whatever hold she had on me. I used every ounce of my demon slayer mojo, but my hands didn't budge.

"You stay put. I'll come get you when it's time for the end of the world."

I stiffened.

"Kidding," she added. "That'll take at least another week. I'll come get you once we ax North America, give or take Panama."

"Panama is in Central America," I said, my voice raising two octaves at the end. Call it the natural response of a teacher, or more likely, the only thing my brain could grasp at that moment. I felt bad enough about Phil and Dimitri. I couldn't be responsible for the end of North America. And Central America. And . . . oh geez. How many billions of people were we talking about?

Damn the creature, she beamed—proud of what she was about to do. "You stay here," she said, stepping past me, her ankle sideswiping my nose on her way down the hall. "Oh, who am I kidding? Where else are you going to go?"

"What are you going to do to Phil?" Not that there'd be much of a world left for him, but there were worse things to take than someone's life.

She barked out a laugh. "Phil's soul is mine as soon as the turbines shut down. Phil is a pain in the ass. Always resisting." She surveyed me, cold and calculating, as if wondering if there was more to me than what she saw. "The guy almost threw himself over the dam when I told him I needed him to lure you here."

Phil was bait?

The pieces fell together with gut-wrenching clarity. I'd been so proud. So determined to be some great demon slayer—so convinced this whole thing had been about everyone needing my help. It was never about the kick-butt demon slayer blazing into town to ride to the rescue of good ol' Phil. He'd been trying to save *me*.

Shock froze my brain. "You needed him to sabotage the dam," I said, almost to myself.

"Oh come on. Axing a dam is nothing compared to capturing demon slayer power. We need six hundred sixty-six she-demons—and you—in order to open the gates of Hell."

My jaw locked as I stared at her, not wanting to comprehend.

It really was about my power. Dimitri hadn't needed to flee Vegas. I did.

"And now I'll take this little number." I winced as she ripped Dimitri's protective necklace from my throat. He'd used it to find me before. Now if he tracked the necklace, he'd find . . . her.

"Pretty," she said, twirling it around her finger. "And it'd be almost impossible to remove if your big lug of a griffin wasn't almost dry. Pity. He was tasty." She sighed, remembering, before turning her icy blue eyes back on me. "I'll be back for your power soon."

I battled to free my hands as Serena's boots clattered down the hallway and up a metal staircase. I had to get out of here. At least my friends would have missed me by now. And Dimitri. I cringed to think of what he was going through right now. They wouldn't know what had happened to me—or where on Earth or in the underworld to look.

Meanwhile, there was no way to stop the concert or the blackout—not in the next twenty minutes. Phil was completely brainwashed and overloading the turbine timing systems, blowing power to the dam. And Serena, well, she was about to get everything she wanted.

I yanked at my hands until my wrists screamed in protest.

"Mother fudrucker!"

Dimitri should be in Greece right now—putting his family back together. He worked his whole life to do that. Instead, he'd put it off to help me. I'd rewarded him by muddying his pure griffin blood, serving him up as a snack for the demons, stealing all of his energy and now—failing at the one thing we'd sacrificed everything to do.

Sure, he'd come willingly, but that almost made it worse. I loved his loyalty and his courage and—dang—everything about him. He was like the light of a smoldering fire, warm and affirming. The man I wanted with me when things got rough, or to simply curl up with at the end of a long day. But I had to wonder if he'd have been better off if he'd never met me.

It was my fault. Dimitri, Phil, everyone had trusted me to do the right thing and I'd let them down. I buried my face in the black T-shirt he'd given me and inhaled his rich, warm scent, wishing I could see him one last time.

I'd lose my lover, my fairy godfather, my life and everything else that lived and breathed. All because I'd thought I could do this on my own.

Now who was going to save me?

# CHAPTER TWENTY-SEVEN

"Joe!" I hollered with all of my strength. My voice echoed down the pitch-black hallway. "Joe!"

I didn't know exactly where I was inside the sixty million tons of concrete that made up Hoover Dam, but I knew Joe wasn't going anywhere.

Neither was I, if Serena got her way. My stomach roiled at the thought.

"Joe!" I yelled, over and over again until I grew hoarse. I felt the demons clamoring with excitement. With every pleading, desperate word, I yanked at my hands until my wrists screamed in protest and my back nearly gave out.

"Joe. I. Need. You. Now. Joe. I. Need—"

The magical world lurched as the fluorescent lights above me sputtered and died. Blackness chilled me. An orange emergency beacon pitched an oasis of light at the far end of the hall and my concrete tomb grew much, much too silent. I braced myself, knowing this was the intake of breath before the scream.

Maybe Serena's plan wouldn't work. Maybe America wasn't watching Ricardo Zarro or everyone was at dinner or it wasn't really true what they said about blackouts. Maybe not enough people would make love, or the succubi would fail to harness the carnal energy or . . . The temperature of the room plummeted at least twenty degrees.

Succubi. I felt their power grow. I closed my eyes and could almost *see* it. The back of my throat constricted as hordes of succubi pounded on the walls deep below the old prison. My stomach felt hollow. The iron weakened. The demons raged. And I knew it was only a matter of time.

Didn't mean we wouldn't go down fighting.

"Joe!" I started to panic. Where was he? Ghosts traveled fast.

Twenty demons burst through the portal at once and the shock of it almost took the breath out of me.

"Joe!"

My stomach flip-flopped as the demons swarmed. They piled on top of each other, through each other. At least forty more made it though. I could hardly count them all.

God, what was happening to Dimitri?

I'd failed tonight. Dots hovered in front of my eyes as I stared at the dark marble floor in front of me. Sweat trickled down my spine as I racked my brain for something, anything to do.

No one came.

They were coming fast. "A hundred and twelve!"

Maybe, if I tried hard enough, I could reach Phil. Never mind that it had barely worked before Serena married Phil, took over his free will and tasked him with an integral part of her plan for world domination. It was better than counting the demons flooding through the portal.

Sweat tickled between my eyes. I cocked my head

and wiped my forehead on my shoulder. Cripes. I still wore Dimitri's T-shirt. His musky scent short-circuited my brain and drilled warmth straight through me.

I had to do this—for him and for everybody. I closed my eyes and pictured my fairy godfather.

"Phil?" I called, pleaded really. I focused every ounce of strength and concentration into finding him. Maybe I could break through.

"Phil." I clenched my jaw and willed him to answer. Through the soupy, murky distance between our minds, I scrambled for him. I ached for him. Last time, I'd found him in a hurry. This time, I couldn't locate a trace of my quirky, funny, teddy bear of a guardian. The man who'd fought to protect me had disappeared from the astral plane as if he'd never existed.

I braced myself as Max's demons broke free in a rush of bodies, tumbling, clawing, lashing out at whatever they could reach. They roiled toward the city, fracturing off along the way. The bitter taste of sulfur practically choked me.

Add the demons from the portal and we had one hundred eighty. Make that one hundred eighty-eight. No way I could recapture that many demons, or stop the destruction.

*No more.* I couldn't watch. I forced my eyes open. I had to get away, even if it meant taking comfort in a deserted, dimly lit hallway. But I should have known it wouldn't be that easy. This place had changed too.

Yellow vapor clouded the light from the sconces and the stench of sulfur lingered. I could see my breath in front of me, as the hellish smog wound through my lungs. I renewed my battle against the forces that kept my hands pinned in the floor, now icy with the power of Hades. I couldn't feel my hands any longer, but I knew I had to get out of there.

Now.

Fear surged through me. It was survival at its most basic. Because they were coming for me next.

I pulled until my wrists stretched nearly out of their sockets and thought, hoped, prayed I felt one move. This had to work because, frankly, nothing else had.

However late, I had truly believed Joe would arrive, or Grandma and Dimitri. Or maybe Phil would find the strength to defeat the demons that held him, however impossible it seemed. I refused to think Serena would win.

But she did.

"Three hundred." And counting.

The demons rushed me in a wave of sulfur and rot. I could feel their leathery bodies, see the black shadowy figures surrounding me. Bony hands grabbed at my hair and clothes. They slipped under my arms, yanked me out of the floor and straight up.

My toes left the floor as we hurtled straight up into the air. "Blazes!" Pain lanced through my head as they smacked it up against the ceiling.

I breathed too close to one of them, inhaling the stench, and the back of my throat watered. They smacked my head against the ceiling again and my vision blurred.

"Halt!" ordered a raspy voice as they practically smothered me with their frigid bodies. "It's human. It can't pass through."

Talons dug into my arms and I cringed at the multitude of icy hands pressing the top of my head against the concrete ceiling, as if they didn't quite believe I could be so supernaturally inept. Acidic breath singed the back of my neck.

My freed wrists ached and cold, dark, freezing air prickled my face as they rushed me down the hall. My toes never quite touched the floor as we darted around a corner and up a flight of stairs. So this was it. Serena was strong enough to kill me and take my power. Most likely, my Uncle Phil was already dead. They'd drain Dimitri. The Red Skulls would be fighting a losing battle for their lives.

We burst into the control room and I winced against the glare. A second power source, most likely a backup generator, had kept the lights blazing and the control panels lit. Engineers' stations lined three of the four walls, all the chairs empty, save one. Phil slumped over the control panels, his bulbous nose at rest next to a flashing orange button.

My fairy godfather wasn't dead. Not yet, anyway. I could feel it.

I wondered if anyone else knew that.

Windows along the fourth wall overlooked a massive sunken room with six truck-sized generators, each of them silent. Serena watched them, knowing I was there.

It ticked me off.

It was bad enough to be powerless, weaponless— without her rubbing it in.

I had to figure out a way to destroy her before the demon army reached six hundred sixty-six. Because after the gates of hell opened, well, I didn't know what could stop them.

Five hundred and one.

Triumphant, Serena flipped her pageboy haircut and strolled straight for me.

Son of a mother. I wasn't surprised, but I had a hard time containing the dread. She wore Dimitri's emerald.

She followed my gaze. "Oh, this old thing?" she said, her French-tipped nails lingering over the teardrop-shaped stone at the hollow of her throat. "He's not coming. For all I know, someone else finished him off. He was quite tasty."

My stomach hitched. I wanted to kill her.

I needed to force my emotions down or I'd never be able to focus. I had a job to do. Plain and simple. No telling how I'd destroy Serena, recapture the succubi and save Phil, but I knew I had to try.

Five hundred eighty-two.

A blue bubble formed in Serena's palm, pulsing with a life of its own. Claws erupted from her fingers and her hands took on their true, skeletal form. I took an involuntary step backward and into a wall of freezing cold demons. They shoved me forward and I almost stumbled.

Serena rubbed at the bubble with a taloned finger. "Don't worry, sweetheart. You won't feel a thing." The bubble grew to the size of a basketball. "Besides, you scream too much and I'll send you to the third layer of hell with Max's other slayer."

I stiffened. "*You* took her?"

Serena winked. "Turned her. Same difference, really." Demons seized my arms. "Now, hold still." Serena gripped the bubble, wound back like a boxer and slammed it into my chest. Ice tore through my veins and at the same time I felt like I'd collided with a live electrical wire. Energy flooded my system and I realized, to my utter horror, that I could use none of it to move. It was like she'd bug-zapped me into complete paralysis.

Six hundred five.

The energy flowed between us in a frigid blue stream as I felt her searching *inside* me.

"Oh you are a fun one." Her perfectly arched brows knit. "I felt you take the mark," she muttered. "Now where did you put it?"

Sweet happy puppies! She must need the mark to get a grip on my power. And I'd gotten rid of it. My knees sagged in relief as the demons at my sides shoved me forward, upward, closer to Serena.

I'd thought I wanted that extra edge, hoped like heck I hadn't needed it. Max's other slayer must have thought the same thing. But while she'd kept her mark, I'd shed Serena's leash.

Now what was I going to do about it?

I swallowed hard, gathered my strength as Serena's power prickled inside me. I knew I had one shot. One. Before I lost the element of surprise.

It was a classic maneuver, like old J. Bennett used to do at the Springdale Country Club pool. He'd reach up, ask you for a hand out of the deep end and then— whammo—he'd yank you in, flip-flops and all.

If he could do it, I could try. Problem was, for this plan to work, for me to seize all her power, I had to free all mine. I had to open myself up to her completely.

*Sacrifice yourself.*

I didn't know what her dark power would do to me. Jaws clenched, I served up everything I had and laid it bare. I'd never felt more raw or vulnerable. To my shock, I felt Phil join me. His presence felt like a warm hand on my back. A steady hum surged through my body as he mingled his life force with mine.

*Please let this work.* I surrounded her energy as it searched me, and braced myself as I chose the precise moment to attack.

Now or never.

I took a deep breath, shot both hands through the blue stream connecting us and grabbed her power at the base of her white minidress. She shrieked as my fingers closed around it. Yeah, well she was going to do a lot worse than that. I kicked her backward and yanked her power into me.

Serena gasped and tried to pull away. I pulled harder, but she'd already started to fall. Wet, red energy flooded my limbs, filling me up. Her sopping power streamed through my fingers and out onto the floor. The more of her power I had, the more I could get until it surged into me. Serena's claws dug into my arms. Ha! They didn't even make a scratch. She couldn't hurt me anymore, and there was nothing she could do. She'd already plunged headfirst into my trap.

It felt amazing.

She stumbled backward as I went back for more, sopping up the remnants until I'd drained her. Then I flung off her measly blue current and shoved her shell of a body to the floor. Strength rushed through me until I was almost giddy with it, drunk on power.

I spun and faced the demons behind me. They'd backed away, but not far enough. I thrust my hands out like Tasers and incinerated them on the spot. No switch stars required.

Good gravy, I could get used to this.

Ohhh, and if I wasn't mistaken, I had a mental map of every demon from here to Panama City. Make that Quito. I could see them, like fire ants scurrying around the mound. And lucky for me, it turned out I could zap them mentally. I squashed the first two, marveling at how I could decide for them not to exist and—whammo. It was almost fun. But I didn't have time to indulge myself.

Nope, I might have been Lizzie the all-powerful, but I was also Lizzie the efficient. I torched the six hundred five in Las Vegas, then exterminated them in waves from here down to the Andes Mountains and out into California, until they were no more than hissing stains on the ground, or in one case, oozing down a circular staircase. Talk about a grand entrance for the ultimate demon slayer. Like a well-aimed can of Raid up into Canada and sweeping the United States until I hit ocean on every front.

To make sure they'd never come back, I incinerated the portal. I had no trouble finding it now—a burning hole between our world and theirs. I could see why a chilly demon would have a hard time passing through. I fried it until it was no more than a churning mass of burnt embers, and to make it even better than before, wrapped it in a double layer of protection so nothing could dig itself out.

I turned to the demon at my feet. Serena had shed the rest of her glamour. A leathery thing lay in place of the petite brunette. Hair sprouted in wiry clumps from her chin and blackened skull. Her cadaver-like hands scratched feebly at the industrial linoleum. I drove my hand forward to finish her and with a rush of shock, yanked my shot at the last minute.

Phil was still attached to Serena.

My wayward power surge zapped a gaping hole in one of the monitoring panels. Sparks zipped across the engineers' board along the left wall. I raced for Phil, lifting him off the panel as live wires crackled and the whole thing started to smoke.

God bless America.

We had to figure this out. Fast. I didn't want Serena melting into the floorboards with my uncle in tow. And I wasn't sure how the succubi had managed to keep everyone official out of Hoover Dam, but I didn't expect to have the same kind of luck. No way I could explain the blown-out turbines or the scorched control board or the fried demon holes in the floor.

With Serena damaged, I could feel Phil's strength building.

"Hey," I held his head in my hands and brushed his thinning gray comb-over out of his eyes. "I need you to think. She's got you. Is there a way to pull away from a succubus?"

His eyes fluttered and he sniffed. "I don't know."

I glanced back at Serena. She'd pulled herself to her knees, glaring at us with red eyes. Cripes! I couldn't squash her and I doubt she'd be willing to disclose the proper dose of power for a knockout blow.

He shivered.

"Come on, Phil."

His blue eyes opened and he looked at me the way

I'd always wished my parents would. He cleared his throat and on a rasp, said, "Have I ever told you how proud I am of you?"

My heart squeezed. "Not the time."

Serena slowly rose to her clawlike feet. She took an uneven step forward. "You want your uncle back? You let me go."

Impossible. Serena was too dangerous. Besides, there had to be another way. I had to break her hold on him.

She began to shimmer. "Give me my power or I leave and take him with me."

Holy schniekes.

I didn't want to have to make that choice.

Phil's fingers closed in around my arm, his grip surprisingly strong. "Help me up. Now."

I pulled him to his feet. "Do you have your soul?" I asked, my fingers tracing along his chest, like I could feel it. It seemed like he did. I detected a presence, warm and steady. Still, I had to be sure.

"I have it," Phil said.

He leaned over and kissed me on the cheek before he launched himself into the live wires on the control panel.

"Oh my God! Phil!" His body jerked and sputtered. I dragged him away from the controls, raw electricity shooting up and down my arms. Without my new powers, I had no doubt it would have fried me. Even with them, my limbs burned with shock. I stumbled backward with Phil and we both hit the floor.

Serena cackled. I hit her between her eyes with a jolt of power and rolled my fairy godfather onto his back. I couldn't even see where the current had entered. My fingers danced up and down his neck, searching for a pulse.

I lowered my shaking fingers. My fairy godfather was dead.

Phil didn't have to die to get us out of this. There should have been a better way. He'd already sacrificed himself once to try to save me. How many times did my fairy godfather have to give up his life for me?

Heaven above, he actually looked happy. God, I felt like I'd failed him. I could save the entire West Coast, but I couldn't save my own fairy godfather.

I spent a quiet moment with the man who'd shared my struggles since childhood, the man who'd watched me grow into a demon slayer. He'd trusted me to see this through until the end, bet his life on it. I wouldn't let him down. Worse, I didn't know if he was completely free before he died. Serena could have damned him and I'd never know.

"Where is he?" I demanded.

The power churned inside of me. And I thought the dark mark was bad.

Serena skittered away from me like a locust and hissed, struggling to stand.

I zapped her hard. "Tell me where he is!"

She snarled. "You know he's mine."

Rage bit me to the core. I didn't know if she was telling the truth or not. It didn't matter. She'd never willingly give him back to me and now she was going to die.

I aimed a killer surge at her chest

She screamed as the blast hit her. The most powerful she-demon to hit the West Coast went up in a shower of blue flame, fighting as her body melted into nothingness. I hit her with a blast to the neck to shut her up. Her head rolled from her body, silent except for the hiss and crackle of the obsidian fire.

The old Lizzie might have felt regret, at least for her suffering as the shell fought and kicked. But I didn't feel the slightest bit of shame. I enjoyed it.

I stood, marveling at how I could have probably flown if I'd wanted. Black energy raged inside me. I swallowed, fighting back the stark terror, doing my best to ignore my pounding heart. Hand to my chest, I felt Serena's hellish force merge with my demon slayer powers, twisting together until I could barely distinguish the difference.

I stood above the smoking pit of acid that had been Serena, her power thrumming from my toenails to my fingertips. And that's when a cold realization struck. Serena might have gotten me after all. I didn't own her energy. It owned me.

# Chapter Twenty-eight

"Lizzie!" Pirate's voice echoed down the hallway. "I'm here for you, Lizzie!"

Oh no—what was Pirate doing here?

"Stay away!" I leapt over the remains of the demons and slammed the one and only door to the control room. Fear churned in my stomach. And worse—rage. My new powers screamed for an outlet. I released a fraction of it, enough to break the door lock. Instead the keyhole disappeared and the doorknob melted clean off.

*No, no, no.*

I folded my arms over my chest and swallowed hard, trying not to panic. So I wouldn't be leaving this room for a while. At least no one else could get in. Not until I could get a handle on this.

"What the hell?" Dimitri pounded on the door.

"You're alive." Relief flooded me, followed by a stinging fear. Holy smokes—was I about to fry everyone I loved?

"Lizzie!" Dimitri hollered, rattling the door down to its hinges. "What's wrong?"

Thank heaven, he sounded like his old self again.

My entire body shaking, I battled the urge to rip the

door open and show him exactly what was wrong with me.

"I'm compromised," I said, opting for the shorter version of *I took on demon powers and now I might kill you . . . and my little dog too.*

Dimitri let out a string of curse words while Pirate scratched frantically on the other side of the door.

"What'd they do to you?"

I could practically feel his green eyes boring through the door.

"Nothing." I did it to them. "I took Serena's power," I said, eyes widening as my fingertips began to glow blue. "All of it."

I was answered in the worst possible way—by silence.

Oh no. I couldn't do this by myself.

Who was I kidding? *I had to do this by myself.*

"I think it's getting worse," I told him. My hands took on a horrible, tingling pallor. Blue bubbles erupted from each of my fingertips. "Holy shit!"

"What?" Dimitri demanded, smashing into the other side of the door. He ground something against it. "Pirate, go get Gertie. She's casting wards down by the intake room."

Sure, they didn't want any more demons down here, but . . . "Grandma's wards won't find me, will they?" I'd seen her weave them before—she used a trajectory that would fling the lesser evils straight back to hell. Of course it didn't work on demons, but I had no idea what Grandma's wards would do to me. I couldn't get pitched into hell on the back swing, not like this.

"Lizzie, you're not evil."

I needed to hear that. Even if I wasn't sure I believed it.

"Stand back," Dimitri commanded.

Shaking, I did what he asked. The blue bubbles on my fingertips grew to the size of softballs. Okay, screw the idea of not needing help. "Hurry!"

The entire door fell from its hinges and smacked into the floor in front of me.

Dimitri burst into the room, bronze sword in hand. The poor man still hadn't found time to replace his shirt. He swallowed hard when he saw me. He ripped the protective rags off of his wrists and clutched my head in his hands.

"Steady, Lizzie," he said, his fingers mashing into my hair and his breath warm against my face. I couldn't look at him. My hands, they were getting worse.

He began speaking to me in an ancient language, or maybe it was Greek. His words took on a lilting, almost hypnotic tone. I didn't know it if it was what he was saying, or how he said it, but I felt a calm invade my body. I gasped for breath. God, it felt good to have him here.

"That's it," he said, running his fingers through my hair.

I fought it. I'm not sure if some part of me wanted the power or the anger, but I couldn't let it go. "I think she might have taken Phil with her."

His breath hitched, but his stream of comfort remained unbroken. "I'm not going to lie to you. Your fairy godfather may be gone forever."

Tears clouded my vision.

He made me look at him. The tiny lines around his eyes crinkled as he seemed to see me straight down to my soul. "It was his choice," he said, tracing his thumb over my lower jaw, "he's a fighter, Lizzie, like you. Phil made it possible for you to be standing here right now. Now it's up to you to take what he's given you. Ask yourself, Lizzie. What are you going to do with his gift?"

I knew what I should say, but I didn't want to say it. "I don't know."

His eyes refused to leave mine. "Accept what I'm offering you."

I could barely find my voice. "What is this? Magic?"

He guided a stray lock of hair from my forehead and tucked it behind my ear. "Some would call it that. I prefer to think of it as a reminder."

The tears flowed freely now. I looked into his beautiful face, so full of love and understanding. I felt his warm hands, steady on my shoulders and I knew what I had to do. I closed my eyes and in my mind's eye, I saw my black anger, my hostility, the frustration I felt at my complete and utter failure to save the one person in my life who'd always been there for me. I took it and merged it with the blackness that was Serena's power. But it was too heavy. And it didn't want to leave.

"Let me in," Dimitri said.

I could feel his unwavering presence in front of me and it took everything I had not to wrap myself up in it like a warm blanket.

"Lizzie." He folded my hands in his.

What? "No." I wasn't about to tangle him in this. It was my mistake and I'd fix it.

"I'm part demon slayer, Lizzie. And a big believer in fate."

Oh my word, his *things happen for a reason* speech

flooded my mind. I couldn't believe how he'd actually forgiven me for tainting his pure griffin blood and now I was equally speechless that he'd take on vengeful black power with me.

I rested my forehead on his shoulder "It's—" I began, desperate for his help, terrified that if I let it loose, it would consume him in front of me.

"I know." Fingers on my chin, he guided me up to him and kissed me, warm and deep. The intimacy of that one kiss shocked me. I let it flow over me, opening myself completely for the second time that night. I shivered as some of the awful, heavy burden flowed from me into him. He took a sharp breath when it hit him. I almost panicked. I instinctively tried to pull back, but he clutched my hands and squeezed.

"Together, now," he whispered against my lips before kissing me long and hard.

I let him in. As his power surged into me, and mine into him, I let him see all of me—the good, the bad, everything. I was exhausted from hiding, from fighting, from doing everything on my own. I let go of the need to keep control, and from the one thought that had terrified me from the start—that if he saw everything, he might not want me anymore.

He savored me, pushed me, blanketed me and comforted me in ways I'd never imagined. If we got through this, *please let us survive this,* I didn't want to be alone anymore.

"Ready?" he whispered, hot against my ear.

Goose bumps shivered down my arms. "Yes." As long as I had Dimitri, I'd be ready for anything.

We used the power like an immense blowtorch. I visualized it as clear as if we stood at the edge of hell itself. We harnessed the power of Serena, countless succubi and the whole of the energy generated tonight and aimed it straight at the gates of hell, incinerating countless demons and subdemons on the surface layer. Then we did our best to seal the whole thing from the outside. Let the locusts dig their way out. I poured out my entire arsenal until I'd spent everything.

Dimitri held back. His eyes glowed green, then orange.

Oh no. I couldn't handle it if he'd corrupted himself. "What are you doing?" I demanded.

He fired backward into the dam. "I'm opening up a pathway for the ghosts," he said, groaning with the effort.

Dang it, he shouldn't have tried to do that on his own. "I thought ghosts had to go to the light."

"That's one way," he said, releasing a breath that I hadn't even realized he was holding. He blinked a few times, recovering, as his eyes went from orange to a rich chocolate brown. "It's usually the only choice. But you had a trace of Phil's goodness in that mass of power. I used it to open up a pathway to help them." He gazed down at me, so warm and sure. "After all, if one of your preschoolers was afraid to take on a flight of stairs, would you wait until they found the courage, or would you carry them?"

Like he carried me—the sheer relief of knowing I wasn't alone was almost enough to make me want to curl up on the floor and sleep for a year. Instead, I drew even closer to the man who'd saved me in more ways than one.

I used my thumb to swipe away a trickle of sweat on his neck, marveling that he'd stuck with me—that he'd chosen me—through everything. "How do you know so much?" I asked.

He pulled me close. "Stick with me and you'll find out."

I held him, running my hands down his back. Pain shot down my fingertips and I noticed for the first time that they throbbed. I swallowed hard and risked a glance. My hands were whole again, except for raw sores on the ends of my fingers.

Before I could even think of what to say, Dimitri lowered his mouth to mine and I stopped trying to think. I sank into him and savored his warmth and his goodness.

The man had saved me in more ways than one.

He pulled back slightly, long before I was ready to let him go. "Now about that emerald," he whispered.

We found it under a chair near the control board. I dragged it out and glowed with relief when I felt the heat of the green stone against my fingers. It shone with life and energy.

Dimitri took it and placed it in the center of my palm. "I offer you the protection of the Helios clan, freely given, freely taken."

Its energy whispered to me. The familiar warmth rested against my skin where it belonged.

A thin, bronze chain snaked from the tip of the teardrop and circled my wrist. "I accept." My body ached from exhaustion, not to mention sheer relief. Still, I couldn't help but grin. "Freely."

Something hard loosened inside of me as the chain wound up my arm and circled my chest, until the emerald hung from my neck, where it belonged.

"What did you do to me before?" I asked him.

He kissed me on the forehead. "I helped you find your strength. You had it all along, Lizzie. We all do. It's just sometimes we forget."

"Yeah," I said, leaning against the rock that was Dimitri, "I was a little stressed out."

"That's why I'll always be here."

He was right. I could always lean on Dimitri. He brought out the best in me, whether we were reclaiming my soul, or walking along a moonlit path with gargoyles circling overhead. He was mine again. And he was whole.

I found my empty utility belt in a pile of filth that was probably a demon about twenty minutes before. My switch stars were nearby, along with the powders and crystals I kept in the pouches attached to the belt. I was in the middle of capturing an entire pile of sandy pink granules when a tiny creature screeched from under a small mountain of ash.

Soot flying, he burst from the wreckage, a furless hamster-type creature. I started to reach for him until I saw he had fangs and black dinosaur-type spikes along his back. "What the . . . ?" He shrieked and, as fast as his scrabbly legs would take him, made a beeline for the back pouch of my utility belt.

The creature burrowed into the belt, his rear end wriggling until there was no more of him to be seen.

"Mystery solved," Dimitri said.

I glanced up at him. "Hardly." I gathered up the last few crystals. I'd tackle my powers before worrying about the mysterious creature that lived in the back of my utility belt.

"You should call him Harry," Dimitri said, giving me a hand and helping me up.

"Why not?" I said, feeling the little guy settle himself in. It was better than Fang.

I talked Dimitri into taking back his shirt before we headed up the main elevator. He carried Phil as the doors closed and the car jerked to a start. I held Phil's soft, wide hand as the scent of cinnamon filled the small space. Through my exhaustion, I tried to memorize this moment the best that I could. It might be the last time I saw Phil. There was no telling what fairies, or half fairies, did for funerals.

As for how I'd tell Grandma, I didn't know. My emotions were too raw. I squeezed his hand hard and hoped I'd find the words. I could hardly believe it myself that he was gone.

The elevator opened up into an art deco foyer that led to the outside. Finally, we could get Phil out of this place. I forced myself back into warrior mode, just in case. With a deep breath and switch stars at the ready, I pushed through a set of brass doors.

I about fell backward as Pirate flung himself into my arms, licking everywhere he could reach, which would have been really bad had we been under attack.

"Dang, Lizzie. I leave to get a Twinkie and you disappear on me."

Relief surged through me. "Are you okay, sweetie?" Hands shaking, I inspected my wriggling dog by the light of a hovering Skeep. "Meko? What's going on out here?"

The Hoover Dam backed up to Lake Mead and towered over the river on the other side. Witches lined the sweeping highway at its crest, their Harleys at the ready behind them.

The Skeep dipped and glowed brighter. "Many apologies. I'm Tiko, an associate of Meko. We've been called here to fetch supplies for your rescue."

Harleys crisscrossed the bridge every which way, their supernaturally bright front lights cutting through the night in every direction.

Grandma barreled out of the shadows, a Smucker's jar in each hand. "God damn it, Lizzie. You scared the crap out of me! Oh good. Dimitri. We need you to fly up and—" She screeched to a halt when she saw Dimitri holding Phil's limp body. "Oh no."

"Grandma, I didn't mean—" This was not how I wanted her to find out.

"What?" Frieda asked, seconds behind Grandma. She stopped when she saw. "Oh dang, girl. I am so sorry."

Grandma took Phil's hand and for once, she had nothing to say.

"He sacrificed himself for me," I told her, taking comfort against a bit of unwashed dog.

Grandma nodded, her eyes reddening. "I'd like a moment," she said, hoarse. Frieda brought us a blanket and we laid Phil right inside the doors. My heart broke a little when the doors clicked closed behind her. I should have done more.

Dimitri wrapped his arms around me from the back and I closed my eyes, savoring the closeness. The warm desert air scattered my bangs over my forehead. I chose to focus on that, rather than on my pounding head or wrung-out body.

Pirate nosed the crook of my elbow. "You okay, Lizzie?"

"I will be," I said, ruffling his fur between my aching fingers. *Keep it together, Lizzie.* I couldn't afford to fall apart now.

Frieda's heels clacked on the sidewalk. "I know you want to see me as much as a skunk at a lawn party, but we really do need Dimitri."

"Lizzie?" He ran his hands along my arms.

"I'm fine," I said, pulling away first. It was good to know he could fly again.

He kissed me on the head and followed Frieda toward the edge of the dam to get what looked to be a trapped gargoyle off a clock tower. I stood with my dog, too exhausted to move, waiting for Grandma, mourning Phil, wondering how it had come to this.

Biker witches scattered along the roadway over the dam. The cars that usually traveled Ala Meda Boulevard were conspicuously absent.

"Well, look who decided to join the fight after all," a deep voice rumbled.

I about fell over as the angelic blond hunter strolled into the light. He looked like he'd been run over by a truck. "Max," I gaped. I couldn't believe he was here. "How?"

He crossed his arms in front of his chest and scowled down at me. "My job wasn't done."

My body surged into high alert mode. I was tempted to touch him and make sure he was real. But it had to be Max. I didn't sense any demonic imposters. Besides, we'd fried or captured every demon within a three-thousand-mile radius.

"Is she dead?" Max asked.

Oh yes. Definitely Max. "Serena's a demonic grease stain on the floor. Now, if you don't mind me asking, what are you doing here?"

"Did you think I'd stand by and watch Serena take you?"

Frankly, I didn't think the man did a day of standing in his life.

Max delivered a biting stare. "Killing demons on my own wouldn't have solved anything if you screwed up. I told you we needed a slayer to beat her."

This coming from the person who had encouraged me to keep the dark mark. "I'm glad you made it out," I told him. And I was.

Dimitri crunched up the road. I'd been so focused on Max I hadn't even heard him coming. He reached out for Max and I prepared for the fight.

Instead, Dimitri clapped the hunter on the shoulder like an old friend. "Good to see you, buddy."

Buddy? What on earth had happened since I'd been captured?

Dimitri noticed my confusion and grinned. "We needed Max to get inside the dam. You should have seen the barriers the demons set up."

I couldn't believe it. I stared at Dimitri, then Max, the tension draining out of me. "You two actually worked together?"

"I helped," Pirate said, squirming in my arms. "Joe got Ezra, who got Sid, who got Dimitri. But then nobody understood the message."

"Ghosts are horrible at getting facts right," said Max. "That's why I don't trust any of them."

"But I understood," Pirate said, his tail thwumping my arm. "Ezra and I've been playing lots of Scrabble.

I know how he thinks. See that's the trick. You study your opponent like a hunting dog. Sniff out their weaknesses and—whammo!—thirty-six-point word."

I kissed Pirate on the head. "Ghosts and dogs. I never would have guessed."

Bob wheeled up, his antidemonic quilt bits flapping in his spokes. "Hey, Lizzie. Glad to see you're not dead."

"Me too," I said. "I don't mean to sound ungrateful, but what are you guys doing here?"

Bob huffed. "Saving you. What else?"

Max nodded. "Your witches have a gift for focusing power."

"Red Skulls have always been that way," said Bob. "We get into trouble and it's trouble times ten. Frieda works a water spell and it's the Vegas flood of '99." He grimaced. "Talk about a mess. But you need to intensify a power like Max's, we can do that too." He chuckled at the look on my face, which must have reflected my pure and utter astonishment. "And, Ms. Lizzie, when we felt your power grow, we helped you aim your magic."

I leaned my back against the concrete wall of the dam. Here I thought I had to do everything on my own. I was the Demon Slayer of Dalea, for goodness sake. I'd just assumed that power came with complete and utter responsibility. First Dimitri helped save me, and now the witches had my back. And Max. I didn't know what to say. This whole time, I'd imagined the Red Skulls as a liability, and Max as someone not to be trusted. Come to think of it, I still wasn't sure if I trusted Max.

"I really did need you guys as much as you needed me," I said. It felt strange to even say it out loud.

"Ding, ding, ding! Finally!" Grandma clapped me on the back, forcing humor through reddened eyes. "You don't have to know everything, sport. Nobody does. Not even me."

"I never thought you'd be the type to go all After School Special on me," I said.

She wrapped an arm around my shoulder and gave a long sigh. "Shut up. And next time, remember to trust yourself and your friends."

I nodded, knowing she was right. Trust my friends, the Red Skulls, the witches who tempted the demons themselves to help me. It felt good to be a part of something bigger than myself. I straightened out my bustier and, despite the rigors of the night, walked a little taller in my pink zipper pants. I was a Red Skull and proud of it.

*Excerpt from* The Dangerous Book for Demon Slayers:
*Sacrifice Yourself: This is the third Truth of the demon
slayer. Most take it to mean self-sacrifice in the face of
great danger, looking beyond who you are and what you
want. But it can also mean something that seems much
simpler, but is actually much harder in practice—letting
go of what you think you need, thereby opening yourself up to the things, and people, that have the power to
make you truly happy.*

# CHAPTER TWENTY-NINE

We buried Uncle Phil in green linen pants and a
matching Hawaiian shirt. Grandma said that's how
he dressed before Serena had him running around in
a white wedding tux. I had to admit, it looked more
like him. She even tucked a can of Pabst Blue Ribbon
into his casket.

I wished I had something to give him, a token of
how much he'd meant to me. I couldn't think of anything that would do justice to the years he'd spent
watching over me, or for what he did in the end.

The night before the funeral, I wriggled out of Dimitri's arms. I sat on the steps of our cabin and wrote Phil
a letter. I told him all of the things I wish we could
have talked about when he was alive. And I told him
how it broke my heart to lose him.

I tucked it into his shirt pocket before the graveside
ceremony at St. Christopher's Cemetery. Witches, fairies and who knew what else clustered in uneven rows
amid a desert field of headstones. I held Grandma's

hand while Dimitri stood on the other side of me, his arm wrapped around my waist. I marveled at how Uncle Phil's funeral turned out to be a typical ceremony in every way, except when Sid reached out to catch Father Hamilton's prayer book a second before the good reverend dropped it.

I couldn't shake the feeling that I'd let Phil down. He'd been willing to sacrifice for me, but did he *have* to? I wasn't sure what I could have done to keep him from being used as bait. My original sin was in being a demon slayer in the first place. There had to be something else afterward, some other series of choices that would have kept him from making the ultimate sacrifice. I fully intended to berate myself until I came up with an entire list, alphabetized.

Afterward, as we walked to the car, I caught a hint of cinnamon in the air. I squeezed Dimitri's hand. "Can I have a minute?"

Dimitri walked Grandma back to the Harleys while I traced my way over to a small garden wall where the air was particularly sweet. My heart swelled, hoping desperately for any sign Phil was okay.

As I rounded the wall, however, my hopes sank. Pungent, dead flowers assaulted my senses. They lay in half-wilted heaps, tossed aside from earlier funerals, left to rot in this corner of the cemetery.

I couldn't help it. Images of my fairy godfather in his grave skimmed the surface of my mind. "I'm sorry Phil," I said, watching the once-sweet flowers. "I'll figure out what I did wrong, and next time I'll do better. I promise."

"I think you did just fine this time."

I whirled around, my heart hammering in my chest.

"Phil?" He had a faint glow around the edges. Not exactly a ghost, but . . .

"Stop being so hard on yourself, Lizzie. Of course, you're a demon slayer, but believe it or not, you're only human."

Tears blurred my vision and I let them come. "I'm sorry."

"I know. I read the letter. All twelve pages, or I would have been here sooner."

I wanted to hug him so hard. "Do you have your soul?" I asked, hoping—praying.

He tapped the center of his chest. "Got her right here." His face fell slightly. "It's not that bad, Lizzie. Look," he said, floating a foot off the ground. "My basketball game has improved. I got to meet Elvis. And I know where they buried Jimmy Hoffa."

I snarfed, half sniveling, half laughing. "I can't believe I'm going to lose you before I even got to know you."

"Watch and be amazed." he levitated another foot off the ground and twirled. "Brian Boitano skating spectacular," he said, ending in a figure eight.

"Now you're showing off."

His eyes crinkled as he smiled.

I found myself returning it—damn the man—and wiped my nose on my wrist. "You were supposed to be off the job when I turned thirty."

He chuckled. "Just because you're all grown up, doesn't mean I can let you go."

And here I thought I'd come to Vegas to save him.

His bulbous nose widened as he smiled. "Glad I could do this for you, pumpkin."

He'd always been doing things for me, from fairy beans under my pillow to dragging me out of Lake Newman when I was eight. I couldn't lose him. "I just found you."

Phil grinned. "Don't think of it as losing a fairy godfather, so much as gaining a guardian angel."

He couldn't. He wouldn't. "You'll be back?" I asked, voice hitching, almost afraid to hope.

He nodded, entirely too pleased about the whole thing. "Told you. I have a hard time letting go. And tell your Grandma thanks for the brew."

I had so much more to tell him, I realized as he faded away. It hurt to lose him, even temporarily. Still, over the pungent aroma of dying flowers, I detected a whiff of cinnamon. He'd been there to save me—in big ways and small. He'd sat through my five-hour-long dance recitals, left fairy beans under my pillow and the more I thought about it, I wondered if he hadn't been the one who barged up to my corner lemonade stand and demanded old Mr. Steele pay me the full nickel, even though we'd run out of ice. Uncle Phil, it seemed, always knew when to show up. And he'd always be with me, no matter what.

We held the funeral reception in the lodge next to the petting zoo. The building sagged and most of the walls needed paint. There was little furniture, save for wooden benches and tables. Tire tracks ran up and down the stairs, but I had a feeling the Red Skulls were responsible for those.

The Red Skulls mingled with the fairies. Plus, we'd found Phil's address book and asked his friends from the bowling league, plus his boss at work. Luckily, Mr. Reed had no idea what had happened at the dam. I could thank the Red Skulls—again—for that.

The murmur of the crowd echoed through the spartan room.

"You going to turn this into a biker bar?" I asked Grandma as I handed her a cup of punch.

"Nah," she said, pausing for a large gulp. "This doesn't feel like home. We're going to hit the road, head south somewhere."

I sipped my own punch and nearly choked as acid burned my throat. "What is this?" I asked, my voice an octave higher.

"Mmm," Grandma tipped the paper cup to her lips again, savoring. "Not a clue. Ant Eater doesn't share her recipes."

That's not all Ant Eater had kept to herself. She hadn't let poor Sid out of the corner the entire afternoon. Worse, the short, stocky fairy sported a Harley Davidson do-rag over his balding head. And, "Why is he wearing leather chaps?"

Grandma shrugged. "Life on the road can chafe your thighs."

Oh my word. Ant Eater and Sid? They'd kill each other.

Grandma took another swallow. "What? Now you can tell the immediate future?"

Sid saw me and broke away from Ant Eater with— ew—a kiss to her cheek.

"I got something for you," he said, unfolding a piece of paper from his back pocket.

The gold seal of the Department of Intramagical Affairs decorated the right corner. "A full demon slayer license?" I asked, swelling with pride and relief. "You mean I don't have to take the test?"

Sid rolled his eyes. "Stopping a demon invasion wasn't enough of a test? You earned it. But don't go flaunting it in front of Officer Ly or she'll have you back on that ladder faster than you can say 'crash landing.'"

Like I ever wanted to see the Dragon Lady again.

Dimitri wrapped his arm around my shoulders, warm and inviting. "Come here. You have to see this."

I followed him to the front room. Next to a charred spot on the hardwood, Pirate stood behind a line of white plastic forks.

"Look at this, Lizzie. One! Two! Three! Four! Five! Six! Six forks! Want me to do it again? One! Two! . . ."

I hardly knew what to think. "Did Ezra teach you that?"

"No-sir-ee-bob. Dimitri taught me!" Dimitri rubbed Pirate between the ears and my dog closed his eyes with pleasure.

I stared at my dog. Was he imitating? It had to be. "Dogs can't count."

Dimitri grinned. "Not with that attitude."

He stood and wrapped his arm around my waist. "I figured now that Pirate's going to be a world traveler, he needs to learn a few new things."

The griffin had a point. I yanked him closer and dragged my fingertips along his side, pleased at the little shiver I felt run through him. "So we're finally headed to Greece?"

He ran his hand along my spine, trailing a line of kisses up my neck. "The sooner the better."

At last I'd meet his sisters, sip a little ouzo, help unravel the secrets that brought Dimitri to me in the first place. "I love you," I said.

He grinned. "Finally."

# ☐ **YES!**

Sign me up for the Love Spell Book Club and send my
FREE BOOKS! If I choose to stay in the club, I will pay
only $8.50* each month, a savings of $6.48!

NAME: _____

ADDRESS: _____

TELEPHONE: _____

EMAIL: _____

☐ I want to pay by credit card.

☐ **VISA**      ☐ **MasterCard**      ☐ **DISCOVER**

ACCOUNT #: _____

EXPIRATION DATE: _____

SIGNATURE: _____

Mail this page along with $2.00 shipping and handling to:
**Love Spell Book Club**
**PO Box 6640**
**Wayne, PA 19087**
Or fax (must include credit card information) to:
**610-995-9274**
You can also sign up online at **www.dorchesterpub.com**.
*Plus $2.00 for shipping. Offer open to residents of the U.S. and Canada only.
Canadian residents please call 1-800-481-9191 for pricing information.
If under 18, a parent or guardian must sign. Terms, prices and conditions subject to
change. Subscription subject to acceptance. Dorchester Publishing reserves the right
to reject any order or cancel any subscription.